THE HAND OF FU-MANCHU

THE HAND OF FU-MANCHU

SAX ROHMER

TITAN BOOKS

THE HAND OF FU-MANCHU
Print edition ISBN: 9780857686053
E-book edition ISBN: 9780857686718

Published by Titan Books
A division of Titan Publishing Group Ltd
144 Southwark St London SE1 0UP

First edition: May 2012
10 9 8 7 6 5 4 3 2 1

First published as a novel in the UK as *The Si-Fan Mysteries*, Methuen, 1917
First published as a novel in the US as *The Hand of Fu-Manchu*, McBride, 1917

Frontispiece illustration by J. C. Coll, detail from an illustration for "The Clue of the Pigtail", first appearing in *Collier's Weekly*, March 1, 1913. Special thanks to Dr. Lawrence Knapp for the illustrations as they appeared on "The Page of Fu-Manchu" – http://www.njedge.net/~knapp/FuFrames.htm

A CIP catalogue record for this title is available from the British Library.

Printed and bound in India by Replika Press Pvt. Ltd.

"I looked into that still, awful face, into those unnatural green eyes."

CHAPTER ONE

THE TRAVELER FROM TIBET

"Who's there?" I called sharply.

I turned and looked across the room. The window had been widely opened when I entered, and a faint fog haze hung in the apartment, seeming to veil the light of the shaded lamp. I watched the closed door intently, expecting every moment to see the knob turn. But nothing happened.

"Who's there?" I cried again, and, crossing the room, I threw open the door.

The long corridor without, lighted only by one inhospitable lamp at a remote end, showed choked and yellowed with this same fog so characteristic of London in November. But nothing moved to right nor left of me. The New Louvre Hotel was in some respects yet incomplete, and the long passage in which I stood, despite its marble facings, had no air of comfort or good cheer; palatial it was, but inhospitable.

I returned to the room, reclosing the door behind me, then for some five minutes or more I stood listening for a repetition of that mysterious sound, as of something that both dragged and tapped, which already had arrested my attention. My vigilance went unrewarded. I had closed the window to exclude the yellow mist, but subconsciously I was aware of its encircling presence, walling me in, and now I found myself in such a silence as I had known in deserts but could scarce have deemed possible in fog-bound London, in the heart of the world's metropolis, with the traffic of the Strand below me upon one side and the restless life of the river upon the other.

It was easy to conclude that I had been mistaken, that my nervous system was somewhat overwrought as a result of my hurried return from Cairo—from Cairo where I had left behind me many a fondly cherished hope. I addressed myself again to the task of unpacking my steamer-trunk and was so engaged when again a sound in the corridor outside brought me upright with a jerk.

A quick footstep approached the door, and there came a muffled rapping upon the panel.

This time I asked no question, but leapt across the room and threw the door open. Nayland Smith stood before me, muffled up in a heavy traveling coat, and with his hat pulled down over his brows.

"At last!" I cried, as my friend stepped in and quickly reclosed the door.

Smith threw his hat upon the settee, stripped off the great-coat, and pulling out his pipe began to load it in feverish haste.

"Well," I said, standing amid the litter cast out from the trunk, and watching him eagerly, "what's afoot?"

Nayland Smith lighted his pipe, carelessly dropping the match-end upon the floor at his feet.

"God knows what *is* afoot this time, Petrie!" he replied. "You and I have lived no commonplace lives; Dr. Fu-Manchu has seen to that; but if I am to believe what the Chief has told me today, even stranger things are ahead of us!"

I stared at him wonder-stricken.

"That is almost incredible," I said; "terror can have no darker meaning than that which Dr. Fu-Manchu gave to it. Fu-Manchu is dead, so what have we to fear?"

"We have to fear," replied Smith, throwing himself into a corner of the settee, "the Si-Fan!"

I continued to stare, uncomprehendingly.

"The Si-Fan—"

"I always knew and you always knew," interrupted Smith in his short, decisive manner, "that Fu-Manchu, genius that he was, remained nevertheless the servant of another or others. He was not the head of that organization which dealt in wholesale murder, which aimed at upsetting the balance of the world. I even knew the name of one, a certain mandarin, and member of the Sublime Order of the White Peacock, who was his immediate superior. I had never dared to guess at the identity of what I may term the Head Center."

He ceased speaking, and sat gripping his pipe grimly between his teeth, whilst I stood staring at him almost fatuously. Then—

"Evidently you have much to tell me," I said, with forced calm.

I drew up a chair beside the settee and was about to sit down.

"Suppose you bolt the door," jerked my friend.

I nodded, entirely comprehending, crossed the room and shot the little nickel bolt into its socket.

"Now," said Smith as I took my seat, "the story is a fragmentary one in which there are many gaps. Let us see what we know. It seems that the despatch which led to my sudden recall (and incidentally yours) from Egypt to London and which only reached me as I was on the point of embarking at Suez for Rangoon, was prompted by the arrival here of Sir Gregory Hale, whilom attaché at the British

Embassy, Peking. So much, you will remember, was conveyed in my instructions."

"Quite so."

"Furthermore, I was instructed, you'll remember, to put up at the New Louvre Hotel; therefore you came here and engaged this suite whilst I reported to the chief. A stranger business is before us, Petrie, I verily believe, than any we have known hitherto. In the first place, Sir Gregory Hale is here—"

"Here?"

"In the New Louvre Hotel. I ascertained on the way up, but not by direct inquiry, that he occupies a suite similar to this, and incidentally on the same floor."

"His report to the India Office, whatever its nature, must have been a sensational one."

"He has made no report to the India Office."

"What! made no report?"

"He has not entered any office whatever, nor will he receive any representative. He's been playing at Robinson Crusoe in a private suite here for close upon a fortnight—*id est* since the time of his arrival in London!"

I suppose my growing perplexity was plainly visible, for Smith suddenly burst out with his short, boyish laugh.

"Oh! I told you it was a strange business," he cried.

"Is he mad?"

Nayland Smith's gaiety left him; he became suddenly stern and grim.

"Either mad, Petrie, stark raving mad, or the savior of the Indian Empire—perhaps of all Western civilization. Listen. Sir Gregory Hale, whom I know slightly and who honors me, apparently, with a belief that I am the only man in Europe worthy of his confidence, resigned his appointment at Peking some time ago, and set out upon a private expedition to the Mongolian frontier with the avowed intention of visiting some place in the Gobi Desert. From the time that he actually crossed the frontier he disappeared for nearly six months, to reappear again suddenly and dramatically in London. He buried himself in this hotel, refusing all visitors and only advising the authorities of his return by telephone. He demanded that *I* should be sent to see him; and—despite his eccentric methods—so great is the Chief's faith in Sir Gregory's knowledge of matters Far Eastern, that behold, here I am."

He broke off abruptly and sat in an attitude of tense listening. Then—

"Do you hear anything, Petrie?" he rapped.

"A sort of tapping?" I inquired, listening intently myself the while.

Smith nodded his head rapidly.

We both listened for some time, Smith with his head bent slightly forward and his pipe held in his hands; I with my gaze upon the bolted door. A faint mist still hung in the room, and once I thought I detected a slight sound from the bedroom beyond, which was in darkness. Smith noted me turn my head, and for a moment the pair of us stared into the gap of the doorway. But the silence was complete.

"You have told me neither much nor little, Smith," I said, resuming for some reason, in a hushed voice. "Who or what is this Si-Fan at whose existence you hint?"

Nayland Smith smiled grimly.

"Possibly the real and hitherto unsolved riddle of Tibet, Petrie," he replied—"a mystery concealed from the world behind the veil of Lamaism." He stood up abruptly, glancing at a scrap of paper which he took from his pocket—"Suite Number 14a," he said. "Come along! We have not a moment to waste. Let us make our presence known to Sir Gregory—the man who has dared to raise that veil."

CHAPTER TWO

THE MAN WITH THE LIMP

"Lock the door!" said Smith significantly, as we stepped into the corridor.

I did so and had turned to join my friend when, to the accompaniment of a sort of hysterical muttering, a door further along, and on the opposite side of the corridor, was suddenly thrown open, and a man whose face showed ghastly white in the light of the solitary lamp beyond, literally hurled himself out. He perceived Smith and myself immediately. Throwing one glance back over his shoulder he came tottering forward to meet us.

"My God! I can't stand it any longer!" he babbled, and threw himself upon Smith, who was foremost, clutching pitifully at him for support. "Come and see him, sir—for Heaven's sake come in! I think he's dying; and he's going mad. I never disobeyed an order in my life before, but I can't help myself—I can't help myself!"

"Brace up!" I cried, seizing him by the shoulders as, still clutching at Nayland Smith, he turned his ghastly face to me. "Who are you, and what's your trouble?"

"I'm Beeton, Sir Gregory Hale's man."

Smith started visibly, and his gaunt, tanned face seemed to me to have grown perceptively paler.

"Come on, Petrie!" he snapped. "There's some devilry here."

Thrusting Beeton aside he rushed in at the open door—upon which, as I followed him, I had time to note the number, 14a. It communicated with a suite of rooms almost identical with our own. The sitting-room was empty and in the utmost disorder, but from the direction of the principal bedroom came a most horrible mumbling and gurgling sound—a sound utterly indescribable. For one instant we hesitated at the threshold—hesitated to face the horror beyond; then almost side by side we came into the bedroom....

Only one of the two lamps was alight—that above the bed; and on the bed a man lay writhing. He was incredibly gaunt, so that the suit of tropical twill which he wore hung upon him in folds, showing if such evidence were necessary, how terribly he was fallen away from his constitutional habit. He wore a beard of at least ten days' growth, which served to accentuate the cavitous hollowness of his face. His eyes seemed starting from their sockets as he lay upon his back uttering inarticulate sounds and plucking with skinny fingers at his lips.

Smith bent forward peering into the wasted face; and then started back with a suppressed cry.

"Merciful God! can it be Hale?" he muttered. "What does it mean? what does it mean?"

I ran to the opposite side of the bed, and placing my arms under the writhing man, raised him and propped a pillow at his back. He continued to babble, rolling his eyes from side to side hideously; then by degrees they seemed to become less glazed, and a light of returning sanity entered them. They became fixed; and they were fixed upon Nayland Smith, who bending over the bed, was watching

Sir Gregory (for Sir Gregory I concluded this pitiable wreck to be) with an expression upon his face compound of many emotions.

"A glass of water," I said, catching the glance of the man Beeton, who stood trembling at the open doorway.

Spilling a liberal quantity upon the carpet, Beeton ultimately succeeded in conveying the glass to me. Hale, never taking his gaze from Smith, gulped a little of the water and then thrust my hand away. As I turned to place the tumbler upon a small table the resumed the wordless babbling, and now, with his index finger, pointed to his mouth.

"He has lost the power of speech!" whispered Smith.

"He was stricken dumb, gentlemen, ten minutes ago," said Beeton in a trembling voice. "He dropped off to sleep out there on the floor, and I brought him in here and laid him on the bed. When he woke up he was like that!"

The man on the bed ceased his inchoate babbling and now, gulping noisily, began to make quick nervous movements with his hands.

"He wants to write something," said Smith in a low voice. "Quick! hold him up!" He thrust his notebook, open at a blank page, before the man whose moments were numbered, and placed a pencil in the shaking right hand.

Faintly and unevenly Sir Gregory commenced to write—whilst I supported him. Across the bent shoulders Smith silently questioned me, and my reply was a negative shake of the head.

The lamp above the bed was swaying as if in a heavy draught; I remembered that it had been swaying as we entered. There was no fog in the room, but already from the bleak corridor outside it was entering; murky, yellow clouds steaming in at the open door. Save for the gulping of the dying man, and the sobbing breaths of Beeton, there was no sound. Six irregular lines Sir Gregory Hale scrawled upon the page; then suddenly his body became a dead weight in my arms. Gently I laid him back upon the pillows, gently disengaged his fingers from the notebook, and, my head almost touching Smith's as we both craned forward over the page, read, with great difficulty, the following:—

"Guard my diary.... Tibetan frontier ... Key of India. Beware man ... with the limp. Yellow ... rising. Watch Tibet ... the *Si-Fan*...."

From somewhere outside the room, whether above or below I could not be sure, came a faint, dragging sound, accompanied by a *tap—tap—tap*....

CHAPTER THREE

"SÂKYA MÛNI"

The faint disturbance faded into silence again. Across the dead man's body I met Smith's gaze. Faint wreaths of fog floated in from the outer room. Beeton clutched the foot of the bed, and the structure shook in sympathy with his wild trembling. That was the only sound now; there was absolutely nothing physical so far as my memory serves to signalize the coming of the brown man.

Yet, stealthy as his approach had been, something must have warned us. For suddenly, with one accord, we three turned upon the bed, and stared out into the room from which the fog wreaths floated in.

Beeton stood nearest to the door, but, although he turned, he did not go out, but with a smothered cry crouched back against the bed. Smith it was who moved first, then I followed, and close upon his heels burst into the disordered sitting-room. The outer door had been closed but not bolted, and what with the tinted light, diffused through the silken Japanese shade, and the presence of fog in the room, I was almost tempted to believe myself the victim of a delusion. What I saw or thought I saw was this:—

A tall screen stood immediately inside the door, and around its end, like some materialization of the choking mist, glided a lithe, yellow figure, a slim, crouching figure, wearing a sort of loose robe. An impression I had of jet-black hair, protruding from beneath a little cap, of finely chiseled features and great, luminous eyes, then, with no sound to tell of a door opened or shut, the apparition was gone.

"You saw him, Petrie!—you saw him!" cried Smith.

In three bounds he was across the room, had tossed the screen aside and thrown open the door. Out he sprang into the yellow haze of the corridor, tripped, and, uttering a cry of pain, fell sprawling upon the marble floor. Hot with apprehension I joined him, but he looked up with a wry smile and began furiously rubbing his left shin.

"A queer trick, Petrie," he said, rising to his feet; "but nevertheless effective."

He pointed to the object which had occasioned his fall. It was a small metal chest, evidently of very considerable weight, and it stood immediately outside the door of number 14a.

"That was what he came for, sir! That was what he came for! You were too quick for him!"

Beeton stood behind us, his horror-bright eyes fixed upon the box.

"Eh?" rapped Smith, turning upon him.

"That's what Sir Gregory brought to England," the man ran on almost hysterically; "that's what he's been guarding this past two weeks, night and day, crouching over it with a loaded pistol. That's what cost him his life, sir. He's had no peace, day or night, since he got it...."

We were inside the room again now, Smith bearing the coffer in his arms, and still the man ran on:

"He's never slept for more than an hour at a time, that I know of, for weeks past. Since the day we came here he hasn't spoken to another living soul, and he's lain there on the floor at night with his head on that brass box, and sat watching over it all day.

"'Beeton!' he'd cry out, perhaps in the middle of the night—'Beeton—do you hear that damned woman!' But although I'd begun to think I could hear something, I believe it was the constant strain working on my nerves and nothing else at all.

"Then he was always listening out for someone he called 'the man with the limp.' Five and six times a night he'd have me up to listen with him. 'There he goes, Beeton!' he'd whisper, crouching with his ear pressed flat to the door. 'Do you hear him dragging himself along?'

"God knows how I've stood it as I have; for I've known no peace since we left China. Once we got here I thought it would be better, but it's been worse.

"Gentlemen have come (from the India Office, I believe), but he would not see them. Said he would see no one but Mr. Nayland Smith. He had never lain in his bed until tonight, but what with taking no proper food nor sleep, and some secret trouble that was killing him by inches, he collapsed altogether a while ago, and I carried him in and laid him on the bed as I told you. Now he's dead—now he's dead."

Beeton leant up against the mantelpiece and buried his face in his hands, whilst his shoulders shook convulsively. He had evidently been greatly attached to his master, and I found something very pathetic in this breakdown of a physically strong man. Smith laid his hands upon his shoulders.

"You have passed through a very trying ordeal," he said, "and no man could have done his duty better; but forces beyond your control have proved too strong for you. I am Nayland Smith."

The man spun around with a surprising expression of relief upon his pale face.

"So that whatever can be done," continued my friend, "to carry out your master's wishes, will be done now. Rely upon it. Go into your room and lie down until we call you."

"Thank you, sir, and thank God you are here," said Beeton dazedly, and with one hand raised to his head he went, obediently, to the smaller bedroom and disappeared within.

"Now, Petrie," rapped Smith, glancing around the littered floor, "since I am empowered to deal with this matter as I see fit, and since you are a medical man, we can devote the next half-hour, at any rate, to a strictly confidential inquiry into this most perplexing case. I propose that you examine the body for any evidences that may assist you determining the cause of death, whilst I make a few inquiries here."

I nodded, without speaking, and went into the bedroom. It contained not one solitary item of the dead man's belongings, and in every way bore out Beeton's statement that Sir Gregory had never inhabited it. I bent over Hale, as he lay fully dressed upon the bed.

Saving the singularity of the symptom which had immediately preceded death—viz., the paralysis of the muscles of articulation—I should have felt disposed to ascribe his end to sheer inanition; and a cursory examination brought to light nothing contradictory to that view. Not being prepared to proceed further in the matter at the moment I was about to rejoin Smith, whom I could hear rummaging about amongst the litter of the outer room, when I made a curious discovery.

Lying in a fold of the disordered bed linen were a few petals of some kind of blossom, three of them still attached to a fragment of slender stalk.

I collected the tiny petals, mechanically, and held them in the palm of my hand studying them for some moments before the mystery of their presence there became fully appreciable to me. Then I began to wonder. The petals (which I was disposed to class as belonging to some species of *Curcas* or Physic Nut), though bruised, were fresh, and therefore could not have been in the room for many hours. How had they been introduced, and by whom? Above all, what could their presence there at that time portend?

"Smith," I called, and walked towards the door carrying the mysterious fragments in my palm. "Look what I have found upon the bed."

Nayland Smith, who was bending over an open despatch case which he had placed upon a chair, turned—and his glance fell upon the petals and tiny piece of stem.

I think I have never seen so sudden a change of expression take place in the face of any man. Even in that imperfect light I saw him blanch. I saw a hard glitter come into his eyes. He spoke, evenly, but hoarsely:

"Put those things down—there, on the table; anywhere."

I obeyed him without demur; for something in his manner had chilled me with foreboding.

"You did not break that stalk?"

"No. I found it as you see it."

"Have you smelled the petals?"

I shook my head. Thereupon, having his eyes fixed upon me with the strangest expression in their gray depths, Nayland Smith said a singular thing.

"Pronounce, slowly, the words *'Sâkya Mûni,'*" he directed.

I stared at him, scarce crediting my senses; but—

"I mean it!" he rapped. "Do as I tell you."

"Sâkya Mûni," I said, in ever-increasing wonder.

Smith laughed unmirthfully.

"Go into the bathroom and thoroughly wash your hands," was his next order. "Renew the water at least three times." As I turned to fulfill his instructions, for I doubted no longer his deadly earnestness: "Beeton!" he called.

Beeton, very white-faced and shaky, came out from the bedroom as I entered the bathroom, and whist I proceeded carefully to cleanse my hands I heard Smith interrogating him.

"Have any flowers been brought into the room today, Beeton?"

"Flowers, sir? Certainly not. Nothing has ever been brought in here but what I have brought myself."

"You are certain of that?"

"Positive."

"Who brought up the meals, then?"

"If you'll look into my room here, sir, you'll see that I have enough tinned and bottled stuff to last us for weeks. Sir Gregory sent me out to buy it on the day we arrived. No one else had left or entered these rooms until you came tonight."

I returned to find Nayland Smith standing tugging at the lobe of his left ear in evident perplexity. He turned to me.

"I find my hands over full," he said. "Will you oblige me by telephoning for Inspector Weymouth? Also, I should be glad if you would ask M. Samarkan, the manager, to see me here immediately."

As I was about to quit the room—

"Not a word of our suspicions to M. Samarkan," he added; "not a word about the brass box."

I was far along the corridor ere I remembered that which,

remembered earlier, had saved me the journey. There was a telephone in every suite. However, I was not indisposed to avail myself of an opportunity for a few moments' undisturbed reflection, and, avoiding the lift, I descended by the broad, marble staircase.

To what strange adventure were we committed? What did the brass coffer contain which Sir Gregory had guarded night and day? Something associated in some way with Tibet, something which he believed to be "the key of India" and which had brought in its train, presumably, the sinister "man with a limp."

Who was the "man with the limp"? What was the Si-Fan? Lastly, by what conceivable means could the flower, which my friend evidently regarded with extreme horror, have been introduced into Hale's room, and why had I been required to pronounce the words "Sâkya Mûni"?

So ran my reflections—at random and to no clear end; and, as is often the case in such circumstances, my steps bore them company; so that all at once I became aware that instead of having gained the lobby of the hotel, I had taken some wrong turning and was in a part of the building entirely unfamiliar to me.

A long corridor of the inevitable white marble extended far behind me. I had evidently traversed it. Before me was a heavily curtained archway. Irritably, I pulled the curtain aside, learnt that it masked a glass-paneled door, opened this door—and found myself in a small court, dimly lighted and redolent of some pungent, incense-like perfume.

One step forward I took, then pulled up abruptly. A sound had come to my ears. From a second curtained doorway, close to my right hand, it came—a sound of muffled *tapping*, together with that of something which dragged upon the floor.

Within my brain the words seemed audibly to form: "The man with the limp!"

I sprang to the door; I had my hand upon the drapery ... when a woman stepped out, barring the way!

No impression, not even a vague one, did I form of her costume, save that she wore a green silk shawl, embroidered with raised white figures of birds, thrown over her head and shoulders and draped in such fashion that part of her face was concealed. I was transfixed by the vindictive glare of her eyes, of her huge dark eyes.

They were ablaze with anger—but it was not this expression within them which struck me so forcibly as the fact that they were in some way familiar.

Motionless, we faced one another. Then—

"You go away," said the woman—at the same time extending her arms across the doorway as barriers to my progress.

Her voice had a husky intonation; her hands and arms, which were bare and of old ivory hue, were laden with barbaric jewelry, much of it tawdry silverware of the bazaars. Clearly she was a half-caste of some kind, probably a Eurasian.

I hesitated. The sounds of dragging and tapping had ceased. But the presence of this grotesque Oriental figure only increased my anxiety to pass the doorway. I looked steadily into the black eyes; they looked into mine unflinchingly.

"You go away, please," repeated the woman, raising her right hand and pointing to the door whereby I had entered. "These private rooms. What you doing here?"

Her words, despite her broken English, served to recall to me the fact that I was, beyond doubt, a trespasser! By what right did I presume to force my way into other people's apartments?

"There is someone in there whom I must see," I said, realizing, however, that my chance of doing so was poor.

"You see nobody," she snapped back uncompromisingly. "You go away!"

She took a step towards me, continuing to point to the door. Where had I previously encountered the glance of those splendid, savage eyes?

So engaged was I with this taunting, partial memory, and so sure, if the woman would but uncover her face, of instantly recognizing her, that still I hesitated. Whereupon, glancing rapidly over her shoulder into whatever place lay beyond the curtained doorway, she suddenly stepped back and vanished, drawing the curtains to with an angry jerk.

I heard her retiring footsteps; then came a loud bang. If her object in intercepting me had been to cover the slow retreat of someone she had succeeded.

Recognizing that I had cut a truly sorry figure in the encounter, I retraced my steps.

By what route I ultimately regained the main staircase I have no idea; for my mind was busy with that taunting memory of the two dark eyes looking out from the folds of the green embroidered shawl. Where, and when, had I met their glance before?

To that problem I sought an answer in vain.

The message despatched to New Scotland Yard, I found M. Samarkan, long famous as a *mâitre d'hôtel* in Cairo, and now host of London's newest and most palatial *khan*. Portly, and wearing a gray imperial, M. Samarkan had the manners of a courtier, and the smile of a true Greek.

I told him what was necessary, and no more, desiring him to go to suite 14a without delay and also without arousing unnecessary attention. I dropped no hint of foul play, but M. Samarkan expressed profound (and professional) regret that so distinguished, though unprofitable, a patron should have selected the New Louvre, thus early in its history, as the terminus of his career.

"By the way," I said, "have you Oriental guests with you, at the moment?"

"No, monsieur," he assured me.

"Not a certain Oriental lady?" I persisted.

M. Samarkan slowly shook his head.

"Possibly monsieur has seen one of the *ayahs*? There are several Anglo-Indian families resident in the New Louvre at present."

An *ayah*? It was just possible, of course. Yet ...

CHAPTER FOUR

THE FLOWER OF SILENCE

"We are dealing now," said Nayland Smith, pacing restlessly up and down our sitting-room, "not, as of old, with Dr. Fu-Manchu, but with an entirely unknown quantity—the Si-Fan."

"For Heaven's sake!" I cried, "what is the Si-Fan?"

"The greatest mystery of the mysterious East, Petrie. Think. You know, as I know, that a malignant being, Dr. Fu-Manchu, was for some time in England, engaged in 'paving the way' (I believe those words were my own) for nothing less than a giant Yellow Empire. That dream is what millions of Europeans and Americans term 'the Yellow Peril'! Very good. Such an empire needs must have—"

"An emperor!"

Nayland Smith stopped his restless pacing immediately in front of me.

"Why not an *empress*, Petrie!" he rapped.

His words were something of a verbal thunderbolt; I found myself at loss for any suitable reply.

"You will perhaps remind me," he continued rapidly, "of the lowly place held by women in the East. I can cite notable exceptions, ancient and modern. In fact, a moment's consideration by a hypothetical body of Eastern dynast-makers not of an emperor but of an empress. Finally, there is a persistent tradition throughout the Far East that such a woman will one day rule over the known peoples. I was assured some years ago, by a very learned pundit, that a princess of incalculably ancient lineage, residing in some secret monastery in Tartary or Tibet, was to be the future empress of the world. I believe this tradition, or the extensive group who seek to keep it alive and potent, to be what is called the Si-Fan!"

I was past greater amazement; but—

"This lady can be no longer young, then?" I asked.

"On the contrary, Petrie, she remains always young and beautiful by means of a continuous series of reincarnations; also she thus conserves the collated wisdom of many ages. In short, she is the archetype of Lamaism. The real secret of Lama celibacy is the existence of this immaculate ruler, of whom the Grand Lama is merely a high priest. She has, as attendants, maidens of good family, selected for their personal charms, and rendered dumb in order that they may never report what they see and hear."

"Smith!" I cried, "this is utterly incredible!"

"Her body slaves are not only mute, but blind; for it is death to look upon her beauty unveiled."

I stood up impatiently.

"You are amusing yourself," I said.

Nayland Smith clapped his hands upon my shoulders, in his own impulsive fashion, and looked earnestly into my eyes.

"Forgive me, old man," he said, "if I have related all these fantastic particulars as though I gave them credence. Much of this is legendary, I know, some of it mere superstition, but—I am serious now, Petrie—*part of it is true*."

I stared at the square-cut, sun-tanned face; and no trace of a smile lurked about that grim mouth. "Such a woman may actually exist, Petrie, only in legend; but, nevertheless, she forms the head center of that giant conspiracy in which the activities of Dr. Fu-Manchu were merely a part. Hale blundered on to this stupendous business; and from what I have gathered from Beeton and what I have seen for myself, it is evident that in yonder coffer"—he pointed to the brass chest standing hard by—"Hale got hold of something indispensable to the success of this vast Yellow conspiracy. That he was followed here, to the very hotel, by agents of this mystic Unknown is evident. But," he added grimly, "they have failed in their object!"

A thousand outrageous possibilities fought for precedence in my mind.

"Smith!" I cried, "the half-caste woman whom I saw in the hotel …"

Nayland Smith shrugged his shoulders.

"Probably, as M. Samarkan suggests, an *ayah*!" he said; but there was an odd note in his voice and an odd look in his eyes.

"Then again, I am almost certain that Hale's warning concerning 'the man with the limp' was no empty one. Shall you open the brass chest?"

"At present, decidedly *no*. Hale's fate renders his warning one that I dare not neglect. For I was with him when he died; and they cannot know how much *I* know. How did he die? How did he die? How was the Flower of Silence introduced into his closely guarded room?"

"The Flower of Silence?"

Smith laughed shortly and unmirthfully.

"I was once sent for," he said, "during the time that I was stationed in Upper Burma, to see a stranger—a sort of itinerant Buddhist priest, so I understood, who had desired to communicate some message to me personally. He was dying—in a dirty hut on the outskirts of Manipur, up in the hills. When I arrived I say at a glance that the man was a Tibetan monk. He must have crossed the river and come down through Assam; but the nature of his message I never knew. He had lost the power of speech! He was gurgling, inarticulate, just like poor Hale. A few moments after my arrival he breathed his last. The fellow who had guided me to the place bent over him—I shall always remember the scene—then fell back as though he had stepped upon an adder.

"'He holds the Flower Silence in his hand!' he cried—'the Si-Fan! the Si-Fan!'—and bolted from the hut."

"When I went to examine the dead man, sure enough he held in one hand a little crumpled spray of flowers. I did not touch it with my fingers naturally, but I managed to loop a piece of twine around the stem, and by that means I gingerly removed the flowers and carried them to an orchid-hunter of my acquaintance who chanced to be visiting Manipur.

"Grahame—that was my orchid man's name—pronounced the specimen to be an unclassified species of *jatropha;* belonging to the *Curcas* family. He discovered a sort of hollow thorn, almost like a fang, amongst the blooms, but was unable to surmise the nature of its functions. He extracted enough of a certain fixed oil from the flowers, however, to have poisoned the pair of us!"

"Probably the breaking of a bloom ..."

"Ejects some of this acrid oil through the thorn? Practically the uncanny thing stings when it is hurt? That is my own idea, Petrie. And I can understand how these Eastern fanatics accept their sentence—silence and death—when they have deserved it, at the hands of their mysterious organization, and commit this novel form of *hara-kiri*. But I shall not sleep soundly with that brass coffer in my possession until I know by what means Sir Gregory was induced to touch a Flower of Silence, and by what means it was placed in his room!"

"But, Smith, why did you direct me tonight to repeat the words, 'Sâkya Mûni'?"

Smith smiled in a very grim fashion.

"It was after the episode I have just related that I made the acquaintance of that pundit, some of whose statements I have already quoted for your enlightenment. He admitted that the Flower of Silence was an instrument frequently employed by a certain group, adding that, according to some authorities, one who had touched the flower might escape death by immediately pronouncing the sacred name of Buddha. He was no fanatic himself, however, and, marking my incredulity, he explained that the truth was this;—

"No one whose powers of speech were imperfect could possibly pronounce correctly the words 'Sâkya Mûni.' Therefore, since the first effects of this damnable thing is instantly to tie the tongue, the uttering of the sacred name of Buddha becomes practically a test whereby the victim may learn whether the venom has entered his system or not!"

I repressed a shudder. An atmosphere of horror seemed to be enveloping us, foglike.

"Smith," I said slowly, "we must be on our guard," for at last I had run to earth that elusive memory. "Unless I am strangely mistaken, the 'man' who so mysteriously entered Hale's room and the supposed *ayah* whom I met downstairs are one and the same. Two, at least, of the Yellow group are actually here in the New Louvre!"

The light of the shaded lamp shone down upon the brass coffer on the table beside me. The fog seemed to have cleared from the room somewhat, but since in the midnight stillness I could detect the muffled sounds of sirens from the river and the reports of fog signals from the railways, I concluded that the night was not yet wholly clear of the choking mist. In accordance with a pre-arranged scheme we had decided to guard "the key of India" (whatever it might be) turn and turn about through the night. In a word—we feared to sleep unguarded. Now my watch informed me that four o'clock approached, at which hour I was to arouse Smith and retire to sleep to my own bedroom.

Nothing had disturbed my vigil—that is, nothing definite. True once, about half an hour earlier, I had thought I heard the dragging and tapping sound from somewhere up above me; but since the corridor overhead was unfinished and none of the rooms opening upon it yet habitable, I concluded that I had been mistaken. The stairway at the end of our corridor, which communicated with that above, was still blocked with bags of cement and slabs of marble, in fact.

Faintly to my ears came the booming of London's clocks, beating out the hour of four. But still I sat beside the mysterious coffer, indisposed to awaken my friend any sooner than was necessary, particularly since I felt in no way sleepy myself.

I was to learn a lesson that night: the lesson of strict adherence to a compact. I had arranged to awaken Nayland Smith at four; and because I dallied, determined to finish my pipe ere entering his bedroom, almost it happened that Fate placed it beyond my power ever to awaken him again.

At ten minutes past four, amid a stillness so intense that the creaking of my slippers seemed a loud disturbance, I crossed the room and pushed open the door of Smith's bedroom. It was in darkness, but as I entered I depressed the switch immediately inside the door, lighting the lamp which swung form the center of the ceiling.

Glancing towards the bed, I immediately perceived that there was something different in its aspect, but at first I found this difference difficult to define. I stood for a moment in doubt. Then I realized the nature of the change which had taken place.

A lamp hung above the bed, attached to a movable fitting, which enabled it to be raised or lowered at the pleasure of the occupant. When Smith had retired he was in no reading mood, and he had not even lighted the reading-lamp, but had left it pushed high up against the ceiling.

It was the position of this lamp which had changed. For now it swung so low over the pillow that the silken fringe of the shade almost touched my friend's face as he lay soundly asleep with one lean brown hand outstretched upon the coverlet.

I stood in the doorway staring, mystified, at this phenomenon; I might have stood there without intervening, until intervention had been too late, were it not that, glancing upward toward the wooden block from which ordinarily the pendant hung, I perceived that no block was visible, but only a round, black cavity from which the white flex supporting the lamp swung out.

Then, uttering a hoarse cry which rose unbidden to my lips, I sprang wildly across the room … for now I had seen something else!

Attached to one of the four silken tassels which ornamented the lampshade, so as almost to rest upon the cheek of the sleeping man, was a little corymb of bloom … the *Flower of Silence*!

Grasping the shade with my left hand I seized the flex with my right, and as Smith sprang upright in bed, eyes wildly glaring, I wrenched with all my might. Upward my gaze was set; and I glimpsed a yellow hand, with long, pointed finger nails. There came a loud resounding snap; an electric spark spat venomously from the circular opening above the bed; and, with the cord and lamp still fast in my grip, I went rolling across the carpet—as the other lamp became instantly extinguished.

Dimly I perceived Smith, arrayed in pyjamas, jumping out upon the opposite side of the bed.

"Petrie, Petrie!" he cried, "where are you? what has happened?"

A laugh, little short of hysterical, escaped me. I gathered myself up and made for the lighted sitting-room.

"Quick, Smith!" I said—but I did not recognize my own voice. "Quick—come out of that room."

I crossed to the settee, and shaking in every limb, sank down upon it. Nayland Smith, still wild-eyed, and his face a mask of bewilderment, came out of the bedroom and stood watching me.

"For God's sake what has happened, Petrie?" he demanded, and began clutching at the lobe of his left ear and looking all about the room dazedly.

"The Flower of Silence!" I said; "someone has been at work in the top corridor.... Heaven knows when, for since we engaged these rooms we have not been much away from them ... the same device as in the case of poor Hale.... You would have tried to brush the thing away ..."

A light of understanding began to dawn in my friend's eyes. He drew himself stiffly upright, and in a loud, harsh voice uttered the words: "Sâkya Mûni"—and again: "Sâkya Mûni."

"Thank God!" I said shakily. "I was not too late."

Nayland Smith, with much rattling of glass, poured out two stiff pegs from the decanter. Then—

"Ssh! what's that?" he whispered.

He stood, tense, listening, his head cast slightly to one side.

A very faint sound of shuffling and tapping was perceptible, coming, as I thought, from the incomplete stairway communicating with the upper corridor.

"The man with the limp!" whispered Smith.

He bounded to the door and actually had one hand upon the bolt, when he turned, and fixed his gaze upon the brass box.

"No!" he snapped; "there are occasions when prudence should rule. Neither of us must leave these rooms tonight!"

CHAPTER FIVE

JOHN KI'S

"What is the meaning of Si-Fan?" asked Detective-Sergeant Fletcher.

He stood looking from the window at the prospect below; at the trees bordering the winding embankment; at the ancient monolith which for unnumbered ages had looked across desert sands to the Nile, and now looked down upon another river of many mysteries. The view seemed to absorb his attention. He spoke without turning his head.

Nayland Smith laughed shortly.

"The Si-Fan are the natives of Eastern Tibet," he replied.

"But the term has some other significance, sir?" said the detective; his words were more of an assertion than a query.

"It has," replied my friend grimly. "I believe it to be the name, or perhaps the sigil, of an extensive secret society with branches stretching out into every corner of the Orient."

We were silent for a while. Inspector Weymouth, who sat in a chair near the window, glanced appreciatively at the back of his subordinate, who still stood looking out. Detective-Sergeant Fletcher was one of Scotland Yard's coming men. He had information of the first importance to communicate, and Nayland Smith had delayed his departure upon an urgent errand in order to meet him.

"Your case to date, Mr. Smith," continued Fletcher, remaining with hands locked behind him, staring from the window, "reads something like this, I believe: A brass box, locked, contents unknown, has come into your possession. It stands now upon the table there. It was brought from Tibet by a man who evidently thought that it had something to do with the Si-Fan. He is dead, possibly by the agency of members of this group. No arrests have been made. You know that there are people here in London who are anxious to regain the box. You have theories respecting the identity of some of them, but there are practically no facts."

Nayland Smith nodded his head.

"Exactly!" he snapped.

"Inspector Weymouth, here," continued Fletcher, "has put me in possession of such facts as are known to him, and I believe that I have had the good fortune to chance upon a valuable one."

"You interest me, Sergeant Fletcher," said Smith. "What is the nature of this clue?"

"I will tell you," replied the other, and turned briskly upon his heel to face us.

He had a dark, clean-shaven face, rather sallow complexion, and deep-set, searching eyes. There was decision in the square, cleft chin and strong character in the cleanly chiseled features. His manner was alert.

"I have specialized in Chinese crime," he said; "much of my time is spent amongst our Asiatic visitors. I am fairly familiar with the Easterns who use the port of London, and I have a number of useful acquaintances among them."

Nayland Smith nodded. Beyond doubt Detective-Sergeant Fletcher knew his business.

"To my lasting regret," Fletcher continued, "I never met the late Dr. Fu-Manchu. I understand, sir, that you believe him to have been a high official of this dangerous society? However, I think we may get in touch with some other notabilities; for instance, I'm told that one of the people you're looking for has been described as 'the man with the limp'?"

Smith, who had been about to relight his pipe, dropped the match on the carpet and set his foot upon it. His eyes shone like steel.

"'The man with the limp,'" he said, and slowly rose to his feet—"what do you know of the man with the limp?"

Fletcher's face flushed slightly; his words had proved more dramatic than he had anticipated.

"There's a place down Shadwell way," he replied, "of which, no doubt, you will have heard; it has no official title, but it is known to habitués as the Joy-Shop ."

Inspector Weymouth stood up, his burly figure towering over that of his slighter confrère.

"I don't think you know John Ki's, Mr. Smith," he said. "We keep all those places pretty well patrolled, and until this present business cropped up, John's establishment had never given us any trouble."

"What is this Joy-Shop?" I asked.

"A resort of shady characters, mostly Asiatics," replied Weymouth. "It's a gambling-house, an unlicensed drinking-shop, and even worse—but it's more use to us open than it would be shut."

"It is one of my regular jobs to keep an eye on the visitors to the Joy-Shop," continued Fletcher. "I have many acquaintances who use the place. Needless to add, they don't know my real business! Well, lately several of them have asked me if I know who the man is that hobbles about the place with two sticks. Everybody seems to have heard him, but no one has seen him."

Nayland Smith began to pace the floor restlessly.

"I have heard him myself," added Fletcher, "but never managed to get so much as a glimpse of him. When I learnt about this Si-Fan mystery, I realized that he might very possibly be the man for whom you're looking—and a golden opportunity has cropped up for you to visit the Joy-Shop, and, if our luck remains in, to get a peep behind the scenes."

"I am all attention," snapped Smith.

"A woman called Zarmi has recently put in an appearance at the Joy-Shop. Roughly speaking, she turned up at about the same time as the unseen man with the limp...."

Nayland Smith's eyes were blazing with suppressed excitement; he was pacing quickly up and down the floor, tugging at the lobe of his left ear.

"She is—different in some way from any other woman I have ever seen in the place. She's a Eurasian and good-looking, after a tigerish fashion. I have done my best"—he smiled slightly—"to get in her good books, and up to a point I've succeeded. I was there last night, and Zarmi asked me if I knew what she called a 'strong feller.'

"'These,' she informed me, contemptuously referring to the rest of the company, 'are poor weak Johnnies!'

"I had nothing definite in view at the time, for I had not then heard about your return to London, but I thought it might lead to something anyway, so I promised to bring a friend along tonight. I don't know what we're wanted to do, but ..."

"Count on me!" snapped Smith. "I will leave all details to you and to Weymouth, and I will be at New Scotland Yard this evening in time to adopt a suitable disguise. Petrie"—he turned impetuously to me—"I fear I shall have to go without you; but I shall be in safe company, as you see, and doubtless Weymouth can find you a part in his portion of the evening's program."

He glanced at his watch.

"Ah! I must be off. If you will oblige me, Petrie, by putting the brass box into my smaller portmanteau, whilst I slip my coat on, perhaps Weymouth, on his way out, will be good enough to order a taxi. I shall venture to breathe again once our unpleasant charge is safely deposited in the bank vaults!"

CHAPTER SIX

THE SI-FAN MOVE

A slight drizzling rain was falling as Smith entered the cab which the hall-porter had summoned. The brown bag in his hand contained the brass box which actually was responsible for our presence in London. The last glimpse I had of him through the glass of the closed window showed him striking a match to light his pipe—which he rarely allowed to grow cool.

Oppressed with an unaccountable weariness of spirit, I stood within the lobby looking out upon the grayness of London in November. A slight mental effort was sufficient to blot out that drab prospect and to conjure up before my mind's eye a balcony overlooking the Nile—a glimpse of dusty palms, a white wall overgrown with purple blossoms, and above all the dazzling vault of Egypt. Upon the balcony my imagination painted a figure, limning it with loving details, the figure of Kâramaneh; and I thought that her glorious eyes would be sorrowful and her lips perhaps a little tremulous, as, her arms resting upon the rail of the balcony, she looked out across the smiling river to the domes and minarets of Cairo—and beyond, into the hazy distance; seeing me in dreary, rain-swept London, as I saw her, at Gezîra beneath the cloudless sky of Egypt.

From these tender but mournful reflections I aroused myself, almost angrily, and set off through the muddy streets towards Charing Cross; for I was availing myself of the opportunity to call upon Dr. Murray, who had purchased my small suburban practice when (finally, as I thought at the time) I had left London.

This matter occupied me for the greater part of the afternoon, and I returned to the New Louvre Hotel shortly after five, and seeing no one in the lobby whom I knew, proceeded immediately to our apartment. Nayland Smith was not there, and having made some changes in my attire I descended again and inquired if he had left any message for me.

The booking-clerk informed me that Smith had not returned; therefore I resigned myself to wait. I purchased an evening paper and settled down in the lounge where I had an uninterrupted view of the entrance doors. The dinner hour approached, but still my friend failed to put in an appearance. Becoming impatient, I entered a call-box and rang up Inspector Weymouth.

Smith had not been to Scotland Yard, nor had they received any message from him. Perhaps it would appear that there was little cause for alarm in this, but I, familiar with my friend's punctual and exact habits, became strangely uneasy. I did not wish to make myself ridiculous, but growing restlessness impelled me to institute inquiries regarding the cabman who had driven my friend. The result of these was to increase rather than to allay my fears.

The man was a stranger to the hall-porter, and he was not one of the taximen who habitually stood upon the neighboring rank; no one seemed to have noticed the number of the cab.

And now my mind began to play with strange doubts and fears.

The driver, I recollected, had been a small, dark man, possessing remarkably well-cut olive-hued features. Had he not worn spectacles he would indeed have been handsome, in an effeminate fashion.

I was almost certain, by this time, that he had not been an Englishman; I was almost certain that some catastrophe had befallen Smith. Our ceaseless vigilance had been momentarily relaxed—and this was the result!

At some large bank branches there is a resident messenger. Even granting that such was the case in the present instance, I doubted if the man could help me, unless, as was possible, he chanced to be familiar with my friend's appearance, and had actually seen him there that day. I determined, at any rate, to make the attempt; re-entering the call-box, I asked for the bank's number.

There proved to be a resident messenger, who, after a time, replied to my call. He knew Nayland Smith very well by sight, and as he had been on duty in the public office of the bank at the time that Smith should have arrived, he assured me that my friend had not been there that day!

"Besides, sir," he said, "you say he came to deposit valuables of some kind here?"

"Yes, yes!" I cried eagerly.

"I take all such things down on the lift to the vaults at night, sir, under the supervision of the assistant manager—and I can assure you that nothing of the kind has been left with us today."

I stepped out of the call-box unsteadily. Indeed, I clutched at the door for support.

"What is the meaning of Si-Fan?" Detective-Sergeant Fletcher had asked that morning. None of us could answer him; none of us knew. With a haze seeming to dance between my eyes and the active life in the lobby before me, I realized that the Si-Fan—that unseen, sinister power—had reached out and plucked my friend from the very midst of this noisy life about me, into its own mysterious, deathly silence.

CHAPTER SEVEN

CHINATOWN

"It's no easy matter," said Inspector Weymouth, "to patrol the vicinity of John Ki's Joy-Shop without their getting wind of it. The entrance, as you'll see, is a long, narrow rat-hole of a street running at right angles to the Thames. There's no point, so far as I know, from which the yard can be overlooked; and the back is on a narrow cutting belonging to a disused mill."

I paid little attention to his words. Disguised beyond all chance of recognition even by one intimate with my appearance, I was all impatience to set out. I had taken Smith's place in the night's program; for, every possible source of information having been tapped in vain, I now hoped against hope that some clue to the fate of my poor friend might be obtained at the Chinese den which he had designed to visit with Fletcher.

The latter, who presented a strange picture in his make-up as a sort of half-caste sailor, stared doubtfully at the inspector; then—

"The River Police cutter," he said, "can drop down on the tide and lie off under the Surrey bank. There's a vacant wharf facing the end of the street and we can slip through and show a light there, to let you know we've arrived. You reply in the same way. If there's any trouble, I shall blaze away with this"—he showed the butt of a Service revolver protruding from his hip pocket—"and you can be ashore in no time."

The plan had one thing to commend it, viz., that no one could devise another. Therefore it was adopted, and five minutes later a taxi-cab swung out of the Yard containing Inspector Weymouth and two ruffianly looking companions—myself and Fletcher.

Any zest with which, at another time, I might have entered upon such an expedition, was absent now. I bore with me a gnawing anxiety and sorrow that precluded all conversation on my part, save monosyllabic replies, to questions that I comprehended but vaguely.

At the River Police Depot we found Inspector Ryman, an old acquaintance, awaiting us. Weymouth had telephoned from Scotland Yard.

"I've got a motor-boat at the breakwater," said Ryman, nodding to Fletcher, and staring hard at me.

Weymouth laughed shortly.

"Evidently you don't recognize Dr. Petrie!" he said.

"Eh!" cried Ryman—"Dr. Petrie! why, good heavens, Doctor, I should never have known you in a month of bank holidays! What's afoot, then?"—and he turned to Weymouth, eyebrows raised interrogatively.

"It's the Fu-Manchu business again, Ryman."

"Fu-Manchu! But I thought the Fu-Manchu case was off the books long ago? It was always a mystery to me; never a word in the papers; and we as much in the dark as everybody else—but didn't I hear that the Chinaman, Fu-Manchu, was dead?"

Weymouth nodded.

"Some of his friends seem to be very much alive, though," he said. "It appears that Fu-Manchu, for all his genius—and there's no denying he was a genius, Ryman—was only the agent of somebody altogether bigger."

Ryman whistled softly.

"Has the real head of affairs arrived, then?"

"We find we are up against what is known as the Si-Fan."

At that it came to the inevitable, unanswerable question.

"What is the Si-Fan?"

I laughed, but my laughter was not mirthful. Inspector Weymouth shook his head.

"Perhaps Mr. Nayland Smith could tell you that," he replied; "for the Si-Fan got him today!"

"Got him!" cried Ryman.

"Absolutely! He's vanished! And Fletcher here has found out that John Ki's place is in some way connected with this business."

I interrupted—impatiently, I fear.

"Then let us set out, Inspector," I said, "for it seems to me that we are wasting precious time—and you know what that may mean." I turned to Fletcher. "Where is this place situated, exactly? How do we proceed?"

"The cab can take us part of the way," he replied, "and we shall have to walk the rest. Patrons of John's don't turn up in taxis, as a rule!"

"Then let us be off," I said, and made for the door.

"Don't forget the signal!" Weymouth cried after me, "and don't venture into the place until you've received our reply…."

But I was already outside, Fletcher following; and a moment later we were both in the cab and off into a maze of tortuous streets toward John Ki's Joy-Shop.

With the coming of nightfall the rain had ceased, but the sky remained heavily overcast and the air was filled with clammy mist. It was a night to arouse longings for Southern skies; and when, discharging the cabman, we set out afoot along a muddy and ill-lighted thoroughfare bordered on either side by high brick walls, their monotony occasionally broken by gateways, I felt that the load of depression which had settled upon my shoulders must ere long bear me down.

Sounds of shunting upon some railway siding came to my ears; train whistles and fog signals hooted and boomed. River sounds there were, too, for we were close beside the Thames, that gray old stream which has borne upon its bier many a poor victim of underground London. The sky glowed sullenly red above.

"There's the Joy-Shop, along on the left," said Fletcher, breaking in upon my reflections. "You'll notice a faint light; it's shining out through the open door. Then, here is the wharf."

He began fumbling with the fastenings of a dilapidated gateway beside which we were standing; and a moment later—

"All right—slip through," he said.

I followed him through the narrow gap which the ruinous state of the gates had enabled him to force, and found myself looking under a low arch, with the Thames beyond, and a few hazy lights coming and going on the opposite bank.

"Go steady!" warned Fletcher. "It's only a few paces to the edge of the wharf."

I heard him taking a box of matches from his pocket.

"Here is my electric lamp," I said. "It will serve the purpose better."

"Good," muttered my companion. "Show a light down here, so that we can find our way."

With the aid of the lamp we found our way out on to the rotting timbers of the crazy structure. The mist hung denser over the river, but through it, as through a dirty gauze curtain, it was possible to discern some of the greater lights on the opposite shore. These, without exception, however, showed high up upon the fog curtain; along the water level lay a belt of darkness.

"Let me give them the signal," said Fletcher, shivering slightly and taking the lamp from my hand.

He flashed the light two or three times. Then we both stood watching the belt of darkness that followed the Surrey shore. The tide lapped upon the timbers supporting the wharf and little whispers and gurgling sounds stole up from beneath our feet. Once there was a faint splash from somewhere below and behind us.

"There goes a rat," said Fletcher vaguely, and without taking his gaze from the darkness under the distant shore. "It's gone into the cutting at the back of John Ki's."

He ceased speaking and flashed the lamp again several times. Then, all at once out of the murky darkness into which we were peering, looked a little eye of light—once, twice, thrice it winked at us from low down upon the oily water; then was gone.

"It's Weymouth with the cutter," said Fletcher; "they are ready … now for Jon Ki's."

We stumbled back up the slight acclivity beneath the archway to the street, leaving the ruinous gates as we had found them. Into the uninviting little alley immediately opposite we plunged, and where the faint yellow luminance showed upon the muddy path before us, Fletcher paused a moment, whispering to me warningly.

"Don't speak if you can help it," he said; "if you do, mumble any old jargon in any language you like, and throw in plenty of cursing!"

He grasped me by the arm, and I found myself crossing the threshold of the Joy-Shop—I found myself in a meanly furnished room no more than twelve feet square and very low ceiled, smelling strongly of paraffin oil. The few items of furniture which it contained were but dimly discernible in the light of a common tin lamp which stood upon a packing-case at the head of what looked like cellar steps.

Abruptly, I pulled up; for this stuffy little den did not correspond with pre-conceived ideas of the place for which we were bound. I was about to speak when Fletcher nipped my arm—and out from the shadows behind the packing-case a little bent figure arose!

I started violently, for I had had no idea that another was in the room. The apparition proved to be a Chinaman, and judging from what I could see of him, a very old Chinaman, his bent figure attired in a blue smock. His eyes were almost invisible amidst an intricate map of wrinkles which covered his yellow face.

"Evening, John," said Fletcher—and, pulling me with him, he made for the head of the steps.

As I came abreast of the packing-case, the Chinaman lifted the lamp and directed its light fully upon my face.

Great as was the faith which I reposed in my make-up, a doubt and a tremor disturbed me now, as I found myself thus scrutinized by those cunning old eyes looking out from the mask-like, apish face. For the first time the Chinaman spoke.

"You blinger fliend, Charlie?" he squeaked in a thin, piping voice.

"Him play piecee card," replied Fletcher briefly. "Good fellow, plenty much money."

He descended the steps, still holding my arm, and I perforce followed him. Apparently John's scrutiny and Fletcher's explanation respecting me, together had proved satisfactory; for the lamp was replaced upon the lid of the packing-case, and the little bent figure dropped down again into the shadows from which it had emerged.

"Allee lightee," I heard faintly as I stumbled downward in the wake of Fletcher.

I had expected to find myself in a cellar, but instead discovered that we were in a small square court with the mist of the night about us again. On a doorstep facing us stood a duplicate of the lamp upon the box upstairs. Evidently this was designed to indicate the portals of the Joy-Shop, for Fletcher pushed open the door, whose threshold accommodated the lamp, and the light of the place beyond shone out into our faces. We entered and my companion closed the door behind us.

Before me I perceived a long low room lighted by flaming gas-burners, the jets hissing and spluttering in the draught from the door, for they were entirely innocent of shades or mantles. Wooden tables, their surfaces stained with the marks of countless wet glasses, were ranged about the place, café fashion; and many of these tables accommodated groups, of nondescript nationality for the most part. One or two there were in a distant corner who were unmistakably Chinamen; but my slight acquaintance with the races of the East did not enable me to classify the greater number of those whom I now saw about me. There were several unattractive-looking women present.

Fletcher walked up the center of the place, exchanging nods of recognition with two hang-dog poker-players, and I was pleased to note that our advent had apparently failed to attract the slightest attention. Through an opening on the right-hand side of the room, near the top, I looked into a smaller apartment, occupied exclusively by Chinese. They were playing some kind of roulette and another game which seemed wholly to absorb their interest. I ventured no more than a glance, then passed on with my companion.

"*Fan-tan!*" he whispered in my ear.

Other forms of gambling were in progress at some of the tables; and now Fletcher silently drew my attention to yet a third dimly lighted apartment—this opening out from the left-hand corner of the principal room. The atmosphere of the latter was sufficiently abominable; indeed, the stench was appalling; but a wave of choking vapor met me as I paused for a moment at the threshold of this inner sanctuary. I formed but the vaguest impression of its interior; the smell was sufficient. This annex was evidently reserved for opium-smokers.

Fletcher sat down at a small table near by, and I took a common wooden chair which he thrust forward with his foot. I was looking around at the sordid scene, filled with a bitter sense of my own impotency to aid my missing friend, when that occurred which set my heart beating wildly at once with hope and excitement. Fletcher must have seen something of this in my attitude, for—

"Don't forget what I told you," he whispered. "Be cautious!—be very cautious! …"

CHAPTER EIGHT

ZARMI OF THE JOY-SHOP

Down the center of the room came a girl carrying the only ornamental object which thus far I had seen in the Joy-Shop: a large Oriental brass tray. She was a figure which must have formed a center of interest in any place, trebly so, then, in such a place as this. Her costume consisted in a series of incongruities, whilst the entire effect was barbaric and by no means unpicturesque. She wore high-heeled red slippers, and, as her short gauzy skirt rendered amply evident, black silk stockings. A brilliantly colored Oriental scarf was wound around her waist and knotted in front, its tasseled ends swinging girdle fashion. A sort of chemise—like the *'anteree* of Egyptian women—completed her costume, if I except a number of barbaric ornaments, some of them of silver, with which her hands and arms were bedecked.

But strange as was the girl's attire, it was to her face that my gaze was drawn irresistibly. Evidently, like most of those around us, she was some kind of half-caste; but, unlike them, she was wickedly handsome. I use the adverb *wickedly* with deliberation; for the pallidly dusky, oval face, with the full red lips, between which rested a large yellow cigarette, and the half-closed almond-shaped eyes, possessed a beauty which might have appealed to an artist of one of the modern perverted schools, but which filled me less with admiration than horror. For I *knew* her—I recognized her, from a past, brief meeting; I knew her, beyond all possibility of doubt, to be one of the Si-Fan group!

This strange creature, tossing back her jet-black, frizzy hair, which was entirely innocent of any binding or ornament, advanced along the room towards us, making unhesitatingly for our table, and carrying her lithe body with the grace of a *Ghâzeeyeh*.

I glanced at Fletcher across the table.

"Zarmi!" he whispered.

Again I raised my eyes to the face which now was close to mine, and became aware that I was trembling with excitement....

Heavens! why did enlightenment come too late! Either I was the victim of an odd delusion, or Zarmi had been the driver of the cab in which Nayland Smith had left the New Louvre Hotel!

Zarmi placed the brass tray upon the table and bent down, resting her elbows upon it, her hands upturned and her chin nestling in her palms. The smoke from the cigarette, now held in her fingers, mingled with her disheveled hair. She looked fully into my face, a long, searching look; then her lips parted in the slow, voluptuous smile of the Orient. Without moving her head she turned the wonderful eyes (rendered doubly luminous by the *kohl* with which her lashes and lids were darkened) upon Fletcher.

"What you and your strong friend drinking?" she said softly.

Her voice possessed a faint husky note which betrayed her Eastern parentage, yet it had in it the siren lure which is the ancient heritage of the Eastern woman—a heritage more ancient than the tribe of the *Ghâzeeyeh*, to one of whom I had mentally likened Zarmi.

"Same thing," replied Fletcher promptly; and raising his hand, he idly toyed with a huge gold earring which she wore.

Still resting her elbows upon the table and bending down between us, Zarmi turned her slumbering, half-closed black eyes again upon me, then slowly, languishingly, upon Fletcher. She replaced the yellow cigarette between her lips. He continued to toy with the earring.

Suddenly the girl sprang upright, and from its hiding-place within the silken scarf, plucked out a Malay *krîs* with a richly jeweled hilt. Her eyes now widely opened and blazing, she struck at my companion!

I half rose from my chair, stifling a cry of horror; but Fletcher, regarding her fixedly, never moved … and Zarmi stayed her hand just as the point of the dagger had reached his throat!

"You see," she whispered softly but intensely, "how soon I can kill you."

Ere I had overcome the amazement and horror with which her action had filled me, she had suddenly clutched me by the shoulder, and, turning from Fletcher, had the point of the *krîs* at *my* throat!

"You, too!" she whispered, "you too!"

Lower and lower she bent, the needle point of the weapon pricking my skin, until her beautiful, evil face almost touched mine. Then, miraculously, the fire died out of her eyes; they half closed again and became languishing, luresome *Ghâzeeyeh* eyes. She laughed softly, wickedly, and puffed cigarette smoke into my face.

Thrusting her dagger into her waist-belt, and snatching up the brass tray, she swayed down the room, chanting some barbaric song in her husky Eastern voice.

I inhaled deeply and glanced across at my companion. Beneath the make-up with which I had stained my skin, I knew that I had grown more than a little pale.

"Fletcher!" I whispered, "we are on the eve of a great discovery—that girl …"

I broke off, and clutching the table with both hands, sat listening intently. From the room behind me, the opium-room, whose entrance was less than two paces from where we sat, came a sound of dragging and tapping! Slowly, cautiously, I began to turn my head; when a sudden outburst of simian chattering from the *fan-tan* players drowned that other sinister sound.

"You heard it, Doctor!" hissed Fletcher.

"The man with the limp!" I said hoarsely; "he is in there! Fletcher! I am utterly confused. I believe this place to hold the key to the whole mystery, I believe …"

Fletcher gave me a warning glance—and, turning anew, I saw Zarmi approaching with her sinuous gait, carrying two glasses and jug upon the ornate tray. These she set down upon the table; then stood spinning the salver cleverly upon the point of her index finger and watching us through half-closed eyes.

My companion took out some loose coins, but the girl thrust the proffered payment aside with her disengaged hand, the salver still whirling upon the upraised finger of the other.

"Presently you pay for drink," she said. "You do something for me—eh?"

"Yep," replied Fletcher nonchalantly, watering the rum in the tumblers. "What time?"

"Presently I tell you. You stay here. This one a strong feller?"—indicating myself.

"Sure," drawled Fletcher; "strong as a mule he is."

"All right. I give him one little kiss if he good boy!"

Tossing the tray in the air she caught it, rested its edge upon her hip, turned, and walked away down the room, puffing her cigarette.

"Listen," I said, bending across the table, "it was Zarmi who drove the cab that came for Nayland Smith today!"

"My God!" whispered Fletcher, "then it was nothing less than the hand of Providence that brought us here tonight. Yes! I know how you feel, Doctor!—but we must play our cards as they're dealt to us. We must wait—wait."

Out from the den of the opium-smokers came Zarmi, one hand resting upon her hip and the other uplifted, a smoldering yellow cigarette held between the first and second fingers. With a movement of her eyes she summoned us to join her, then turned and disappeared again through the low doorway.

The time for action was arrived—we were to see behind the scenes of the Joy-Shop! Our chance to revenge poor Smith even if we could not save him. I became conscious of an inward and suppressed excitement; surreptitiously I felt the hilt of the Browning pistol in my pocket. The shadow of the dead Fu-Manchu seemed to be upon me. God! how I loathed and feared that memory!

"We can make no plans," I whispered to Fletcher, as together we rose from the table; "we must be guided by circumstance."

In order to enter the little room laden with those sickly opium fumes we had to lower our heads. Two steps led down into the place, which was so dark that I hesitated, momentarily, peering about me.

Apparently some four or five persons squatted and lay in the darkness about me. Some were couched upon rough wooden shelves ranged around the walls, others sprawled upon the floor, in the center whereof, upon a small tea-chest, stood a smoky brass lamp. The room and its occupants alike were indeterminate, sketchy; its deadly atmosphere seemed to be suffocating me. A sort of choking sound came from one of the bunks; a vague, obscene murmuring filled the whole place revoltingly.

Zarmi stood at the further end, her lithe figure silhouetted against the vague light coming through an open doorway. I saw her raise her hand, beckoning to us.

Circling around the chest supporting the lamp we crossed the foul den and found ourselves in a narrow, dim passageway, but in cleaner air.

"Come," said Zarmi, extending her long, slim hand to me.

I took it, solely for guidance in the gloom, and she immediately drew my arm about her waist, leant back against my shoulder and, raising her pouted red lips, blew a cloud of tobacco smoke fully into my eyes!

Momentarily blinded, I drew back with a muttered exclamation. Suspecting what I did of this tigerish half-caste, I could almost have found it in my heart to return her savage pleasantries with interest.

As I raised my hands to my burning eyes, Fletcher uttered a sharp cry of pain. I turned in time to see the girl touch him lightly on the neck with the burning tip of her cigarette.

"You jealous, eh, Charlie?" she said. "But I love you, too—see! Come along, you strong fellers…."

And away she went along the passage, swaying her hips lithely and glancing back over her shoulders in smiling coquetry.

Tears were still streaming from my eyes when I found myself standing in a sort of rough shed, stone-paved, and containing a variety of nondescript rubbish. A lantern stood upon the floor; and beside it …

The place seemed to be swimming around me, the stone floor to be heaving beneath my feet….

Beside the lantern stood a wooden chest, some six feet long, and having strong rope handles at either end. Evidently the chest had but recently been nailed up. As Zarmi touched it lightly with the pointed toe of her little red slipper I clutched at Fletcher for support.

Fletcher grasped my arm in a vice-like grip. To him, too, had come the ghastly conviction—the gruesome thought that neither of us dared to name.

It was Nayland Smith's coffin that we were to carry!

"Through here," came dimly to my ears, "and then I tell you what to do...."

Coolness returned to me, suddenly, unaccountably. I doubted not for an instant that the best friend I had in the world lay dead there at the feet of the hellish girl who called herself Zarmi, and I knew since it was she, disguised, who had driven him to his doom, that she must have been actively concerned in his murder.

But, I argued, although the damp night air was pouring in through the door which Zarmi now held open, although sound of Thames-side activity came stealing to my ears, we were yet within the walls of the Joy-Shop, with a score or more Asiatic ruffians at the woman's beck and call....

With perfect truth I can state that I retain not even a shadowy recollection of aiding Fletcher to move the chest out on to the brink of the cutting—for it was upon this that the door directly opened. The mist had grown denser, and except a glimpse of slowly moving water beneath me, I could discern little of our surroundings.

So much I saw by the light of a lantern which stood in the stern of a boat. In the bows of this boat I was vaguely aware of the presence of a crouched figure enveloped in rugs—vaguely aware that two filmy eyes regarded me out of the darkness. A man who looked like a lascar stood upright in the stern.

I must have been acting like a man in a stupor; for I was aroused to the realities by the contact of a burning cigarette with the lobe of my right ear!

"Hurry, quick, strong feller!" said Zarmi softly.

At that it seemed as though some fine nerve of my brain, already strained to utmost tension, snapped. I turned, with a wild, inarticulate cry, my fists raised frenziedly above my head.

"You fiend!" I shrieked at the mocking Eurasian, "you yellow fiend of hell!"

I was beside myself, insane. Zarmi fell back a step, flashing a glance from my own contorted face to that, now pale even beneath its artificial tan, of Fletcher.

I snatched the pistol from my pocket, and for one fateful moment the lust of slaying claimed my mind.... Then I turned towards the river, and, raising the Browning, fired shot after shot in the air.

"Weymouth!" I cried. "Weymouth!"

A sharp hissing sound came from behind me; a short, muffled cry ... and something descended, crushing, upon my skull. Like a wild cat Zarmi hurled herself past me and leapt into the boat. One glimpse I had of her pallidly dusky face, of her blazing black eyes, and the boat was thrust off into the waterway ... was swallowed up in the mist.

I turned, dizzily, to see Fletcher sinking to his knees, one hand clutching his breast.

"She got me ... with the knife," he whispered. "But ... don't worry ... look to yourself, and ... *him*...."

He pointed, weakly—then collapsed at my feet. I threw myself upon the wooden chest with a fierce, sobbing cry.

"Smith, Smith!" I babbled, and knew myself no better, in my sorrow, than an hysterical woman. "Smith, dear old man! speak to me! speak to me! ..."

Outraged emotion overcame me utterly, and with my arms thrown across the box, I slipped into unconsciousness.

CHAPTER NINE

FU-MANCHU

Many poignant recollections are mine, more of them bitter than sweet; but no one of them all can compare with the memory of that moment of my awakening.

Weymouth was supporting me, and my throat still tingled from the effects of the brandy which he had forced between my teeth from his flask. My heart was beating irregularly; my mind yet partly inert. With something compound of horror and hope I lay staring at one who was anxiously bending over the inspector's shoulder, watching me.

It was Nayland Smith.

A whole hour of silence seemed to pass, ere speech became possible; then—

"Smith!" I whispered, "are you …"

Smith grasped my outstretched, questing hand, grasped it firmly, warmly; and I saw his gray eyes to be dim in the light of the several lanterns around us.

"Am I alive?" he said. "Dear old Petrie! Thanks to you, I am not only alive, but free!"

My head was buzzing like a hive of bees, but I managed, aided by Weymouth, to struggle to my feet. Muffled sounds of shouting and scuffling reached me. Two men in the uniform of the Thames Police were carrying a limp body in at the low doorway communicating with the infernal Joy-Shop.

"It's Fletcher," said Weymouth, noting the anxiety exprêssed in my face. "His missing lady friend has given him a nasty wound, but he'll pull round all right."

"Thank God for that," I replied, clutched my aching head. "I don't know what weapon she employed in my case, but it narrowly missed achieving her purpose."

My eyes, throughout, were turned upon Smith, for his presence there, still seemed to me miraculous.

"Smith," I said, "for Heaven's sake enlighten me! I never doubted that you were …"

"In the wooden chest!" concluded Smith grimly, "Look!"

He pointed to something that lay behind me. I turned, and saw the box which had occasioned me such anguish. The top had been wrenched off and the contents exposed to view. It was filled with a variety of gold ornaments, cups, vases, silks, and barbaric brocaded raiment; it might well have contained the loot of a cathedral. Inspector Weymouth laughed gruffly at my surprise.

"What is it?" I asked, in a voice of amazement.

"It's the treasure of the Si-Fan, I presume," rapped Smith. "Where it has come from and where it was going to, it must be my immediate business to ascertain."

"Then you …"

"I was lying, bound and gagged, upon one of the upper shelves in the opium den! I heard you and Fletcher arrive. I saw you pass through later with that she-devil who drove the cab today …"

"Then the cab ..."

"The windows were fastened, unopenable, and some anaesthetic was injected into the interior through a tube—that speaking-tube. I know nothing further, except that our plans must have leaked out in some mysterious fashion. Petrie, my suspicions point to high quarters. The Si-Fan score thus far, for unless the search now in progress brings it to light, we must conclude that they have the brass coffer."

He was interrupted by a sudden loud crying of his name.

"Mr. Nayland Smith!" came from somewhere within the Joy-Shop. "This way, sir!"

Off he went, in his quick, impetuous manner, whilst I stood there, none too steadily, wondering what discovery this outcry portended. I had not long to wait. Out by the low doorway come Smith, a grimly triumphant smile upon his face, carrying the missing brass coffer!

He set it down upon the planking before me.

"John Ki," he said, "who was also on the missing list, had dragged the thing out of the cellar where it was hidden, and in another minute must have slipped away with it. Detective Deacon saw the light shining through a crack in the floor. I shall never forget the look John gave us when we came upon him, as, lamp in hand, he bent over the precious chest."

"Shall you open it now?"

"No." He glanced at me oddly. "I shall have it valued in the morning by Messrs. Meyerstein."

He was keeping something back; I was sure of it.

"Smith," I said suddenly, "the man with the limp! I heard him in the place where you were confined! Did you ..."

Nayland Smith clicked his teeth together sharply, looking straightly and grimly into my eyes.

"I *saw* him!" he replied slowly; "and unless the effects of the anaesthetic had not wholly worn off …"

"Well!" I cried.

"The man with the limp is *Dr. Fu-Manchu*!"

CHAPTER TEN

THE TÛLUN-NÛR CHEST

"This box," said Mr. Meyerstein, bending attentively over the carven brass coffer upon the table, "is certainly of considerable value, and possibly almost unique."

Nayland Smith glanced across at me with a slight smile. Mr. Meyerstein ran one fat finger tenderly across the heavily embossed figures, which, like barnacles, encrusted the sides and lid of the weird curio which we had summoned him to appraise.

"What do you think, Lewison?" he added, glancing over his shoulder at the clerk who accompanied him.

Lewison, whose flaxen hair and light blue eyes almost served to mask his Semitic origin, shrugged his shoulders in a fashion incongruous in one of his complexion, though characteristic in one of his name.

"It is as you say, Mr. Meyerstein, an example of early Tûlun-Nûr work," he said. "It may be sixteenth century or even earlier. The Kûren treasure-chest in the Hague Collection has points of similarity, but the workmanship of this specimen is infinitely finer."

"In a word, gentlemen," snapped Nayland Smith, rising from the armchair in which he had been sitting, and beginning restlessly to pace the room, "in a word, you would be prepared to make me a substantial offer for this box?"

Mr. Meyerstein, his shrewd eyes twinkling behind the pebbles of his pince-nez, straightened himself slowly, turned in the ponderous manner of a fat man, and readjusted the pince-nez upon his nose. He cleared his throat.

"I have not yet seen the interior of the box, Mr. Smith," he said.

Smith paused in his perambulation of the carpet and stared hard at the celebrated art dealer.

"Unfortunately," he replied, "the key is missing."

"Ah!" cried the assistant, Lewison, excitedly, "you are mistaken, sir! Coffers of this description and workmanship are nearly always complicated conjuring tricks; they rarely open by any such rational means as lock and key. For instance, the Kûren treasure-chest to which I referred, opens by an intricate process involving the pressing of certain knobs in the design, and the turning of others."

"It was ultimately opened," said Mr. Meyerstein, with a faint note of professional envy in his voice, "by one of Christie's experts."

"Does my memory mislead me," I interrupted, "or was it not regarding the possession of the chest to which you refer, that the celebrated case of 'Hague versus Jacobs' arose?"

"You are quite right, Dr. Petrie," said Meyerstein, turning to me. "The original owner, a member of the Younghusband Expedition, had been unable to open the chest. When opened at Christie's it proved to contain jewels and other valuables. It was a curious case, wasn't it, Lewison?" turning to his clerk.

"Very," agreed the other absently; then—"Have you endeavored to open this box, Mr. Smith?"

Nayland Smith shook his head grimly.

"From its weight," said Meyerstein, "I am inclined to think that the contents might prove of interest. With your permission I will endeavor to open it."

Nayland Smith, tugging reflectively at the lobe of his left ear, stood looking at the expert. Then—

"I do not care to attempt it at present," he said.

Meyerstein and his clerk stared at the speaker in surprise.

"But you would be mad," cried the former, "if you accepted an offer for the box, whilst ignorant of the nature of its contents."

"But I have invited no offer," said Smith. "I do not propose to sell."

Meyerstein adjusted his pince-nez again.

"I am a business man," he said, "and I will make a business proposal: A hundred guineas for the box, cash down, and our commission to be ten per cent on the proceeds of the contents. You must remember," raising a fat forefinger to check Smith, who was about to interrupt him, "that it may be necessary to force the box in order to open it, thereby decreasing its market value and making it a bad bargain at a hundred guineas."

Nayland Smith met my gaze across the room; again a slight smile crossed the lean, tanned face.

"I can only reply, Mr. Meyerstein," he said, "in this way: If I desire to place the box on the market, you shall have first refusal, and the same applies to the contents, if any. For the moment if you will send me a note of your fee, I shall be obliged." He raised his hand with a conclusive gesture. "I am not prepared to discuss the question of sale any further at present, Mr. Meyerstein."

At that the dealer bowed, took up his hat from the table, and prepared to depart. Lewison opened the door and stood aside.

"Good morning, gentlemen," said Meyerstein.

As Lewison was about to follow him—

"Since you do not intend to open the box," he said, turning, his hand upon the door knob, "have you any idea of its contents?"

"None," replied Smith; "but with my present inadequate knowledge of its history, I do not care to open it."

Lewison smiled skeptically.

"Probably you know best," he said, bowed to us both, and retired.

When the door was closed—

"You see, Petrie," said Smith, beginning to stuff tobacco into his briar, "if we are ever short of funds, here's something"—pointing to the Tûlun-Nûr box upon the—"which would retrieve our fallen fortunes."

He uttered one of his rare, boyish laughs, and began to pace the carpet again, his gaze always set upon our strange treasure. What did it contain?

The manner in which it had come into our possession suggested that it might contain something of the utmost value to the Yellow group. For we knew the house of John Ki to be, if not the headquarters, certainly a meeting-place of the mysterious organization the Si-Fan; we knew that Dr. Fu-Manchu used the place—Dr. Fu-Manchu, the uncanny being whose existence seemingly proved him immune from natural laws, a deathless incarnation of evil.

My gaze set upon the box, I wondered anew what strange, dark secrets it held; I wondered how many murders and crimes greater than murder blackened its history.

"Smith," I said suddenly, "now that the mystery of the absence of a keyhole is explained, I am sorely tempted to essay the task of opening the coffer. I think it might help us to a solution of the whole mystery."

"And I think otherwise!" interrupted my friend grimly. "In a word, Petrie, I look upon this box as a sort of hostage by means of which—who knows—we might one day buy our lives from the enemy. I have a sort of fancy, call it superstition if you will, that nothing—not even our miraculous good luck—could save us if once we ravished its secret."

I stared at him amazedly; this was a new phase in his character.

"I am conscious of something almost like a spiritual unrest," he continued. "Formerly you were endowed with a capacity for divining the presence of Fu-Manchu or his agents. Some such second-sight would appear to have visited me now, and it directs me forcibly to avoid opening the box."

His steps as he paced the floor grew more and more rapid. He relighted his pipe, which had gone out as usual, and tossed the match-end into the hearth.

"Tomorrow," he said, "I shall lodge the coffer in a place of greater security. Come along, Petrie, Weymouth is expecting us at Scotland Yard."

CHAPTER ELEVEN

IN THE FOG

"But, Smith," I began, as my friend hurried me along the corridor, "you are not going to leave the box unguarded?"

Nayland Smith tugged at my arm, and, glancing at him, I saw him frowningly shake his head. Utterly mystified, I nevertheless understood that for some reason he desired me to preserve silence for the present. Accordingly I said no more until the lift brought us down into the lobby and we had passed out from the New Louvre Hotel, crossed the busy thoroughfare and entered the buffet of an establishment not far distant. My friend having ordered cocktails—

"And now perhaps you will explain to me the reason for your mysterious behavior?" said I.

Smith, placing my glass before me, glanced about him to right and left, and having satisfied himself that his words could not be overheard—

"Petrie," he whispered, "I believe we are spied upon at the New Louvre."

"What!"

"There are spies of the Si-Fan—of Fu-Manchu—amongst the hotel servants! We have good reason to believe that Dr. Fu-Manchu at one time was actually in the building, and we have been compelled to draw attention to the state of the electric fitting in our apartments, which enables any one in the corridor above to spy upon us."

"Then why do you stay?"

"For a very good reason, Petrie, and the same that prompts me to retain the Tûlun-Nûr box in my own possession rather than to deposit it in the strongroom of my bank."

"I begin to understand."

"I trust you do, Petrie; it is fairly obvious. Probably the plan is a perilous one, but I hope, by laying myself open to attack, to apprehend the enemy—perhaps to make an important capture."

Setting down my glass, I stared in silence at Smith.

"I will anticipate your remark," he said, smiling dryly. "I am aware that I am not entitled to expose *you* to these dangers. It is *my* duty and I must perform it as best I can; you, as a volunteer, are perfectly entitled to withdraw."

As I continued silently to stare at him, his expression changed; the gray eyes grew less steely, and presently, clapping his hand upon my shoulder in his impulsive way—

"Petrie!" he cried, "you know I had no intention of hurting your feelings, but in the circumstances it was impossible for me to say less."

"You have said enough, Smith," I replied shortly. "I beg of you to say no more."

He gripped my shoulder hard, then plunged his hand into his pocket and pulled out the blackened pipe.

"We see it through together, then, though God knows whither it will lead us."

"In the first place," I interrupted, "since you have left the chest unguarded—"

"I locked the door."

"What is a mere lock where Fu-Manchu is concerned?"

Nayland Smith laughed almost gaily.

"Really, Petrie," he cried, "sometimes I cannot believe that you mean me to take you seriously. Inspector Weymouth has engaged the room immediately facing our door, and no one can enter or leave the suite unseen by him."

"Inspector Weymouth?"

"Oh! for once he has stooped to a disguise: spectacles, and a muffler which covers his face right up to the tip of his nose. Add to this a prodigious overcoat and an asthmatic cough, and you have a picture of Mr. Jonathan Martin, the occupant of room number 239."

I could not repress a smile upon hearing this description.

"Number 239," continued Smith, "contains two beds, and Mr. Martin's friend will be joining him there this evening."

Meeting my friend's questioning glance, I nodded comprehendingly.

"Then what part do *I* play?"

"Ostensibly we both leave town this evening," he explained; "but I have a scheme whereby you will be enabled to remain behind. We shall thus have one watcher inside and two out."

"It seems almost absurd," I said incredulously, "to expect any member of the Yellow group to attempt anything in a huge hotel like the New Louvre, here in the heart of London!"

Nayland Smith, having lighted his pipe, stretched his arms and stared me straight in the face.

"Has Fu-Manchu never attempted outrage, murder, in the heart of London before?" he snapped.

The words were sufficient. Remembering black episodes of the past (one at least of them had occurred not a thousand yards from the very spot upon which we now stood), I knew that I had spoken folly.

Certain arrangements were made then, including a visit to Scotland Yard; and a plan—though it sounds anomalous—at once elaborate and simple, was put into execution in the dusk of the evening.

London remained in the grip of fog, and when we passed along the corridor communicating with our apartments, faint streaks of yellow vapor showed in the light of the lamp suspended at the further end. I knew that Nayland Smith suspected the presence of some spying contrivance in our rooms, although I was unable to conjecture how this could have been managed without the connivance of the management. In pursuance of his idea, however, he extinguished the lights a moment before we actually quitted the suite. Just within the door he helped me to remove the somewhat conspicuous check traveling-coat which I wore. With this upon his arm he opened the door and stepped out into the corridor.

As the door slammed upon his exit, I heard him cry: "Come along, Petrie! we have barely five minutes to catch our train."

Detective Carter of New Scotland Yard had joined him at the threshold, and muffled up in the gray traveling-coat was now hurrying with Smith along the corridor and out of the hotel. Carter, in build and features, was not unlike me, and I did not doubt that anyone who might be spying upon our movements would be deceived by this device.

In the darkness of the apartment I stood listening to the retreating footsteps in the corridor. A sense of loneliness and danger assailed me. I knew that Inspector Weymouth was watching and listening from the room immediately opposite; that he held Smith's key; that I could summon him to my assistance, if necessary, in a matter of seconds.

Yet, contemplating the vigil that lay before me in silence and darkness, I cannot pretend that my frame of mind was buoyant. I could not smoke; I must make no sound.

As pre-arranged, I cautiously removed my boots, and as cautiously tiptoed across the carpet and seated myself in an armchair. I determined there to await the arrival of Mr. Jonathan Martin's friend, which I knew could not now be long delayed.

The clocks were striking eleven when he arrived, and in the perfect stillness of that upper corridor. I heard the bustle which heralded his approach, heard the rap upon the door opposite, followed by a muffled "Come in" from Weymouth. Then, as the door was opened, I heard the sound of a wheezy cough.

A strange cracked voice (which, nevertheless, I recognized for Smith's) cried, "Hullo, Martin!—cough no better?"

Upon that the door was closed again, and as the retreating footsteps of the servant died away, complete silence—that peculiar silence which comes with fog—descended once more upon the upper part of the New Louvre Hotel.

CHAPTER TWELVE

THE VISITANT

That first hour of watching, waiting, and listening in the lonely quietude passed drearily; and with the passage of every quarter—signalized by London's muffled clocks—my mood became increasingly morbid. I peopled the silent rooms opening out of that wherein I sat, with stealthy, murderous figures; my imagination painted hideous yellow faces upon the draperies, twitching yellow hands protruding from this crevice and that. A score of times I started nervously, thinking I heard the pad of bare feet upon the floor behind me, the suppressed breathing of some deathly approach.

Since nothing occurred to justify these tremors, this apprehensive mood passed; I realized that I was growing cramped and stiff, that unconsciously I had been sitting with my muscles nervously tensed. The window was open a foot or so at the top and the blind was drawn; but so accustomed were my eyes now to peering through the darkness, that I could plainly discern the yellow oblong of the window, and though very vaguely, some of the appointments of the room—the Chesterfield against one wall, the lampshade above my head, the table with the Tûlun-Nûr box upon it.

There was fog in the room, and it was growing damply chill, for we had extinguished the electric heater some hours before. Very few sounds penetrated from outside. Twice or perhaps thrice people passed along the corridor, going to their rooms; but, as I knew, the greater number of the rooms along that corridor were unoccupied.

From the Embankment far below me, and from the river, faint noises came at long intervals it is true; the muffled hooting of motors, and yet fainter ringing of bells. Fog signals boomed distantly, and train whistles shrieked, remote and unreal. I determined to enter my bedroom, and, risking any sound which I might make, to lie down upon the bed.

I rose carefully and carried this plan into execution. I would have given much for a smoke, although my throat was parched; and almost any drink would have been nectar. But although my hopes (or my fears) of an intruder had left me, I determined to stick to the rules of the game as laid down. Therefore I neither smoked nor drank, but carefully extended my weary limbs upon the coverlet, and telling myself that I could guard our strange treasure as well from there as from elsewhere … slipped off into a profound sleep.

Nothing approaching in acute and sustained horror to the moment when next I opened my eyes exists in all my memories of those days.

In the first place I was aroused by the shaking of the bed. It was quivering beneath me as though an earthquake disturbed the very foundations of the building. I sprang upright and into full consciousness of my lapse…. My hands clutching the coverlet on either side of me, I sat staring, staring, staring … at *that* which peered at me over the foot of the bed.

I knew that I had slept at my post; I was convinced that I was now widely awake; yet I *dared* not admit to myself that what I saw was other than a product of my imagination. I dared not admit the physical quivering of the bed, for I could not, with sanity, believe its cause to be anything human. But what I saw, yet could not credit seeing, was this:

A ghostly white face, which seemed to glisten in some faint reflected light from the sitting-room beyond, peered over the bedrail; gibbered at me demoniacally. With quivering hands this nightmare horror, which had intruded where I believed human intrusion to be all but impossible, clutched the bedposts so that the frame of the structure shook and faintly rattled....

My heart leapt wildly in my breast, then seemed to suspend its pulsations and to grow icily cold. My whole body became chilled horrifically. My scalp tingled: I felt that I must either cry out or become stark raving mad!

For this clammily white face, those staring eyes, that wordless gibbering, and the shaking, shaking, shaking of the bed in the clutch of the nameless visitant—prevailed, refused to disperse like the evil dream I had hoped it all to be; manifested itself, indubitably, as something tangible—objective....

Outraged reason deprived me of coherent speech. Past the clammy white face I could see the sitting-room illuminated by a faint light; I could even see the Tûlun-Nûr box upon the table immediately opposite the door.

The thing which shook the bed was actual, existent—to be counted with!

Further and further I drew myself away from it, until I crouched close up against the head of the bed. Then, as the thing reeled aside, and—merciful Heaven!—made as if to come around and approach me yet closer, I uttered a hoarse cry and hurled myself out upon the floor and on the side remote from that pallid horror which I thought was pursuing me.

I heard a dull thud … and the thing disappeared from my view, yet—and remembering the supreme terror of that visitation I am not ashamed to confess it—I dared not move from the spot upon which I stood, I dared not make to pass that which lay between me and the door.

"Smith!" I cried, but my voice was little more than a hoarse whisper—"Smith! Weymouth!"

The words became clearer and louder as I proceeded, so that the last—"Weymouth!"—was uttered in a sort of falsetto scream.

A door burst open upon the other side of the corridor. A key was inserted in the lock of the door. Into the dimly lighted arch which divided the bedroom from the sitting-room, sprang the figure of Nayland Smith!

"Petrie! Petrie!" he called—and I saw him standing there looking from left to right.

Then, ere I could reply, he turned, and his gaze fell upon whatever lay upon the floor at the foot of the bed.

"My God!" he whispered—and sprang into the room.

"Smith! Smith!" I cried, "what is it? what is it?"

He turned in a flash, as Weymouth entered at his heels, saw me, and fell back a step; then looked again down at the floor.

"God's mercy!" he whispered, "I thought it was you—I thought it was you!"

Trembling violently, my mind a feverish chaos, I moved to the foot of the bed and looked down at what lay there.

"Turn up the light!" snapped Smith.

Weymouth reached for the switch, and the room became illuminated suddenly.

Prone upon the carpet, hands outstretched and nails dug deeply into the pile of the fabric, lay a dark-haired man having his head twisted sideways so that the face showed a ghastly pallid profile against the rich colorings upon which it rested. He wore no coat, but a sort of dark gray shirt and black trousers. To add to the incongruity of his attire, his feet were clad in drab-colored shoes, rubber-soled.

I stood, one hand raised to my head, looking down upon him, and gradually regaining control of myself. Weymouth, perceiving something of my condition, silently passed his flask to me; and I gladly availed myself of this.

"How in Heaven's name did he get in?" I whispered.

"How, indeed!" said Weymouth, staring about him with wondering eyes.

Both he and Smith had discarded their disguises; and, a bewildered trio, we stood looking down upon the man at our feet. Suddenly Smith dropped to his knees and turned him flat upon his back. Composure was nearly restored to me, and I knelt upon the other side of the white-faced creature whose presence there seemed so utterly outside the realm of possibility, and examined him with a consuming and fearful interest; for it was palpable that, if not already dead, he was dying rapidly.

He was a slightly built man, and the first discovery that I made was a curious one. What I had mistaken for dark hair was a wig! The short black mustache which he wore was also factitious.

"Look at this!" I cried.

"I am looking," snapped Smith.

He suddenly stood up, and entering the room beyond, turned on the light there. I saw him staring at the Tûlun-Nûr box, and I knew what had been in his mind. But the box, undisturbed, stood upon the table as we had left it. I saw Smith tugging irritably at the lobe of his ear, and staring from the box towards the man beside whom I knelt.

"For God's sake, what does it mean?" said Inspector Weymouth in a voice hushed with wonder. "How did he get in? What did he come for?—and what has happened to him?"

"As to what has happened to him," I replied, "unfortunately I cannot tell you. I only know that unless something can be done his end is not far off."

"Shall we lay him on the bed?"

I nodded, and together we raised the slight figure and placed it upon the bed where so recently I had lain.

As we did so, the man suddenly opened his eyes, which were glazed with delirium. He tore himself from our grip, sat bolt upright, and holding his hands, fingers outstretched, before his face, stared at them frenziedly.

"The golden pomegranates!" he shrieked, and a slight froth appeared on his blanched lips. "The golden pomegranates!"

He laughed madly, and fell back inert.

"He's dead!" whispered Weymouth; "he's dead!"

Hard upon his words came a cry from Smith:

"Quick! Petrie!—Weymouth!"

CHAPTER THIRTEEN

THE ROOM BELOW

I ran into the sitting-room, to discover Nayland Smith craning out of the now widely opened window. The blind had been drawn up, I did not know by whom; and, leaning out beside my friend, I was in time to perceive some bright object moving down the gray stone wall. Almost instantly it disappeared from sight in the yellow banks below.

Smith leapt around in a whirl of excitement.

"Come in, Petrie!" he cried, seizing my arm. "You remain here, Weymouth; don't leave these rooms whatever happens!"

We ran out into the corridor. For my own part I had not the vaguest idea what we were about. My mind was not yet fully recovered from the frightful shock which it had sustained; and the strange words of the dying man—"the golden pomegranates"—had increased my mental confusion. Smith apparently had not heard them, for he remained grimly silent, as side by side we raced down the marble stairs to the corridor immediately below our own.

Although, amid the hideous turmoil to which I had awakened, I had noted nothing of the hour, evidently the night was far advanced.

Not a soul was to be seen from end to end of the vast corridor in which we stood ... until on the right-hand side and about halfway along, a door opened and a woman came out hurriedly, carrying a small handbag.

She wore a veil, so that her features were but vaguely distinguished, but her every movement was agitated; and this agitation perceptibly increased when, turning, she perceived the two of us bearing down upon her.

Nayland Smith, who had been audibly counting the doors along the corridor as we passed them, seized the woman's arm without ceremony, and pulled her into the apartment she had been on the point of quitting, closing the door behind us as we entered.

"Smith!" I began, "for Heaven's sake what are you about?"

"You shall see, Petrie!" he snapped.

He released the woman's arm, and pointing to an armchair nearby—

"Be seated," he said sternly.

Speechless with amazement, I stood, with my back to the door, watching this singular scene. Our captive, who wore a smart walking costume and whose appearance was indicative of elegance and culture, so far had uttered no word of protest, no cry.

Now, whilst Smith stood rigidly pointing to the chair, she seated herself with something very like composure and placed the leather bag upon the floor beside her. The room in which I found myself was one of a suite almost identical with our own, but from what I had gathered in a hasty glance around, it bore no signs of recent tenancy. The window was widely opened, and upon the floor lay a strange-looking contrivance apparently made of aluminum. A large grip, open, stood beside it, and from this some portions of a black coat and other garments protruded.

"Now, madame," said Nayland Smith, "will you be good enough to raise your veil?"

Silently, unprotestingly, the woman obeyed him, raising her gloved hands and lifting the veil from her face.

The features revealed were handsome in a hard fashion, but heavily made-up. Our captive was younger than I had hitherto supposed; a blonde; her hair artificially reduced to the so-called Titian tint. But, despite her youth, her eyes, with the blackened lashes, were full of a world weariness. Now she smiled cynically.

"Are you satisfied," she said, speaking unemotionally, "or," holding up her wrists, "would you like to handcuff me?"

Nayland Smith, glancing from the open grip and the appliance beside it to the face of the speaker, began clicking his teeth together, whereby I knew him to be perplexed. Then he stared across at me.

"You appear bemused, Petrie," he said, with a certain irritation. "Is this what mystifies you?"

Stooping, he picked up the metal contrivance, and almost savagely jerked open the top section. It was a telescopic ladder, and more ingeniously designed than anything of the kind I had seen before. There was a sort of clamp attached to the base, and two sharply pointed hooks at the top.

"For reaching windows on an upper floor," snapped my friend, dropping the thing with a clatter upon the carpet. "An American device which forms part of the equipment of the modern hotel thief!"

He seemed to be disappointed—fiercely disappointed; and I found his attitude inexplicable. He turned to the woman—who sat regarding him with that fixed cynical smile.

"Who are you?" he demanded; "and what business have you with the Si-Fan?"

The woman's eyes opened more widely, and the smile disappeared from her face.

"The Si-Fan!" she repeated slowly. "I don't know what you mean, Inspector."

"I am not an inspector," snapped Smith, "and you know it well enough. You have one chance—your last. To whom were you to deliver the box? When and where?"

But the blue eyes remained upraised to the grim tanned face with a look of wonder in them, which, if assumed, marked the woman a consummate actress.

"Who are you?" she asked in a low voice, "and what are you talking about?"

Inactive, I stood by the door watching my friend, and his face was a fruitful study in perplexity. He seemed upon the point of an angry outburst, then, staring intently into the questioning eyes upraised to his, he checked the words he would have uttered and began to click his teeth together again.

"You are some servant of Dr. Fu-Manchu!" he said.

The girl frowned with a bewilderment which I could have sworn was not assumed. Then—

"You said I had one chance a moment ago," she replied. "But if you referred to my answering any of your questions, it is no chance at all. We have gone under, and I know it. I am not complaining; it's all in the game. There's a clear enough case against us, and I am sorry"—suddenly, unexpectedly, her eyes became filled with tears, which coursed down her cheeks, leaving little wakes of blackness from the make-up upon her lashes. Her lips trembled, and her voice shook. "I am sorry I let him do it. He'd never done anything—not anything big like this—before, and he never would have done if he had not met me…."

The look of perplexity upon Smith's face was increasing with every word that the girl uttered.

"You don't seem to know me," she continued, her emotion growing momentarily greater, "and I don't know you; but they will know me at Bow Street. I urged him to do it, when he told me about the box today at lunch. He said that if it contained half as much as the Kûren treasure-chest, we could sail for America and be on the straight all the rest of our lives."

And now something which had hitherto been puzzling me became suddenly evident. I had not removed the wig worn by the dead man, but I knew that he had fair hair, and when in his last moments he had opened his eyes, there had been in the contorted face something faintly familiar.

"Smith!" I cried excitedly, "it is Lewison, Meyerstein's clerk! Don't you understand? Don't you understand?"

Smith brought his teeth together with a snap and stared me hard in the face.

"I do, Petrie. I have been following a false scent. I do!"

The girl in the chair was now sobbing convulsively.

"He was tempted by the possibility of the box containing treasure," I ran on, "and his acquaintance with this—lady—who is evidently no stranger to felonious operations, led him to make the attempt with her assistance. But"—I found myself confronted by a new problem—"what caused his death?"

"His ... *death*!"

As a wild, hysterical shriek the words smote upon my ears. I turned, to see the girl rise, tottering, from her seat. She began groping in front of her, blindly, as though a darkness had descended.

"You did not say he was dead?" she whispered, "not dead!—not ..."

The words were lost in a wild peal of laughter. Clutching at her throat she swayed and would have fallen had I not caught her in my arms. As I laid her insensible upon the settee I met Smith's glance.

"I think I know that, too, Petrie," he said gravely.

CHAPTER FOURTEEN

THE GOLDEN POMEGRANATES

"What was it that he cried out?" demanded Nayland Smith abruptly. "I was in the sitting-room and it sounded to me like 'pomegranates'!"

We were bending over Lewison; for now, the wig removed, Lewison it proved unmistakably to be, despite the puffy and pallid face.

"He said 'the golden pomegranates,'" I replied, and laughed harshly. "They were words of delirium and cannot possibly have any bearing upon the manner of his death."

"I disagree."

He strode out into the sitting-room.

Weymouth was below, supervising the removal of the unhappy prisoner, and together Smith and I stood looking down at the brass box. Suddenly—

"I propose to attempt to open it," said my friend.

His words came as a complete surprise.

"For what reason?—and why have you so suddenly changed your mind?"

"For a reason which I hope will presently become evident," he said; "and as to my change of mind, unless I am greatly mistaken, the wily old Chinaman from whom I wrested this treasure was infinitely more clever than I gave him credit for being!"

Through the open window came faintly to my ears the chiming of Big Ben. The hour was a quarter to two. London's pulse was dimmed now, and around about us that great city slept as soundly as it ever sleeps. Other sounds came vaguely through the fog, and beside Nayland Smith I sat and watched him at work upon the Tûlun-Nûr box.

Every knob of the intricate design he pushed, pulled and twisted; but without result. The night wore on, and just before three o'clock Inspector Weymouth knocked upon the door. I admitted him, and side by side the two of us stood watching Smith patiently pursuing his task.

All conversation had ceased, when, just as the muted booming of London's clocks reached my ears again and Weymouth pulled out his watch, there came a faint click … and I saw that Smith had raised the lid of the coffer!

Weymouth and I sprang forward with one accord, and over Smith's shoulders peered into the interior. There was a second lid of some dull, black wood, apparently of great age, and fastened to it so as to form knobs or handles was an exquisitely carved pair of *golden pomegranates*!

"They are to raise the wooden lid, Mr. Smith!" cried Weymouth eagerly.

"Look! there is a hollow in each to accommodate the fingers!"

"Aren't you going to open it?" I demanded excitedly—"aren't you going to open it?"

"Might I invite you to accompany me into the bedroom yonder

for a moment?" he replied in a tome of studied reserve. "You also, Weymouth?"

Smith leading, we entered the room where the dead man lay stretched upon the bed.

"Note the appearance of his fingers," directed Nayland Smith.

I examined the peculiarity to which Smith had drawn my attention. The dead man's fingers were swollen extraordinarily, the index finger of either hand especially being oddly discolored, as though bruised from the nail upward. I looked again at the ghastly face, then, repressing a shudder, for the sight was one not good to look upon, I turned to Smith, who was watching me expectantly with his keen, steely eyes.

From his pocket the took out a knife containing a number of implements, amongst them a hook-like contrivance.

"Have you a button-hook, Petrie," he asked, "or anything of that nature?"

"How will this do?" said the inspector, and he produced a pair of handcuffs. "They were not wanted," he added significantly.

"Better still," declared Smith.

Reclosing his knife, he took the handcuffs from Weymouth, and, returning to the sitting-room, opened them widely and inserted two steel points in the hollows of the golden pomegranates. He pulled. There was a faint sound of moving mechanism and the wooden lid lifted, revealing the interior of the coffer. It contained three long bars of lead—and nothing else!

Supporting the lid with the handcuffs—

"Just pull the light over here, Petrie," said Smith.

I did as he directed.

"Look into these two cavities where one is expected to thrust one's fingers!"

Weymouth and I craned forward so that our heads came into contact.

"My God!" whispered the inspector, "we know now what killed him!"

Visible, in either little cavity against the edge of the steel handcuff, was the point of a needle, which evidently worked in an exquisitely made socket through which the action of raising the lid caused it to protrude. Underneath the lid, midway between the two pomegranates, as I saw by slowly moving the lamp, was a little receptacle of metal communicating with the base of the hollow needles.

The action of lifting the lid not only protruded the points but also operated the hypodermic syringe!

"Note," snapped Smith—but his voice was slightly hoarse.

He removed the points of the bracelets. The box immediately reclosed with no other sound than a faint click.

"God forgive him," said Smith, glancing toward the other room, "for he died in my stead!—and Dr. Fu-Manchu scores an undeserved failure!"

CHAPTER FIFTEEN

ZARMI REAPPEARS

"Come in!" I cried.

The door opened and a page-boy entered.

"A cable for Dr. Petrie."

I started up from my chair. A thousand possibilities—some of a sort to bring dread to my heart—instantly occurred to me. I tore open the envelope and, as one does, glanced first at the name of the sender.

It was signed "Kâramaneh!"

"Smith!" I said hoarsely, glancing over the massage, "Kâramaneh is on her way to England. She arrives by the *Nicobar* tomorrow!"

"Eh?" cried Nayland Smith, in turn leaping to his feet. "She had no right to come alone, unless—"

The boy, open-mouthed, was listening to our conversation, and I hastily thrust a coin into his hand and dismissed him. As the door closed—

"Unless what, Smith?" I said, looking my friend squarely in the eyes.

"Unless she has learnt something, or—is flying away from someone!"

My mind set in a whirl of hopes and fears, longings and dreads.

"What do you mean, Smith?" I asked. "This is the place of danger, as we know to our cost; she was safe in Egypt."

Nayland Smith commenced one of his restless perambulations, glancing at me from time to time and frequently tugging at the lobe of his ear.

"*Was* she safe in Egypt?" he rapped. "We are dealing, remember, with the Si-Fan, which, if I am not mistaken, is a sort of Eleusinian Mystery holding some kind of dominion over the Eastern mind, and boasting initiates throughout the Orient. It is almost certain that there is an Egyptian branch, or group—call it what you will—of the damnable organization."

"But Dr. Fu-Manchu—"

"Dr. Fu-Manchu—for he lives, Petrie! my own eyes bear witness to the fact—Dr. Fu-Manchu is a sort of delegate from the headquarters. His prodigious genius will readily enable him to keep in touch with every branch of the movement, East and West."

He paused to knock out his pipe into an ashtray and to watch me for some moments in silence.

"He may have instructed his Cairo agents," he added significantly.

"God grant she get to England in safety," I whispered. "Smith! can we make no move to round up the devils who defy us, here in the very heart of civilized England? Listen. You will not have forgotten the wild-cat Eurasian Zarmi?"

Smith nodded. "I recall the lady perfectly!" he snapped.

"Unless my imagination has been playing me tricks, I have seen her twice within the last few days—once in the neighborhood of this hotel and once in a cab in Piccadilly."

"You mentioned the matter at the time," said Smith shortly; "but although I made inquiries, as you remember, nothing came of them."

"Nevertheless, I don't think I was mistaken. I feel in my very bones that the Yellow hand of Fu-Manchu is about to stretch out again. If only we could apprehend Zarmi."

Nayland Smith lighted his pipe with care.

"If only we could, Petrie!" he said; "but, damn it!"—he dashed his left fist into the palm of his right hand—"we are doomed to remain inactive. We can only await the arrival of Kâramaneh and see if she has anything to tell us. I must admit that there are certain theories of my own which I haven't yet had an opportunity of testing. Perhaps in the near future such an opportunity may arise."

How soon that opportunity was to arise neither of us suspected then; but Fate is a merry trickster, and even as we spoke of these matters events were brewing which were to lead us along strange paths.

With such glad anticipations as my pen cannot describe, their gladness not unmixed with fear, I retired to rest that night, scarcely expecting to sleep, so eager was I for the morrow. The musical voice of Kâramaneh seemed to ring in my ears; I seemed to feel the touch of her soft hands and to detect, as I drifted into the borderland betwixt reality and slumber, that faint, exquisite perfume which from the first moment of my meeting with the beautiful Eastern girl, had become to me inseparable from her personality.

It seemed that sleep had but just claimed me when I was awakened by someone roughly shaking my shoulder. I sprang upright, my mind alert to sudden danger. The room looked yellow and dismal, illuminated as it was by a cold light of dawn which crept through the window and with which competed the luminance of the electric lamps.

Nayland Smith stood at my bedside, partially dressed!

"Wake up, Petrie!" he cried; "your instincts serve you better than my reasoning. Hell's afoot, old man! Even as you predicted it, perhaps in that same hour, the yellow fiends were at work!"

"What, Smith, what!" I said, leaping out of bed; "you don't mean—"

"Not that, old man," he replied, clapping his hand upon my shoulder; "there is no further news of *her*, but Weymouth is waiting outside. Sir Baldwin Frazer has disappeared!"

I rubbed my eyes hard and sought to clear my mind of the vapors of sleep.

"Sir Baldwin Frazer!" I said, "of Half-Moon Street? But what—"

"God knows *what*," snapped Smith; "but our old friend Zarmi, or so it would appear, bore him off last night, and he has completely vanished, leaving practically no trace behind."

Only a few sleeping servants were about as we descended the marble stairs to the lobby of the hotel where Weymouth was awaiting us.

"I have a cab outside from the Yard," he said. "I came straight here to fetch you before going on to Half-Moon Street."

"Quite right!" snapped Smith; "but you are sure the cab is from the Yard? I have had painful experience of strange cabs recently!"

"You can trust this one," said Weymouth, smiling slightly. "It has carried me to the scene of many a crime."

"Hem!" said Smith—"a dubious recommendation."

We entered the waiting vehicle and soon were passing through the nearly deserted streets of London. Only those workers whose toils began with the dawn were afoot at that early hour, and in the misty gray light the streets had an unfamiliar look and wore an aspect of sadness in ill accord with the sentiments which now were stirring within me. For whatever might be the fate of the famous mental specialist, whatever the mystery before us—even though

Dr. Fu-Manchu himself, malignantly active, threatened our safety—Kâramaneh would be with me again that day—Kâramaneh, my beautiful wife to be!

So selfishly occupied was I with these reflections that I paid little heed to the words of Weymouth, who was acquainting Nayland Smith with the facts bearing upon the mysterious disappearance of Sir Baldwin Frazer. Indeed, I was almost entirely ignorant upon the subject when the cab pulled up before the surgeon's house in Half-Moon Street.

Here, where all else spoke of a city yet sleeping or but newly awakened, was wild unrest and excitement. Several servants were hovering about the hall eager to glean any scrap of information that might be obtainable; wide-eyed and curious, if not a little fearful. In the somber dining-room with its heavy oak furniture and gleaming silver, Sir Baldwin's secretary awaited us. He was a young man, fair-haired, clean-shaven and alert; but a real and ever-present anxiety could be read in his eyes.

"I am sorry," he began, "to have been the cause of disturbing you at so early an hour, particularly since this mysterious affair may prove to have no connection with the matters which I understand are at present engaging your attention."

Nayland Smith raised his hand deprecatingly.

"We are prepared, Mr. Logan," he replied, "to travel to the uttermost ends of the earth at all times, if by doing so we can obtain even a meager clue to the enigma which baffles us."

"I should not have disturbed Mr. Smith," said Weymouth, "if I had not been pretty sure that there was Chinese devilry at work here: nor should I have told you as much as I have, Mr. Logan," he added, a humorous twinkle creeping into his blue eyes, "if I had thought you could not be of use to us in unraveling our case!"

"I quite understand that," said Logan, "and now, since you have voted for the story first and refreshments afterward, let me tell you what little I know of the matter."

"Be as brief as you can," snapped Nayland Smith, starting up from the chair in which he had been seated and beginning restlessly to pace the floor before the open fireplace—"as brief as is consistent with clarity. We have learnt in the past that an hour or less sometimes means the difference between—"

He paused, glancing at Sir Baldwin's secretary.

"Between life and death," he added.

Mr. Logan started perceptibly.

"You alarm me, Mr. Smith," he declared; "for I can conceive of no earthly manner in which this mysterious Eastern organization of which Inspector Weymouth speaks, could profit by the death of Sir Baldwin."

Nayland Smith suddenly turned and stared grimly at the speaker.

"I call it death," he said harshly, "to be carried off to the interior of China, to be made a mere slave, having no will but the great and evil man who already—already, mark you!—has actually accomplished such things."

"But Sir Baldwin—"

"Sir Baldwin Frazer," snapped Smith, "is the undisputed head of his particular branch of surgery. Dr. Fu-Manchu may have what he deems useful employment for such skill as his. But," glancing at the clock, "we are wasting time. Your story, Mr. Logan."

"It was about half-past twelve last night," began the secretary, closing his eyes as if he were concentrating his mind upon certain past events, "when a woman came here and inquired for Sir Baldwin. The butler informed her that Sir Baldwin was entertaining friends and that he could receive no professional visitors until the morning. She was so insistent, however, absolutely declining to go away, that I was sent for—I have rooms in the house—and I came down to interview her in the library."

"Be very accurate, Mr. Logan," interrupted Smith, "in your description of this visitor."

"I shall do my best," pursued Logan, closing his eyes again in concentrated thought. "She wore evening dress, of a fantastic kind, markedly Oriental in character, and had large gold rings in her ears. A green embroidered shawl, with raised figures of white birds as a design, took the place of a cloak. It was certainly of Eastern workmanship, possibly Arab; and she wore it about her shoulders with one corner thrown over her head—again, something like a *burnous*. She was extremely dark, had jet-black, frizzy hair and very remarkable eyes, the finest of their type I have ever seen. She possessed beauty of a sort, of course, but without being exactly vulgar, it was what I may term *ostentatious*; and as I entered the library I found myself at a loss to define her exact place in society—you understand what I mean?"

We all nodded comprehendingly and awaited with intense interest the resumption of the story. Mr. Logan had vividly described the Eurasian Zarmi, the creature of Dr. Fu-Manchu.

"When the woman addressed me," he continued, "my surmise that she was some kind of half-caste, probably a Eurasian, was confirmed by her broken English. I shall not be misunderstood"—a slight embarrassment became perceptible in his manner—"if I say that the visitor quite openly tried to bewitch me; and since we are all human, you will perhaps condone my conduct when I add that she succeeded, in a measure, inasmuch as I consented to speak to Sir Baldwin, although he was actually playing bridge at the time.

"Either my eloquence, or, to put it bluntly, the extraordinary fee which the woman offered, resulted in Sir Baldwin's agreeing to abandon his friends and accompany the visitor in a cab which was waiting to see the patient."

"And who was the patient?" rapped Smith.

"According to the woman's account, the patient was her mother, who had met with a street accident a week before. She gave the name of the consultant who had been called in, and who, she stated, had advised the opinion of Sir Baldwin. She represented that the matter was urgent, and that it might be necessary to perform an operation immediately in order to save the patient's life."

"But surely," I interrupted, in surprise, "Sir Baldwin did not take his instruments?"

"He took his case with him—yes," replied Logan; "for he in turn yielded to the appeals of the visitor. The very last words that I heard him speak as he left the house were to assure her that no such operation could be undertaken at such short notice in that way."

Logan paused, looking around at us a little wearily.

"And what aroused your suspicions?" said Smith.

"My suspicions were aroused at the very moment of Sir Baldwin's departure, for as I came out onto the steps with him I noticed a singular thing."

"And that was?" snapped Smith.

"Directly Sir Baldwin had entered the cab the woman got out," replied Logan with some excitement in his manner, "and reclosing the door took her seat beside the driver of the vehicle—which immediately moved off."

Nayland Smith glanced significantly at me.

"The cab trick again, Petrie!" he said; "scarcely a doubt of it." Then, to Logan: "Anything else?"

"This," replied the secretary: "I thought, although I could not be sure, that the face of Sir Baldwin peered out of the window for a moment as the cab moved away from the house, and that there was a strange expression upon it, almost a look of horror. But of course as there was no light in the cab and the only illumination was that from the open door, I could not be sure."

"And now tell Mr. Smith," said Weymouth, "how you got confirmation of your fears."

"I felt very uneasy in my mind," continued Logan, "for the whole thing was so irregular, and I could not rid my memory of the idea of Sir Baldwin's face looking out from the cab window. Therefore I rang up the consultant whose name our visitor had mentioned."

"Yes?" cried Smith eagerly.

"He knew nothing whatever of the matter," said Logan, "and had no such case upon his books! That of course put me in a dreadful state of mind, but I was naturally anxious to avoid making a fool of myself and therefore I waited for some hours before mentioning my suspicions to anyone. But when the morning came and no message was received I determined to communicate with Scotland Yard. The rest of the mystery it is for you, gentlemen, to unravel."

CHAPTER SIXTEEN

I TRACK ZARMI

"What does it mean?" said Nayland Smith wearily, looking at me through the haze of tobacco smoke which lay between us. "A well-known man like Sir Baldwin Frazer is decoyed away—undoubtedly by the woman Zarmi; and up to the present moment not so much as a trace of him can be found. It is mortifying to think that with all the facilities of New Scotland Yard at our disposal we cannot trace that damnable cab! We cannot find the headquarters of the group—we cannot *move*! To sit here inactive whilst Sir Baldwin Frazer—God knows for what purpose!—is perhaps being smuggled out of the country, is maddening—maddening!" Then, glancing quickly across to me: "To think ..."

I rose from my chair, head averted. A tragedy had befallen me which completely overshadowed all other affairs, great and small. Indeed, its poignancy was not yet come to its most acute stage; the news was too recent for that. It had numbed my mind; dulled the pulsing life within me.

The S.S. *Nicobar*, of the Oriental Navigation Line, had arrived at Tilbury at the scheduled time. My heart leaping joyously in my bosom, I had hurried on board to meet Kâramaneh.

I have sustained some cruel blows in my life; but I can state with candor that this which now befell me was by far the greatest and the most crushing I had ever been called upon to bear; a calamity dwarfing all others which I could imagine.

She had left the ship at Southampton—and had vanished completely.

"Poor old Petrie," said Smith, and clapped his hands upon my shoulders in his impulsive sympathetic way. "Don't give up hope! We are not going to be beaten!"

"Smith," I interrupted bitterly, "what chance have we? What chance have we? We know no more than a child unborn where these people have their hiding-place, and we haven't a shadow of a clue to guide us to it."

His hands resting upon my shoulders and his gray eyes looking straightly into mine.

"I can only repeat, old man," said my friend, "don't abandon hope. I must leave you for an hour or so, and, when I return, possibly I may have some news."

For long enough after Smith's departure I sat there, companioned only by wretched reflections; then, further inaction seemed impossible; to move, to be up and doing, to be seeking, questing, became an imperative necessity. Muffled in a heavy traveling coat I went out into the wet and dismal night, having no other plan in mind than that of walking on through the rain-swept streets, on and always on, in an attempt, vain enough, to escape from the deadly thoughts that pursued me.

Without having the slightest idea that I had done so, I must have walked along the Strand, crossed Trafalgar Square, proceeded up the Haymarket to Piccadilly Circus, and commenced to trudge along at the Oriental rugs displayed in Messrs. Liberty's window, when an incident aroused me from the apathy of sorrow in which I was sunken.

"Tell the cab feller to drive to the north side of Wandsworth Common," said a woman's voice—a voice speaking in broken English, a voice which electrified me, had me alert and watchful in a moment.

I turned, as the speaker, entering a taxi-cab that was drawn up by the pavement, gave these directions to the door-porter, who with open umbrella was in attendance. Just one glimpse I had of her as she stepped into the cab, but it was sufficient. Indeed, the voice had been sufficient; but that sinuous shape and that lithe swaying movement of the hips removed all doubt.

It was Zarmi!

As the cab moved off I ran out into the middle of the road, where there was a rank, and sprang into the first taxi waiting there.

"Follow the cab ahead!" I cried to the man, my voice quivering with excitement. "Look! you can see the number! There can be no mistake. But don't lose it for your life! It's worth a sovereign to you!"

The man, warming to my mood, cranked his engine rapidly and sprang to the wheel. I was wild with excitement now, and fearful lest the cab ahead should have disappeared; but fortune seemingly was with me for once, and I was not twenty yards behind when Zarmi's cab turned the first corner ahead. Through the gloomy street, which appeared to be populated solely by streaming umbrellas, we went. I could scarcely keep my seat; every nerve in my body seemed to be dancing—twitching. Eternally I was peering ahead; and when, leaving the well-lighted West End thoroughfares, we came to the comparatively gloomy streets of the suburbs, a hundred times I thought we had lost the track. But always in the pool of light cast by some friendly lamp, I would see the quarry again speeding on before us.

At a lonely spot bordering the common the vehicle which contained Zarmi stopped. I snatched up the speaking-tube.

"Drive on," I cried, "and pull up somewhere beyond! Not too far!"

The man obeyed, and presently I found myself standing in what was now become a steady downpour, looking back at the headlights of the other cab. I gave the driver his promised reward.

"Wait for ten minutes," I directed; "then if I have not returned, you need wait no longer."

I strode along the muddy, unpaved path, to the spot where the cab, now discharged, was being slowly backed away into the road. The figure of Zarmi, unmistakable by reason of the lithe carriage, was crossing in the direction of a path which seemingly led across the common. I followed at a discreet distance. Realizing the tremendous potentialities of this rencontre I seemed to rise to the occasion; my brain became alert and clear; every faculty was at its brightest. And I felt serenely confident of my ability to make the most of the situation.

Zarmi went on and on along the lonely path. Not another pedestrian was in sight, and the rain walled in the pair of us. Where comfort-loving humanity sought shelter from the inclement weather, we two moved out there in the storm, linked by a common enmity.

I have said that my every faculty was keen, and have spoken of my confidence in my own alertness. My condition, as a matter of fact, must have been otherwise, and this belief in my powers merely symptomatic of the fever which consumed me; for, as I was to learn, I had failed to take the first elementary precaution necessary in such case. I, who tracked another, had not counted upon being tracked myself! ...

A bag or sack, reeking of some sickly perfume, was dropped silently, accurately, over my head from behind; it was drawn closely about my throat. One muffled shriek, strangely compound of fear and execration, I uttered. I was stifling, choking … I staggered—and fell….

CHAPTER SEVENTEEN

I MEET DR. FU-MANCHU

My next impression was of a splitting headache, which, as memory remounted its throne, brought up a train of recollections. I found myself to be seated upon a heavy wooden bench set flat against a wall, which was covered with a kind of straw matting. My hands were firmly tied behind me. In the first agony of that reawakening I became aware of two things.

I was in an operating-room, for the most conspicuous item of its furniture was an operating-table! Shaded lamps were suspended above it; and instruments, antiseptics, dressings, etc., were arranged upon a glass-topped table beside it. Secondly, I had a companion.

Seated upon a similar bench on the other side of the room, was a heavily built man, his dark hair splashed with gray, as were his short, neatly trimmed beard and mustache. He, too, was pinioned; and he stared across the table with a glare in which a sort of stupefied wonderment predominated, but which was not free from terror.

It was Sir Baldwin Frazer!

"Sir Baldwin!" I muttered, moistening my parched lips with my tongue—"Sir Baldwin!—how—"

"It is Dr. Petrie, is it not?" he said, his voice husky with emotion. "Dr. Petrie!—my dear sir, in mercy tell me—what does this mean? I have been kidnapped—drugged; made the victim of an inconceivable outrage at the very door of my own house…."

I stood up unsteadily.

"Sir Baldwin," I interrupted, "you ask me what it means. It means that we are in the hands of Dr. Fu-Manchu!"

Sir Baldwin stared at me wildly; his face was white and drawn with anxiety.

"Dr. Fu-Manchu!" he said; "but my dear sir, this name conveys nothing to me—nothing!" His manner momentarily was growing more distrait. "Since my captivity began I have been given the use of a singular suite of rooms in this place, and received, I must confess, every possible attention. I have been waited upon by the she-devil who lured me here, but not one word other than a species of coarse badinage has she spoken to me. At times I have been tempted to believe that the fate which frequently befalls the specialist had befallen me? You understand?"

"I quite understand," I replied dully. "There have been times in the past when I, too, have doubted my sanity in my dealings with the group who now hold us in their power."

"But," reiterated the other, his voice rising higher and higher, "what does it mean, my dear sir? It is incredible—fantastic! Even now I find it difficult to disabuse my mind of that old, haunting idea."

"Disabuse it at once, Sir Baldwin," I said bitterly. "The facts are as you see them; the explanation, at any rate in your own case, is quite beyond me. I was tracked …"

"Hush! someone is coming!"

We both turned and stared at an opening before which hung a sort of gaudily embroidered mat, as the sound of dragging footsteps, accompanied by a heavy tapping, announced the approach of *someone.*

The mat was pulled aside by Zarmi. She turned her head, flashing around the apartment a glance of her black eyes, then held the drapery aside to admit the entrance of another....

Supporting himself by the aid of two heavy walking sticks and painfully dragging his gaunt frame along, *Dr. Fu-Manchu entered*!

I think I have never experienced in my life a sensation identical to that which now possessed me. Although Nayland Smith had declared that Fu-Manchu was alive, yet I would have sworn upon oath before any jury summonable that he was dead; for with my own eyes I had seen the bullet enter his skull. Now, whilst I crouched against the matting-covered wall, teeth tightly clenched and my very hair quivering upon my scalp, he dragged himself laboriously across the room, the sticks going *tap—tap—tap* upon the floor, and the tall body, enveloped in a yellow robe, bent grotesquely, gruesomely, with every effort which he made. He wore a surgical bandage about his skull and its presence seemed to accentuate the height of the great domelike brow, to throw into more evil prominence the wonderful, Satanic countenance of the man. His filmed eyes turning to right and left, he dragged himself to a wooden chair that stood beside the operating-table and sank down upon it, breathing sibilantly, exhaustedly.

Zarmi dropped the curtain and stood before it. She had discarded the dripping overall which she had been wearing when I had followed her across the common, and now stood before me with her black, frizzy hair unconfined and her beautiful, wicked face uplifted in a sort of cynical triumph. The big gold rings in her ears glittered strangely in the light of the electric lamps. She wore a garment which looked like a silken shawl wrapped about her in a wildly picturesque fashion, and, her hands upon her hips, leant back against the curtain glancing defiantly from Sir Baldwin to myself.

Those moments of silence which followed the entrance of the Chinese doctor live in my memory and must live there for ever. Only the labored breathing of Fu-Manchu disturbed the stillness of the place. Not a sound penetrated to the room, no one uttered a word; then—

"Sir Baldwin Frazer," began Fu-Manchu in that indescribable voice, alternating between the sibilant and the guttural, "you were promised a certain fee for your services by my servant who summoned you. It shall be paid and the gift of my personal gratitude be added to it."

He turned himself with difficulty to address Sir Baldwin; and it became apparent to me that he was almost completely paralyzed down one side of his body. Some little use he could make of his hand and arm, for he still clutched the heavy carven stick, but the right side of his face was completely immobile; and rarely had I seen anything more ghastly than the effect produced upon that wonderful, Satanic countenance. The mouth, from the center of the thin lips, opened only to the left, as he spoke; in a word, seen in profile from where I sat, or rather crouched, it was the face of a dead man.

Sir Baldwin Frazer uttered no word, but, crouching upon the bench even as I crouched, stared—horror written upon every lineament—at Dr. Fu-Manchu. The latter continued:—

"Your experience, Sir Baldwin, will enable you readily to diagnose my symptoms. Owing to the passage of a bullet along a portion of the third left frontal into the postero-parietal convolution—upon which, from its lodgment in the skull, it continues to press—hemiplegia of the right side has supervened. Aphasia is present also…."

The effort of speech was ghastly. Beads of perspiration dewed Fu-Manchu's brow, and I marveled at the iron will of the man, whereby alone he forced his half-numbed brain to perform its function. He seemed to select his words elaborately and by this monstrous effort of will to compel his partially paralyzed tongue to utter them. Some of the syllables were slurred; but nevertheless distinguishable. It was a demonstration of sheer *force* unlike any I had witnessed, and it impressed me unforgettably.

"The removal of this injurious particle," he continued, "would be an operation which I myself could undertake to perform successfully upon another. It is a matter of some delicacy as you, Sir Baldwin, and"—slowly, horribly, turning the half-dead and half-living head towards me—"you, Dr. Petrie, will appreciate. In the event of clumsy surgery, death may supervene; failing this, permanent hemiplegia—or"—the film lifted from the green eyes, and for a moment they flickered with transient horror—"idiocy! Any one of three of my pupils whom I might name could perform this operation with ease, but their services are not available. Only one English surgeon occurred to me in this connection, and you, Sir Baldwin"—again he slowly turned his head—"were he. Dr. Petrie will act as anaesthetist, and, your duties completed, you shall return to your home richer by the amount stipulated. I have suitably prepared myself for the operation, and I can assure you of the soundness of my heart. I may advise you, Dr. Petrie"—again turning to me—"that my constitution is inured to the use of opium. You will make due allowance for this. Mr. Li-King-Su, a graduate of Canton, will act as dresser."

He turned laboriously to Zarmi. She clapped her hands and held the curtain aside. A perfectly immobile Chinaman, whose age I was unable to guess, and who wore a white overall, entered, bowed composedly to Frazer and myself and began in a matter-of-fact way to prepare the dressings.

CHAPTER EIGHTEEN

QUEEN OF HEARTS

"Sir Baldwin Frazer," said Fu-Manchu, interrupting a wild outburst from the former, "your refusal is dictated by insufficient knowledge of your surroundings. You find yourself in a place strange to you, a place to which no clue can lead your friends; in the absolute power of a man—myself—who knows no law other than his own and that of those associated with him. Virtually, Sir Baldwin, you stand in China; and in China we know how to *exact* obedience. You will not refuse, for Dr. Petrie will tell you something of my *wire jackets* and my *files*...."

I saw Sir Baldwin Frazer blanch. He could not know what I knew of the significance of those words—"my wire jackets, my files"—but perhaps something of my own horror communicated itself to him.

"You will not *refuse*," continued Fu-Manchu softly; "my only fear for you is that the operation my prove unsuccessful! In that event not even my own great clemency could save you, for by virtue of your failure I should be powerless to intervene." He paused for some moments, staring directly at the surgeon. "There are those within sound of my voice," he added sibilantly, "who would flay you alive in the lamentable event of your failure, who would cast your flayed body"—he paused, waving one quivering fist above his head, and his voice rose in a sudden frenzied shriek—"to the rats—to the rats!"

Sir Baldwin's forehead was bathed in perspiration now. It was an incredible and a gruesome situation, a nightmare become reality. But, whatever my own case, I could see that Sir Baldwin Frazer was convinced, I could see that his consent would no longer be withheld.

"You, my dear friend," said Fu-Manchu, turning to me and resuming his studied and painful composure of manner, "will also consent...."

Within my heart of hearts I could not doubt him; I knew that my courage was not of a quality high enough to sustain the frightful ordeals summoned up before my imagination by those words—"my files, my wire jackets!"

"In the event, however, of any little obstinancy," he added, "another will plead with you."

A chill like that of death descended upon me—as, for the second time, Zarmi clapped her hands, pulled the curtain aside and Kâramaneh was thrust into the room!

There comes a blank in my recollections. Long after Kâramaneh had been plucked out again by the two muscular brown hands which clutched her shoulders from the darkness beyond the doorway, I seemed to see her standing there, in her close-fitting traveling dress. Her hair was unbound, disheveled, her lovely face pale to the lips—and her eyes, her glorious, terror-bright eyes, looked fully into mine.

Not a word did she utter, and I was stricken dumb as one who has plucked the Flower of Silence. Only those wondrous eyes seemed to look into my soul, searing, consuming me.

Fu-Manchu had been speaking for some time ere my brain began again to record his words.

"—and this magnanimity," came dully to my ears, "extends to you, Dr. Petrie, because of my esteem. I have little cause to love Kâramaneh"—his voice quivered furiously—"but she can yet be of use to me, and I would not harm a hair of her beautiful head—except in the event of your obstinacy. Shall we then determine your immediate future upon the turn of a card, as the gamester within me, within every one of my race, suggests?"

"Yes, yes!" came hoarsely.

I fought mentally to restore myself to a full knowledge of what was happening, and I realized that the last words had come from the lips of Sir Baldwin Frazer.

"Dr. Petrie," Frazer said, still in the same hoarse and unnatural voice, "what else can we do? At least take the chance of recovering your freedom, for how otherwise can you hope to serve—your friend…."

"God knows!" I said dully; "do as you wish"—and cared not to what I had agreed.

Plunging his hand beneath his white overall, the Chinaman who had been referred to as Li-King-Su calmly produced a pack of cards, unemotionally shuffled them and extended the pack to me.

I shook my head grimly, for my hands were tied. Picking up a lancet from the table, the Chinaman cut the cords which bound me, and again extended the pack. I took a card and laid it on my knee without even glancing at it. Fu-Manchu, with his left hand, in turn selected a card, looked at it and then turned its face towards me.

"It would seem, Dr. Petrie," he said calmly, "that you are fated to remain here as my guest. You will have the felicity of residing beneath the same roof with Kâramaneh."

The card was the Knave of Diamonds.

Conscious of a sudden excitement, I snatched up the card from my knee. It was the Queen of Hearts! For a moment I tasted exultation, then I tossed it upon the floor. I was not fool enough to suppose that the Chinese doctor would pay his debt of honor and release me.

"Your star above mine," said Fu-Manchu, his calm unruffled. "I place myself in your hands, Sir Baldwin."

Assisted by his unemotional compatriot, Fu-Manchu discarded the yellow robe, revealing himself in a white singlet in all his gaunt ugliness, and extended his frame upon the operating-table.

Li-King-Su ignited the large lamp over the head of the table, and from his case took out a trephine.

"Other points for your guidance from my own considerable store of experience"—Fu-Manchu was speaking—"are written out clearly in the notebook which lies upon the table...."

His voice, now, was toneless, emotionless, as though his part in the critical operation about to be performed were that of a spectator. No trace of nervousness, of fear, could I discern; his pulse was practically normal.

How I shuddered as I touched his yellow skin! How my very soul rose up in revolt! ...

"There is the bullet!—quick! ... Steady, Petrie!"

Sir Baldwin Frazer, keen, cool, deft, was metamorphosed, was the enthusiastic, brilliant surgeon whom I knew and revered, and another than the nerveless captive who, but a few minutes ago, had stared, panic-stricken, at Dr. Fu-Manchu.

Although I had met him once or twice professionally, I had never hitherto seen him operate; and his method was little short of miraculous. It was stimulating, inspiring. With unerring touch he whittled madness, death, from the very throne of reason, of life.

Now was the crucial moment of his task … and, with its coming, every light in the room suddenly failed—went out!

"My God!" whispered Frazer, in the darkness, "quick! quick! lights! a match!—a candle!—something, anything!"

There came a faint click, and a beam of white light was directed, steadily, upon the patient's skull. Li-King-Su—unmoved—held an electric torch in his hand!

Frazer and I set to work, in a fierce battle to fend off Death, who already outstretched his pinions over the insensible man—to fend off Death from the arch-murderer, the enemy of the white races, who lay there at our mercy! …

"It seems you want a pick-me-up!" said Zarmi. Sir Baldwin Frazer collapsed into the cane armchair. Only a matting curtain separated us from the room wherein he had successfully performed perhaps the most wonderful operation of his career.

"I could not have lasted out another thirty seconds, Petrie!" he whispered. "The events which led up to it had exhausted my nerves and I had no reserve to call upon. If that last …"

He broke off, the sentence uncompleted, and eagerly seized the tumbler containing brandy and soda, which the beautiful, wicked-eyed Eurasian passed to him. She turned, and prepared a drink for me, with the insolent *insouciance* which had never deserted her.

I emptied the tumbler at a draught.

Even as I set the glass down I realized, too late, that it was the first drink I had ever permitted to pass my lips within an abode of Dr. Fu-Manchu….

I started to my feet.

"Frazer!" I muttered—"we've been drugged! we ..."

"You sit down," came Zarmi's husky voice, and I felt her hands upon my breast, pushing me back into my seat. "You very tired ... you go to sleep...."

"Petrie! Dr. Petrie!"

The words broke in through the curtain of unconsciousness. I strove to arouse myself. I felt cold and wet. I opened my eyes—and the world seemed to be swimming dizzily about me. Then a hand grasped my arm, roughly.

"Brace up! Brace up, Petrie—and thank God you are alive! ..."

I was sitting beside Sir Baldwin Frazer on a wooden bench, under a leafless tree, from the ghostly limbs whereof rain trickled down upon me! In the gray light, which, I thought, must be the light of dawn, I discerned other trees about us and an open expanse, tree-dotted, stretching into the misty grayness.

"Where are we?" I muttered—"Where ..."

"Unless I am greatly mistaken," replied my bedraggled companion, "and I don't think I am, for I attended a consultation in this neighborhood less than a week ago, we are somewhere on the west side of Wandsworth Common!"

He ceased speaking; then uttered a suppressed cry. There came a jangling of coins, and dimly I saw him to be staring at a canvas bag of money which he held.

"Merciful heavens!" he said, "am I mad—or did I *really* perform that operation? And can this be my fee? ..."

I laughed loudly, wildly, plunging my wet, cold hands into the pockets of my rain-soaked overcoat. In one of them, my fingers came in contact with a piece of cardboard. It had an unfamiliar feel, and I pulled it out, peering at it in the dim light.

"Well, I'm damned!" muttered Frazer—"then I'm not mad, after all!"

It was the Queen of Hearts!

CHAPTER NINETEEN

"ZAGAZIG"

Fully two weeks elapsed ere Nayland Smith's arduous labors at last met with a slight reward. For a moment, the curtain of mystery surrounding the Si-Fan was lifted, and we had a glimpse of that organization's elaborate mechanism. I cannot better commence my relation of the episodes associated with the Zagazig's cryptogram than from the moment when I found myself bending over a prostrate form extended upon the table in the inspector's room at the River Police Depot. It was that of a man who looked like a Lascar, who wore an ill-fitting slop-shop suit of blue, soaked and stained and clinging hideously to his body. His dank black hair was streaked upon his low brow; and his face, although it was notable for a sort of evil leer, had assumed in death another and more dreadful expression.

Asphyxiation had accounted for his end beyond doubt, but there were marks about his throat of clutching fingers, his tongue protruded, and the look in the dead eyes was appalling.

"He was amongst the piles upholding the old wharf at the back of the Joy-Shop?" said Smith tersely, turning to the police officer in charge.

"Exactly!" was the reply. "The in-coming tide had jammed him right up under a cross-beam."

"What time was that?'

"Well, at high tide last night. Hewson, returning with the ten o'clock boat, noticed the moonlight glittering upon the knife."

The knife to which the inspector referred possessed a long curved blade of a kind with which I had become terribly familiar in the past. The dead man still clutched the hilt of the weapon in his right hand, and it now lay with the blade resting crosswise upon his breast. I stared in a fascinated way at this mysterious and tragic flotsam of old Thames.

Glancing up, I found Nayland Smith's gray eyes watching me.

"You see the mark, Petrie?" he snapped.

I nodded. The dead man upon the table was a Burmese dacoit!

"What do you make of it?" I said slowly.

"At the moment," replied Smith, "I scarcely know what to make of it. You are agreed with the divisional surgeon that the man—unquestionably a dacoit—died, not from drowning, but from strangulation. From evidence we have heard, it would appear that the encounter which resulted in the body being hurled in the river, actually took place upon the wharf-end beneath which he was found. And we know that a place formerly used by the Si-Fan group—in other words, by Dr. Fu-Manchu—adjoins the wharf. I am tempted to believe that this"—he nodded towards the ghastly and sinister object upon the table—"was a servant of the Chinese doctor. In other words, we see before us one whom Fu-Manchu has rebuked for some shortcoming."

I shuddered coldly. Familiar as I should have been with the methods of the dread Chinaman, with his callous disregard of human suffering, of human life, of human law, I could not reconcile my ideas—the ideas of a modern, ordinary middle-class practitioner—with these Far Eastern devilries which were taking place in London.

Even now I sometimes found myself doubting the reality of the whole thing; found myself reviewing the history of the Eastern doctor and of the horrible group of murderers surrounding him, with an incredulity almost unbelievable in one who had been actually in contact not only with the servants of the Chinaman, but with the sinister Fu-Manchu himself. Then, to restore me to grips with reality, would come the thought of Kâramaneh, of the beautiful girl whose love had brought me seemingly endless sorrow and whose love for me had brought her once again into the power of that mysterious, implacable being.

This thought was enough. With its coming, fantasy vanished; and I knew that the dead dacoit, his great curved knife yet clutched in his hand, the Yellow menace hanging over London, over England, over the civilized world, the absence, the heart-breaking absence, of Kâramaneh—all were real, all were true, all were part of my life.

Nayland Smith was standing staring vaguely before him and tugging at the lobe of his left ear.

"Come along!" he snapped suddenly. "We have no more to learn here: The clue to the mystery must be sought elsewhere."

There was that in his manner whereby I knew that his thoughts were far away, as we filed out from the River Police Depot to the cab which awaited us. Pulling from his overcoat pocket a copy of a daily paper—

"Have you seen this, Weymouth?" he demanded.

With a long, nervous index finger he indicated a paragraph on the front page which appeared under the heading of "Personal." Weymouth bent frowningly over the paper, holding it close to his eyes, for this was a gloomy morning and the light in the cab was poor.

"Such things don't enter into my sphere, Mr. Smith," he replied, "but no doubt the proper department at the Yard have seen it."

"I *know* they have seen it!" snapped Smith; "but they have also been unable to read it!"

Weymouth looked up in surprise.

"Indeed," he said. "You are interested in this, then?"

"Very! Have you any suggestion to offer respecting it?"

Moving from my seat I, also, bent over the paper and read, in growing astonishment, the following:—

ZAGAZIG—Z,—a—•g•—*a*;—z:—*I*—*g*,*z*,—*a*,—*g*•—*a*,z;—*I*;—g:—
z•a•g•A—*z*;i—:*g*;—Z,—*a*;—*g*•a•z•*i*;—G;—z—,a•g—:*a*•—z•*I*;—
g:—z•—*a*•*g*;—a—:Z—,i•g:z,a•*g*,—a:z,*i*—:g•

"This is utterly incomprehensible! It can be nothing but some foolish practical joke! It consists merely of the word 'Zagazig' repeated six or seven times—which can have no possible significance!"

"Can't it!" snapped Smith.

"Well," I said, "what has Zagazig to do with Fu-Manchu, or to do with us?"

"Zagazig, my dear Petrie, is a very unsavory Arab town in Lower Egypt, as you know!"

He returned the paper to the pocket of his overcoat, and, noting my bewildered glance, burst into one of his sudden laughs.

"You think I am talking nonsense," he said; "but, as a matter of fact, that message in the paper has been puzzling me since it appeared—yesterday morning—and at last I think I see the light."

He pulled out his pipe and began rapidly to load it.

"I have been growing careless of late, Petrie," he continued; and no hint of merriment remained in his voice. His gaunt face was drawn grimly, and his eyes glittered like steel. "In future I must avoid going out alone at night as much as possible."

Inspector Weymouth was staring at Smith in a puzzled way; and certainly I was every whit as mystified as he.

"I am disposed to believe," said my friend, in his rapid, incisive way, "that the dacoit met his end at the hands of a tall man, possibly dark and almost certainly clean-shaven. If this missing personage wears, on chilly nights, a long tweed traveling coat and affects soft gray hats of the Stetson pattern, I shall not be surprised."

Weymouth stared at me in frank bewilderment.

"By the way, Inspector," added Smith, a sudden gleam of inspiration entering his keen eyes—"did I not see that the S.S. *Andaman* arrived recently?"

"The Oriental Navigation Company's boat?" inquired Weymouth in a hopeless tone. "Yes. She docked yesterday evening."

"If Jack Forsyth is still chief officer, I shall look him up," declared Smith. "You recall his brother, Petrie?"

"Naturally; since he was done to death in my presence," I replied; for the words awoke memories of one of Dr. Fu-Manchu's most ghastly crimes, always associated in my mind with the cry of a night-hawk.

"The divine afflatus should never be neglected," announced Nayland Smith didactically, "wild though its promptings may seem."

CHAPTER TWENTY

THE NOTE ON THE DOOR

I saw little of Nayland Smith for the remainder of that day. Presumably he was following those "promptings" to which he had referred, though I was unable to conjecture whither they were leading him. Then, towards dusk he arrived in a perfect whirl, figuratively sweeping me off my feet.

"Get your coat on, Petrie!" he cried; "you forget that we have a most urgent appointment!"

Beyond doubt I had forgotten that we had any appointment whatever that evening, and some surprise must have shown upon my face, for—

"Really you are becoming very forgetful!" my friend continued. "You know we can no longer trust the phone. I have to leave certain instructions for Weymouth at the rendezvous!"

There was a hidden significance in his manner, and, my memory harking back to an adventure which we had shared in the past, I suddenly glimpsed the depths of my own stupidity.

He suspected the presence of an eavesdropper! Yes! incredible though it might appear, we were spied upon in the New Louvre;

agents of the Si-Fan, of Dr. Fu-Manchu, were actually within the walls of the great hotel!

We hurried out into the corridor, and descended by the lift to the lobby. M. Samarkan, long famous as *maître d'hôtel* of one of Cairo's fashionable *khans*, and now principal of the New Louvre, greeted us with true Greek courtesy. He trusted that we should be present at some charitable function or other to be held at the hotel on the following evening.

"If possible, M. Samarkan—if possible," said Smith. "We have many demands upon our time." Then, abruptly, to me: "Come, Petrie, we will walk as far as Charing Cross and take a cab from the rank there."

"The hall-porter can call you a cab," said M. Samarkan, solicitous for the comfort of his guests.

"Thanks," snapped Smith; "we prefer to walk a little way."

Passing along the Strand, he took my arm, and speaking close to my ear—

"That place is alive with spies, Petrie," he said; "or if there are only a few of them they are remarkably efficient!"

Not another word could I get from him, although I was eager enough to talk; since one dearer to me than all else in the world was in the hands of the damnable organization we knew as the Si-Fan; until, arrived at Charing Cross, he walked out to the cab rank, and—

"Jump in!" he snapped.

He opened the door of the first cab on the rank.

"Drive to J— Street, Kennington," he directed the man.

In something of a mental stupor I entered and found myself seated beside Smith. The cab made off towards Trafalgar Square, then swung around into Whitehall.

"Look behind!" cried Smith, intense excitement expressed in his voice—"look behind!"

I turned and peered through the little square window.

The cab which had stood second upon the rank was closely following us!

"We are tracked!" snapped my companion. "If further evidence were necessary of the fact that our every movement is watched, here it is!"

I turned to him, momentarily at a loss for words; then—

"Was this the object of our journey?" I said. "Your reference to a 'rendezvous' was presumably addressed to a hypothetical spy?

"Partly," he replied. "I have a plan, as you will see in a moment."

I looked again from the window in the rear of the cab. We were now passing between the House of Lords and the back of Westminster Abbey ... and fifty yards behind us the pursuing cab was crossing from Whitehall! A great excitement grew up within me, and a great curiosity respecting the identity of our pursuer.

"What is the place for which we are bound, Smith?" I said rapidly.

"It is a house which I chanced to notice a few days ago, and I marked it as useful for such a purpose as our present one. You will see what I mean when we arrive."

On we went, following the course of the river, then turned over Vauxhall Bridge and on down Vauxhall Bridge Road into a very dreary neighborhood where gasometers formed the notable feature of the landscape.

"That's the Oval just beyond," said Smith suddenly, "and—here we are."

In a narrow *cul-de-sac* which apparently communicated with the boundary of the famous cricket ground, the cabman pulled up. Smith jumped out and paid the fare.

"Pull back to that court with the iron posts," he directed the man, "and wait there for me." Then: "Come on, Petrie!" he snapped.

Side by side we entered the wooden gate of a small detached house, or more properly cottage, and passed up the tiled path towards a sort of side entrance which apparently gave access to the tiny garden. At this moment I became aware of two things; the first, that the house was an empty one, and the second, that someone—someone who had quitted the second cab (which I had heard pull up at no great distance behind us) was approaching stealthily along the dark and uninviting street, walking upon the opposite pavement and taking advantage of the shadow of a high wooden fence which skirted it for some distance.

Smith pushed the gate open, and I found myself in a narrow passageway in almost complete darkness. But my friend walked confidently forward, turned the angle of the building and entered the miniature wilderness which once had been a garden.

"In here, Petrie!" he whispered.

He seized me by the arm, pushed open a door and thrust me forward down two stone steps into absolute darkness.

"Walk straight ahead!" he directed, still in the same intense whisper, "and you will find a locked door having a broken panel. Watch through the opening for any one who may enter the room beyond, but see that your presence is not detected. Whatever I say or do, don't stir until I actually rejoin you."

He stepped back across the floor and was gone. One glimpse I had of him, silhouetted against the faint light of the open door, then the door was gently closed, and I was left alone in the empty house.

Smith's methods frequently surprised me, but always in the past I had found that they were dictated by sound reasons. I had no doubt that an emergency unknown to me dictated his present course, but it was with my mind in a wildly confused condition, that I groped for and found the door with the broken panel and that I stood there in the complete darkness of the deserted house listening.

I can well appreciate how the blind develop an unusually keen sense of hearing; for there, in the blackness, which (at first) was entirely unrelieved by any speck of light, I became aware of the fact, by dint of tense listening, that Smith was retiring by means of some gateway at the upper end of the little garden, and I became aware of the fact that a lane or court, with which this gateway communicated, gave access to the main road.

Faintly, I heard our discharged cab backing out from the *cul-de-sac*; then, from some nearer place, came Smith's voice speaking loudly.

"Come along, Petrie!" he cried; "there is no occasion for us to wait. Weymouth will see the note pinned on the door."

I started—and was about to stumble back across the room, when, as my mind began to work more clearly, I realized that the words had been spoken as a ruse—a favorite device of Nayland Smith's.

Rigidly I stood there, and continued to listen.

"All right, cabman!" came more distantly now; "back to the New Louvre—jump in, Petrie!"

The cab went rattling away … as a faint light became perceptible in the room beyond the broken panel.

Hitherto I had been able to detect the presence of this panel only by my sense of touch and by means of a faint draught which blew through it; now it suddenly became clearly perceptible. I found myself looking into what was evidently the principal room of the house—a dreary apartment with tatters of paper hanging from the walls and litter of all sorts lying about upon the floor and in the rusty fireplace.

Someone had partly raised the front window and opened the shutters. A patch of moonlight shone down upon the floor immediately below my hiding-place and furthermore enabled me vaguely to discern the disorder of the room.

A bulky figure showed silhouetted against the dirty panes. It was that of a man who, leaning upon the window sill, was peering intently in. Silently he had approached, and silently had raised the sash and opened the shutters.

For thirty seconds or more he stood so, moving his head from right to left … and I watched him through the broken panel, almost holding my breath with suspense. Then, fully raising the window, the man stepped into the room, and, first reclosing the shutters, suddenly flashed the light of an electric lamp all about the place. I was enabled to discern him more clearly, this mysterious spy who had tracked us from the moment that we had left the hotel.

He was a man of portly build wearing a heavy fur-lined overcoat and having a soft felt hat, the brim turned down so as to shade the upper part of his face. Moreover, he wore his fur collar turned up, which served further to disguise him, since it concealed the greater part of his chin. But the eyes which now were searching every corner of the room, the alert, dark eyes, were strangely familiar. The black mustache, the clear-cut, aquiline nose, confirmed the impression.

Our follower was M. Samarkan, manager of the New Louvre.

I suppressed a gasp of astonishment. Small wonder that our plans had leaked out. This was a momentous discovery indeed.

And as I watched the portly Greek who was not only one of the most celebrated *mâitres d'hôtel* in Europe, but also a creature of Dr. Fu-Manchu, he cast the light of his electric lamp upon a note attached by means of a drawing-pin to the inside of the room door. I immediately divined that my friend must have pinned the note in its place earlier in the day; even at that distance I recognized Smith's neat, illegible writing.

Samarkan quickly scanned the message scribbled upon the white page; then, exhibiting an agility uncommon in a man of his bulk, he threw open the shutters again, having first replaced his lamp in his pocket, climbed out into the little front garden, reclosed the window, and disappeared!

A moment I stood, lost to my surroundings, plunged in a sea of wonderment concerning the damnable organization which, its tentacles extending I knew not whither, since new and unexpected limbs were ever coming to light, sought no less a goal than Yellow dominion of the world! I reflected how one man—Nayland Smith—alone stood between this powerful group and the realization of their project … when I was aroused by a hand grasping my arm in the darkness!

I uttered a short cry, of which I was instantly ashamed, for Nayland Smith's voice came:—

"I startled you, eh, Petrie?"

"Smith," I said, "how long have you been standing there?"

"I only returned in time to see our Fenimore Cooper friend retreating through the window," he replied; "but no doubt you had a good look at him?"

"I had!" I answered eagerly. "It was Samarkan!"

"I thought so! I have suspected as much for a long time."

"Was this the object of our visit here?"

"It was one of the objects," admitted Nayland Smith evasively.

From some place not far distant came the sound of a restarted engine.

"The other," he added, "was this: to enable M. Samarkan to read the note which I had pinned upon the door!"

CHAPTER TWENTY-ONE

THE SECOND MESSAGE

"Here you are, Petrie," said Nayland Smith—and he tossed across the table the folded copy of a morning paper. "This may assist you in your study of the first Zagazig message."

I set down my cup and turned my attention to the "Personal" column on the front page of the journal. A paragraph appeared therein conceived as follows:—

ZAGAZIG—Z,—a—•g•—*a;*—z:—I:—*g;z,*•—*a,g;*—A—*z;i*—:G,—z:—*a;*g—A,z—*i;*—g•z,•*A;g,*a•Z—•*i;g,*z:a,*g*—:a z i g•

I stared across at my friend in extreme bewilderment.

"But, Smith!" I cried, "these messages are utterly meaningless!"

"Not at all," he rapped back. "Scotland Yard thought they were meaningless at first, and I must admit that they suggested nothing to me for a long time; but the dead dacoit was the clue to the first, Petrie, and the note pinned upon the door of the house near the Oval is the clue to the second."

Stupidly I continued to stare at him until he broke into a grim smile.

"Surely you understand?" he said. "You remember where the dead Burman was found?"

"Perfectly."

"You know the street along which, ordinarily, one would approach the wharf?"

"Three Colt Street?"

"Three Colt Street, exactly. Well, on the night that the Burman met his end I had an appointment in Three Colt Street with Weymouth. The appointment was made by phone, from the New Louvre! My cab broke down and I never arrived. I discovered later that Weymouth had received a telegram purporting to come from me, putting off the engagement."

"I am aware of all this!"

Nayland Smith burst into a loud laugh.

"But *still* you are fogged!" he cried. "Then I'm hanged if I'll pilot you any farther! You have all the facts before you. There lies the first Zagazig message; here is the second; and you know the context of the note pinned upon the door? It read, if you remember, 'Remove patrol from Joy-Shop neighborhood. Have a theory. Wish to visit place alone on Monday night after one o'clock.'"

"Smith," I said dully, "I have a heavy stake upon this murderous game."

His manner changed instantly; the tanned face grew grim and hard, but the steely eyes softened strangely. He bent over me, clapping his hands upon my shoulders.

"I know it, old man," he replied; "and because it may serve to keep your mind busy during hours when otherwise it would be engaged with profitless sorrows, I invite you to puzzle out this business for yourself. You have nothing else to do until late tonight, and you can work undisturbed, here, at any rate!"

His words referred to the fact that, without surrendering our suite at the New Louvre Hotel, we had gone upon a visit, of indefinite duration, to a mythical friend; and now were quartered in furnished chambers adjoining Fleet Street.

We had remained at the New Louvre long enough to secure confirmation of our belief that a creature of Fu-Manchu spied upon us there; and now we only awaited the termination of the night's affair to take such steps as Smith might consider politic in regard to the sardonic Greek who presided over London's newest and most palatial hotel.

Smith setting out for New Scotland Yard in order to make certain final arrangements in connection with the business of the night, I began closely to study the mysterious Zagazig messages, determined not to be beaten, and remembering the words of Edgar Allan Poe—the strange genius to whom we are indebted for the first workable system of deciphering cryptograms: "It may well be doubted whether human ingenuity can construct an enigma of the kind which human ingenuity may not, by proper application, resolve."

The first conclusion to which I was borne was this: that the letters comprising the word "Zagazig" were designed merely to confuse the reader, and might be neglected; since, occurring as they did in regular sequence, they could possess no significance. I became quite excited upon making the discovery that the *punctuation marks* varied in almost every case!

I immediately assumed that these constituted the cipher; and, seeking for my key-letter, *e* (that which most frequently occurs in the English language), I found the sign of a full stop to appear more frequently than any other in the first message, namely ten times, although it only occurred thrice in the second. Nevertheless, I was hopeful … until I discovered that in two cases it appeared three times *in succession*!

There is no word in English, nor, so far as I am aware, in any language, where this occurs, either in regard to *e* or any other letter!

That unfortunate discovery seemed so wholly to destroy the very theory upon which I relied, that I almost abandoned my investigation there and then. Indeed, I doubt if I ever should have proceeded were it not that by a piece of pure guesswork I blundered on to a clue.

I observed that certain letters, at irregularly occurring intervals, were set in capital, and I divided up the message into corresponding sections, in the hope that the capitals might indicate the commencements of words. This accomplished, I set out upon a series of guesses, basing these upon Smith's assurance that the death of the dacoit afforded a clue to the first message and the note which he (Smith) had pinned upon the door a clue to the second.

Such being my system—if I can honor my random attempts with the title—I take little credit to myself for the fortunate result. In short, I determined (although *e* twice occurred where *r* should have been!) that the first message from the thirteenth letter, onwards to the twenty-seventh (*id est: I;*—g:—*z*•a•g•A•*z;*i—*;g;*—Z,—*a;*—*g*•a•z•*i;*—) read:—

"Three Colt Street."

Endeavoring, now, to eliminate the *e* where *r* should appear, I made another discovery. The presence of a letter in *italics* altered the value of the sign which followed it!

From that point onward the task became child's-play, and I should merely render this account tedious if I entered into further details. Both messages commenced with the name "Smith" as I early perceived, and half an hour of close study gave me the complete sentences, thus:—

1. *Smith passing Three Colt Street twelve-thirty Wednesday.*

2. *Smith going Joy-Shop after one Monday.*

The word "Zagazig" was completed, always, and did not necessarily terminate with the last letter occurring in the cryptographic message. A subsequent inspection of this curious code has enabled Nayland Smith, by a process of simple deduction, to compile the entire alphabet employed by Dr. Fu-Manchu's agent, Samarkan, in communicating with his awful superior. With a little patience, any one of my readers my achieve the same result (and I should be pleased to hear from those who succeed!).

This, then was the outcome of my labors; and although it enlightened me to some extent, I realized that I still had much to learn.

The dacoit, apparently, had met his death at the very hour when Nayland Smith should have been passing along Three Colt Street—a thoroughfare with an unsavory reputation. Who had killed him?

Tonight, Samarkan advised the Chinese doctor, Smith would again be in the same dangerous neighborhood. A strange thrill of excitement swept through me. I glanced at my watch. Yes! It was time for me to repair, secretly, to my post. For I, too, had business on the borders of Chinátown tonight.

CHAPTER TWENTY-TWO

THE SECRET OF THE WHARF

I sat in the evil-smelling little room with its low, blackened ceiling, and strove to avoid making the slightest noise; but the crazy boards creaked beneath me with every movement. The moon hung low in an almost cloudless sky; for, following the spell of damp and foggy weather, a fall in temperature had taken place, and there was a frosty snap in the air tonight.

Through the open window the moonlight poured in and spilled its pure luminance upon the filthy floor; but I kept religiously within the shadows, so posted, however, that I could command an uninterrupted view of the street from the point where it crossed the creek to that where it terminated at the gates of the deserted wharf.

Above and below me the crazy building formerly known as the Joy-Shop and once the nightly resort of the Asiatic riff-raff from the docks—was silent, save for the squealing and scuffling of the rats. The melancholy lapping of the water frequently reached my ears, and a more or less continuous din from the wharves and workshops upon the further bank of the Thames; but in the narrow, dingy streets immediately surrounding the house, quietude reigned and no solitary footstep disturbed it.

Once, looking down in the direction of the bridge, I gave a great start, for a black patch of shadow moved swiftly across the path and merged into the other shadows bordering a high wall. My heart leapt momentarily, then, in another instant, the explanation of the mystery became apparent—in the presence of a gaunt and prowling cat. Bestowing a suspicious glance upward in my direction, the animal slunk away toward the path bordering the cutting.

By a devious route amid ghostly gasometers I had crept to my post in the early dusk, before the moon was risen, and already I was heartily weary of my passive part in the affair of the night. I had never before appreciated the multitudinous sounds, all of them weird and many of them horrible, which are within the compass of those great black rats who find their way to England with cargoes from Russia and elsewhere. From the rafters above my head, from the wall recesses about me, from the floor beneath my feet, proceeded a continuous and nerve-shattering concert, an unholy symphony which seemingly accompanied the eternal dance of the rats.

Sometimes a faint splash from below would tell of one of the revelers taking the water, but save for the more distant throbbing of riverside industry, and rarer note of shipping, the mad discords of this rat saturnalia alone claimed the ear.

The hour was nigh now, when matters should begin to develop. I followed the chimes from the clock of some church nearby—I have never learnt its name; and was conscious of a thrill of excitement when they warned me that the hour was actually arrived....

A strange figure appeared noiselessly, from I knew not where, and stood fully within view upon the bridge crossing the cutting, peering to right and left, in an attitude of listening. It was the figure of a bedraggled old woman, gray-haired, and carrying a large bundle tied up in what appeared to be a red shawl. Of her face I could see little, since it was shaded by the brim of her black bonnet, but she rested her bundle upon the low wall of the bridge, and to my intense surprise, sat down upon it!

She evidently intended to remain there.

I drew back further into the darkness; for the presence of this singular old woman at such a place, and at that hour, could not well be accidental. I was convinced that the first actor in the drama had already taken the stage. Whether I was mistaken or not must shortly appear.

Crisp footsteps sounded upon the roadway; distantly, and from my left. Nearer they approached and nearer. I saw the old woman, in the shadow of the wall, glance once rapidly in the direction of the approaching pedestrian. For some occult reason, the chorus of the rats was stilled. Only that firm and regular tread broke the intimate silence of the dreary spot.

Now the pedestrian came within my range of sight. It was Nayland Smith!

He wore a long tweed overcoat with which I was familiar, and a soft felt hat, the brim pulled down all around in a fashion characteristic of him, and probably acquired during the years spent beneath the merciless sun of Burma. He carried a heavy walking cane which I knew to be a formidable weapon that he could wield to good effect. But, despite the stillness about me, a stillness which had reigned uninterruptedly (save for the *danse macabre* of the rats) since the coming of dusk, some voice within, ignoring these physical evidences of solitude, spoke urgently of lurking assassins; of murderous Easterns armed with those curved knives which sometimes flashed before my eyes in dreams; of a deathly menace which hid in the shadows about me, in the many shadows cloaking the holes and corners of the ramshackle building, draping arches, crannies and portals to which the moonlight could not penetrate.

He was abreast of the Joy-Shop now, and in sight of the ominous old witch huddled upon the bridge. He pulled up suddenly and stood looking at her. Coincident with his doing so, she began to moan and sway her body to right and left as if in pain; then—

"Kind gentleman," she whined in a sing-song voice, "thank God you came this way to help a poor old woman."

"What is the matter?" said Smith tersely, approaching her.

I clenched my fists. I could have cried out; I was indeed hard put to it to refrain from crying out—from warning him. But his injunctions had been explicit, and I restrained myself by a great effort, preserving silence and crouching there at the window, but with every muscle tensed and a desire for action strong upon me.

"I tripped up on a rough stone, sir," whined the old creature, "and here I've been sitting waiting for a policeman or someone to help me, for more than an hour, I have."

Smith stood looking down at her, his arms behind him, and in one gloved hand swinging the cane.

"Where do you live, then?" he asked.

"Not a hundred steps from here, kind gentleman," she replied in the monotonous voice; "but I can't move my left foot. It's only just through the gates yonder."

"What!" snapped Smith, "on the wharf?"

"They let me have a room in the old building until it's let," she explained. "Be helping a poor old woman, and God bless you."

"Come along, then!"

Stooping, Smith placed his arm around her shoulders, and assisted her to her feet. She groaned as if in great pain, but gripped her red bundle, and leaning heavily upon the supporting arm, hobbled off across the bridge in the direction of the wharf gates at the end of the lane.

Now at last a little action became possible, and having seen my friend push open one of the gates and assist the old woman to enter, I crept rapidly across the crazy floor, found the doorway, and, with little noise, for I wore rubber-soled shoes, stole down the stairs into what had formerly been the reception-room of the Joy-Shop, the malodorous sanctum of the old Chinaman, John Ki.

Utter darkness prevailed there, but momentarily flicking the light of a pocket-lamp upon the floor before me, I discovered the further steps that were to be negotiated, and descended into the square yard which gave access to the path skirting the creek.

The moonlight drew a sharp line of shadow along the wall of the house above me, but the yard itself was a well of darkness. I stumbled under the rotting brick archway, and stepped gingerly upon the muddy path that I must follow. One hand pressed to the damp wall, I worked my way cautiously along, for a false step had precipitated me into the foul water of the creek. In this fashion and still enveloped by dense shadows, I reached the angle of the building. Then—at risk of being perceived, for the wharf and the river both were bathed in moonlight—I peered along to the left....

Out onto the paved pathway communicating with the wharf came Smith, shepherding his tottering charge. I was too far away to hear any conversation that might take place between the two, but, unless Smith gave the pre-arranged signal, I must approach no closer. Thus, as one sees a drama upon the screen, I saw what now occurred—occurred with dramatic, lightning swiftness.

Releasing Smith's arm, the old woman suddenly stepped back ... at the instant that another figure, a repellent figure which approached, stooping, apish, with a sort of loping gait, crossed from some spot invisible to me, and sprang like a wild animal upon Smith's back!

It was a Chinaman, wearing a short loose garment of the smock pattern, and having his head bare, so that I could see his pigtail coiled upon his yellow crown. That he carried a cord, I perceived in the instant of his spring, and that he had whipped it about Smith's throat with unerring dexterity was evidenced by the one, short, strangled cry that came from my friend's lips.

Then Smith was down, prone upon the crazy planking, with the ape-like figure of the Chinaman perched between his shoulders—bending forward—the wicked yellow fingers at work, tightening—tightening—tightening the strangling cord!

Uttering a loud cry of horror, I went racing along the gangway which projected actually over the moving Thames waters, and gained the wharf. But, swift as I had been, another had been swifter!

A tall figure (despite the brilliant moon, I doubted the evidence of my sight), wearing a tweed overcoat and a soft felt hat with the brim turned down, sprang up, from nowhere as it seemed, swooped upon the horrible figure squatting, simianesque, between Smith's shoulder-blades, and grasped him by the neck.

I pulled up shortly, one foot set upon the wharf. The new-comer was the double of Nayland Smith!

Seemingly exerting no effort whatever, he lifted the strangler in that remorseless grasp, so that the Chinaman's hands, after one quick convulsive upward movement, hung limply beside him like the paws of a rat in the grip of a terrier.

"You damned murderous swine!" I heard in a repressed, savage undertone. "The knife failed, so now the cord has an innings! Go after your pal!"

Releasing one hand from the neck of the limp figure, the speaker grasped the Chinaman by his loose, smock-like garment, swung him back, once—a mighty swing—and hurled him far out into the river as one might hurl a sack of rubbish!

CHAPTER TWENTY-THREE

ARREST OF SAMARKAN

"As the high gods willed it," explained Nayland Smith, tenderly massaging his throat, "Mr. Forsyth, having just left the docks, chanced to pass along Three Colt Street on Wednesday night at exactly the hour that *I* was expected! The resemblance between us is rather marked and the coincidence of dress completed the illusion. That devilish Eurasian woman, Zarmi, who has escaped us again—of course you recognized her?—made a very natural mistake. Mr. Forsyth, however, made no mistake!"

I glanced at the chief officer of the *Andaman*, who sat in an armchair in our new chambers, contentedly smoking a black cheroot.

"Heaven has blessed me with a pair of useful hands!" said the seaman, grimly, extending his horny palms. "I've an old score against those yellow swine; poor George and I were twins."

He referred to his brother who had been foully done to death by one of the creatures of Dr. Fu-Manchu.

"It beats me how Mr. Smith got on the track!" he added.

"Pure inspiration!" murmured Nayland Smith, glancing aside from the siphon wherewith he now was busy. "The divine afflatus—

and the same whereby Petrie solved the Zagazig cryptogram!"

"But," concluded Forsyth, "I am indebted to you for an opportunity of meeting the Chinese strangler, and sending him to join the Burmese knife expert!"

Such, then, were the episodes that led to the arrest of M. Samarkan, and my duty as narrator of these strange matters now bears me on to the morning when Nayland Smith was hastily summoned to the prison into which the villainous Greek had been cast.

We were shown immediately into the governor's room and were invited by that much-disturbed official to be seated. The news which he had to impart was sufficiently startling.

Samarkan was dead.

"I have Warder Morrison's statement here," said Colonel Warrington, "if you will be good enough to read it—"

Nayland Smith rose abruptly, and began to pace up and down the little office. Through the open window I had a glimpse of a stooping figure in convict garb, engaged in liming the flowerbeds of the prison governor's garden.

"I should like to see this Warder Morrison personally," snapped my friend.

"Very good," replied the governor, pressing a bell-push placed close beside his table.

A man entered, to stand rigidly at attention just within the doorway.

"Send Morrison here," ordered Colonel Warrington.

The man saluted and withdrew. As the door was reclosed, the Colonel sat drumming his fingers upon the table, Nayland Smith walked restlessly about tugging at the lobe of his ear, and I absently watched the convict gardener pursuing his toils. Shortly, sounded a rap at the door, and—

"Come in," cried Colonel Warrington.

A man wearing warder's uniform appeared, saluted the governor, and stood glancing uneasily from the colonel to Smith. The latter had now ceased his perambulations, and, one elbow resting upon the mantelpiece, was staring at Morrison—his penetrating gray eyes as hard as steel. Colonel Warrington twisted his chair around, fixing his monocle more closely in its place. He had the wiry white mustache and fiery red face of the old-style Anglo-Indian officer.

"Morrison," he said, "Mr. Commissioner Nayland Smith has some questions to put to you."

The man's uneasiness palpably was growing by leaps and bounds. He was a tall and intelligent-looking fellow of military build, though spare for his height and of an unhealthy complexion. His eyes were curiously dull, and their pupils interested me, professionally, from the very moment of his entrance.

"You were in charge of the prisoner Samarkan?" began Smith harshly.

"Yes, sir," Morrison replied.

"Were you the first to learn of his death?"

"I was, sir. I looked through the grille in the door and saw him lying on the floor of the cell."

"What time was it?"

"Half-past four A.M."

"What did you do?"

"I went into the cell and then sent for the head warder."

"You realized at once that Samarkan was dead?"

"At once, yes."

"Were you surprised?"

Nayland Smith subtly changed the tone of his voice in asking the last question, and it was evident that the veiled significance of the words was not lost upon Morrison.

"Well, sir," he began, and cleared his throat nervously.

"Yes, or no!" snapped Smith.

Morrison still hesitated, and I saw his underlip twitch. Nayland Smith, taking two long strides, stood immediately in front of him, glaring grimly into his face.

"This is your chance," he said emphatically; "I shall not give you another. You had met Samarkan before?"

Morrison hung his head for a moment, clenching and unclenching his fists; then he looked up swiftly, and the light of a new resolution was in his eyes.

"I'll take the chance, sir," he said, speaking with some emotion, "and I hope, sir"—turning momentarily to Colonel Warrington—"that you'll be as lenient as you can; for I didn't know there was any harm in what I did."

"Don't expect any leniency from me!" cried the Colonel. "If there has been a breach of discipline there will be punishment, rely upon it!"

"I admit the breach of discipline," pursued the man doggedly; "but I want to say, here and now, that I've no more idea than anybody else how the—"

Smith snapped his fingers irritably.

"The facts—the facts!" he demanded. "What you *don't* know cannot help us!"

"Well, sir," said Morrison, clearing his throat again, "when the prisoner, Samarkan, was admitted, and I put him safely into his cell, he told me that he suffered from heart trouble, that he'd had an attack when he was arrested and that he thought he was threatened with another, which might kill him—"

"One moment," interrupted Smith, "is this confirmed by the police officer who made the arrest?"

"It is, sir," replied Colonel Warrington, swinging his chair around and consulting some papers upon his table. "The prisoner was overcome by faintness when the officer showed him the warrant and asked to be given some cognac from the decanter which stood in his room. This was administered, and he then entered the cab which the officer had waiting. He was taken to Bow Street, remanded, and brought here in accordance with someone's instructions."

"*My* instructions," said Smith. "Go on, Morrison."

"He told me," continued Morrison more steadily, "that he suffered from something that sounded to me like apoplexy."

"Catalepsy!" I suggested, for I was beginning to see light.

"That's it, sir! He said he was afraid of being buried alive! He asked me, as a favor, if he should die in prison to go to a friend of his and get a syringe with which to inject some stuff that would do away with all chance of his coming to life again after burial."

"You had no right to talk to the prisoner!" roared Colonel Warrington.

"I know that, sir, but you'll admit that the circumstances were peculiar. Anyway, he died in the night, sure enough, and from heart failure, according to the doctor. I managed to get a couple of hours leave in the evening, and I went and fetched the syringe and a little tube of yellow stuff."

"Do you understand, Petrie?" cried Nayland Smith, his eyes blazing with excitement. "Do you understand?"

"Perfectly."

"It's more than I do, sir," continued Morrison, "but as I was explaining, I brought the little syringe back with me and I filled it from the tube. The body was lying in the mortuary, which you've seen, and the door not being locked, it was easy for me to slip in there for a moment. I didn't fancy the job, but it was soon done. I threw the syringe and the tube over the wall into the lane outside, as I'd been told to do."

"What part of the wall?" asked Smith.

"Behind the mortuary."

"That's where they were waiting!" I cried excitedly. "The building used as a mortuary is quite isolated, and it would not be a difficult matter for someone hiding in the lane outside to throw one of those ladders of silk and bamboo across the top of the wall."

"But, my good sir," interrupted the governor irascibly, "whilst I admit the possibility to which you allude, I do not admit that a dead man, and a heavy one at that, can be carried up a ladder of silk and bamboo! Yet, on the evidence of my own eyes, the body of the prisoner, Samarkan, was removed from the mortuary last night!"

Smith signaled to me to pursue the subject no further; and indeed I realized that it would have been no easy matter to render the amazing truth evident to a man of the colonel's type of mind. But to me the facts of the case were now clear enough.

That Fu-Manchu possessed a preparation for producing artificial catalepsy, of a sort indistinguishable from death, I was well aware. A dose of this unknown drug had doubtless been contained in the cognac (if, indeed, the decanter had held cognac) that the prisoner had drunk at the time of his arrest. The "yellow stuff" spoken of by Morrison I recognized as the antidote (another secret of the brilliant Chinese doctor), a portion of which I had once, some years before, actually had in my possession. The "dead man" had not been carried up the ladder; he had climbed up!

"Now, Morrison," snapped Nayland Smith, "you have acted

wisely thus far. Make a clean breast of it. How much were you paid for the job?"

"Twenty pounds, sir," answered the man promptly, "and I'd have done it for less, because I could see no harm in it, the prisoner being dead, and this his last request."

"And who paid you?"

Now we were come to the nub of the matter, as the change in the man's face revealed. He hesitated momentarily, and Colonel Warrington brought his fist down on the table with a bang. Morrison made a sort of gesture of resignation at that, and—

"When I was in the army, sir, stationed at Cairo," he said slowly, "I regret to confess that I formed a drug habit."

"Opium?" snapped Smith.

"No, sir, hashish."

"Good God! Go on."

"There's a place in Soho, just off Frith Street, where hashish is supplied, and I go there sometimes. Mr. Samarkan used to come, and bring people with him—from the New Louvre Hotel, I believe. That's where I met him."

"The exact address?" demanded Smith.

"Café de l'Egypte. But the hashish is only sold upstairs, and no one is allowed up that isn't known personally to Ismail."

"Who is this Ismail?"

"The proprietor of the café. He's a Greek Jew of Salonica. An old woman used to attend to the customers upstairs, but during the last few months a young one has sometimes taken her place."

"What is she like?" I asked eagerly.

"She has very fine eyes, and that's about all I can tell you, sir, because she wears a yashmak. Last night there were two women there, both veiled, though."

"Two women!"

Hope and fear entered my heart. That Kâramaneh was again in the power of the Chinese doctor I knew to my sorrow. Could it be that the Café de l'Egypte was the place of her captivity?

CHAPTER TWENTY-FOUR

CAFÉ DE L'EGYPTE

I could see that Nayland Smith counted the escape of the prisoner but a trivial matter by comparison with the discovery to which it had led us. That the Soho café should prove to be, if not the headquarters at least a regular resort of Dr. Fu-Manchu, was not too much to hope. The usefulness of such a haunt was evident enough, since it might conveniently be employed as a place of rendezvous for Orientals—and furthermore enable the cunning Chinaman to establish relations with persons likely to prove of service to him.

Formerly, he had used an East End opium den for this purpose, and, later, the resort known as the Joy-Shop. Soho, hitherto, had remained outside the radius of his activity, but that he should have embraced it at last was not surprising; for Soho is the Montmartre of London and a land of many secrets.

"Why," demanded Nayland Smith, "have I never been told of the existence of this place?"

"That's simple enough," answered Inspector Weymouth. "Although we knew of this Café de l'Egypte, we have never had the slightest trouble there. It's a Bohemian resort, where members of the

French Colony, some of the Chelsea art people, professional models, and others of that sort, foregather at night. I've been there myself as a matter of fact, and I've seen people well known in the artistic world come in. It has much the same clientele as, say, the Café Royal, with a rather heavier sprinkling of Hindu students, Japanese, and so forth. It's celebrated for Turkish coffee."

"What do you know of this Ismail?"

"Nothing much. He's a Levantine Jew."

"And something more!" added Smith, surveying himself in the mirror, and turning to nod his satisfaction to the well-known perruquier whose services are sometimes requisitioned by the police authorities.

We were ready for our visit to the Café de l'Egypte, and Smith having deemed it inadvisable that we should appear there openly, we had been transformed, under the adroit manipulation of Foster, into a pair of Futurists oddly unlike our actual selves. No wigs, no false mustaches had been employed; a change of costume and a few deft touches of some watercolor paint had rendered us unrecognizable by our most intimate friends.

It was all very fantastic, very reminiscent of Christmas charades, but the farce had a grim, murderous undercurrent; the life of one dearer to me than life itself hung upon our success; the swamping of the White world by Yellow hordes might well be the price of our failure.

Weymouth left us at the corner of Frith Street. This was no more than a reconnaissance, but—

"I shall be within hail if I'm wanted," said the burly detective; and although we stood not in Chinatown but in the heart of Bohemian London, with popular restaurants about us, I was glad to know that we had so staunch an ally in reserve.

The shadow of the great Chinaman was upon me. That strange, subconscious voice, with which I had become familiar in the past, awoke within me tonight. Not by logic, but by prescience, I knew that the Yellow doctor was near.

Two minutes' walk brought us to the door of the café. The upper half was of glass, neatly curtained, as were the windows on either side of it; and above the establishment appeared the words: "Café de l'Egypte." Between the second and third word was inserted a gilded device representing the crescent of Islâm.

We entered. On our right was a room furnished with marble-topped tables, cane-seated chairs and plush-covered lounges set against the walls. The air was heavy with tobacco smoke; evidently the café was full, although the night was young.

Smith immediately made for the upper end of the room. It was not large, and at first glance I thought that there was no vacant place. Presently, however, I espied two unoccupied chairs; and these we took, finding ourselves facing a pale, bespectacled young man, with long, fair hair and faded eyes, whose companion, a bold brunette, was smoking one of the largest cigarettes I had ever seen, in a gold and amber cigar-holder.

A very commonplace Swiss waiter took our orders for coffee, and we began discreetly to survey our surroundings. The only touch of Oriental color thus far perceptible in the Café de l'Egypte was provided by a red-capped Egyptian behind a narrow counter, who presided over the coffee pots. The patrons of the establishment were in every way typical of Soho, and in the bulk differed not at all from those of the better-known café restaurants.

There were several Easterns present; but Smith, having given each of them a searching glance, turned to me with a slight shrug of disappointment. Coffee being placed before us, we sat sipping the thick, sugary beverage, smoking cigarettes and vainly seeking for some clue to guide us to the inner sanctuary consecrated to hashish. It was maddening to think that Kâramaneh might be somewhere concealed in the building, whilst I sat there, inert amongst this gathering whose conversation was of abnormalities in art, music, and literature.

Then, suddenly, the pale young man seated opposite paid his bill, and with a word of farewell to his companion, went out of the café. He did not make his exit by the door through which we entered, but passed up the crowded room to the counter whereat the Egyptian presided. From some place hidden in the rear, emerged a black-haired, swarthy man, with whom the other exchanged a few words. The pale young artist raised his wide-brimmed hat, and was gone—through a curtained doorway on the left of the counter.

As he opened it, I had a glimpse of a narrow court beyond; then the door was closed again and I found myself thinking of the peculiar eyes of the departed visitor. Even through the thick pebbles of his spectacles, although for some reason I had thought little of the matter at the time, his oddly contracted pupils were noticeable. As the girl, in turn, rose and left the café—but by the ordinary door—I turned to Smith.

"That man ..." I began, and paused.

Smith was watching covertly a Hindu seated at a neighboring table, who was about to settle his bill. Standing up, the Hindu made for the coffee counter, the swarthy man appeared out of the background—and the Asiatic visitor went out by the door opening into the court.

One quick glance Smith gave me, and raised his hand for the waiter. A few minutes later we were out in the street again.

"We must find our way to that court!" snapped my friend. "Let us try back, I noted a sort of alleyway which we passed just before reaching the café."

"You think the hashish den is in some adjoining building?"

"I don't know where it is, Petrie, but I know the way to it!"

Into a narrow, gloomy court we plunged, hemmed in by high walls, and followed it for ten yards or more. An even narrower and less inviting turning revealed itself on the left. We pursued our way, and presently found ourselves at the back of the Café de l'Egypte.

"There's the door," I said.

It opened into a tiny *cul-de-sac*, flanked by dilapidated hoardings, and no other door of any kind was visible in the vicinity. Nayland Smith stood tugging at the lobe of his ear almost savagely.

"Where the devil do they go?" he whispered.

Even as he spoke the words, came a gleam of light through the upper curtained part of the door, and I distinctly saw the figure of a man in silhouette.

"Stand back!" snapped Smith.

We crouched back against the dirty wall of the court, and watched a strange thing happen. The back door of the Café de l'Egypte opened outward, simultaneously a door, hitherto invisible, set at right angles in the hoarding adjoining, opened *inward*!

A man emerged from the café and entered the secret doorway. As he did so, the café door swung back and closed the door in the hoarding!

"Very good!" muttered Nayland Smith. "Our friend Ismail, behind the counter, moves some lever which causes the opening of one door automatically to open the other. Failing his kindly offices, the second exit from the Café de l'Egypte is innocent enough. Now—what is the next move?"

"I have an idea, Smith!" I cried. "According to Morrison, the place in which the hashish may be obtained has no windows but is lighted from above. No doubt it was built for a studio and has a glass roof. Therefore—"

"Come along!" snapped Smith, grasping my arm; "you have solved the difficulty, Petrie."

CHAPTER TWENTY-FIVE

THE HOUSE OF HASHISH

Along the leads from Frith Street we worked our perilous way. From the top landing of a French restaurant we had gained access, by means of a trap, to the roof of the building. Now, the busy streets of Soho were below me, and I clung dizzily to telephone standards and smoke stacks, rarely venturing to glance downward upon the cosmopolitan throng, surging, dwarfish, in the lighted depths.

Sometimes the bulky figure of Inspector Weymouth would loom up grotesquely against the star-sprinkled blue, as he paused to take breath; the next moment Nayland Smith would be leading the way again, and I would find myself contemplating some sheer well of blackness, with nausea threatening me because it had to be negotiated.

None of these gaps were more than a long stride from side to side; but the sense of depth conveyed in the muffled voices and dimmed footsteps from the pavements far below was almost overpowering. Indeed, I am convinced that for my part I should never have essayed that nightmare journey were it not that the musical voice of

Kâramaneh seemed to be calling to me, her little white hands to be seeking mine, blindly, in the darkness.

That we were close to a haunt of the dreadful Chinamen I was persuaded; therefore my hatred and my love cooperated to lend me a coolness and address which otherwise I must have lacked.

"Hullo!" cried Smith, who was leading—"What now?"

We had crept along the crown of a sloping roof and were confronted by the blank wall of a building which rose a story higher than that adjoining it. It was crowned by an iron railing, showing blackly against the sky. I paused, breathing heavily, and seated astride that dizzy perch. Weymouth was immediately behind me, and—

"It's the Café de l'Egypte, Mr. Smith!" he said. "If you'll look up, you'll see the reflection of the lights shining through the glass roof."

Vaguely I discerned Nayland Smith rising to his feet.

"Be careful!" I said. "For God's sake don't slip!"

"Take my hand," he snapped energetically.

I stretched forward and grasped his hand. As I did so, he slid down the slope on the right, away from the street, and hung perilously for a moment over the very *cul-de-sac* upon which the secret door opened.

"Good!" he muttered "There is, as I had hoped, a window lighting the top of the staircase. Ssh!—ssh!"

His grip upon my hand tightened; and there aloft, above the teemful streets of Soho, I sat listening … whilst very faint and muffled footsteps sounded upon an uncarpeted stair, a door banged, and all was silent again, save for the ceaseless turmoil far below.

"Sit tight, and catch!" rapped Smith.

Into my extended hands he swung his boots, fastened together by the laces! Then, ere I could frame any protest, he disengaged his hand from mine, and pressing his body close against the angle of the building, worked his way around to the staircase window, which was invisible from where I crouched.

"Heavens!" muttered Weymouth, close to my ear, "I can never travel that road!"

"Nor I!" was my scarcely audible answer.

In a anguish of fearful anticipation I listened for the cry and the dull thud which should proclaim the fate of my intrepid friend; but no such sounds came to me. Some thirty seconds passed in this fashion, when a subdued call from above caused me to start and look aloft.

Nayland Smith was peering down from the railing on the roof.

"Mind your head!" he warned—and over the rail swung the end of a light wooden ladder, lowering it until it rested upon the crest astride of which I sat.

"Up you come!—then Weymouth!"

Whilst Smith held the top firmly, I climbed up rung by rung, not daring to think of what lay below.

My relief when at last I grasped the railing, climbed over, and found myself upon a wooden platform, was truly inexpressible.

"Come on, Weymouth!" rapped Nayland Smith. "This ladder has to be lowered back down the trap before another visitor arrives!"

Taking short, staccato breaths at every step, Inspector Weymouth ascended, ungainly, that frail and moving stair. Arrived beside me, he wiped the perspiration from his face and forehead.

"I wouldn't do it again for a hundred pounds!" he said hoarsely.

"You don't have to!" snapped Smith.

Back he hauled the ladder, shouldered it, and stepping to a square opening in one corner of the rickety platform, lowered it cautiously down.

"Have you a knife with a corkscrew in it?" he demanded.

Weymouth had one, which he produced. Nayland Smith screwed it into the weather-worn frame, and by that means reclosed the trapdoor softly, then—

"Look," he said, "there is the house of hashish!"

CHAPTER TWENTY-SIX

"THE DEMON'S SELF"

Through the glass panes of the skylight I looked down upon a scene so bizarre that my actual environment became blotted out, and I was mentally translated to Cairo—to that quarter of Cairo immediately surrounding the famous Square of the Fountain—to those indescribable streets, wherefrom arises the perfume of deathless evil, wherein, to the wailing, luresome music of the reed pipe, painted dancing-girls sway in the wild abandon of dances that were ancient when Thebes was the City of a Hundred Gates; I seemed to stand again in el Wasr.

The room below was rectangular, and around three of the walls were divans strewn with garish cushions, whilst highly colored Eastern rugs were spread about the floor. Four lamps swung on chains, two from either of the beams which traversed the apartment. They were fine examples of native perforated brasswork.

Upon the divans some eight or nine men were seated, fully half of whom were Orientals or half-castes. Before each stood a little inlaid table bearing a brass tray; and upon the trays were various boxes, some apparently containing sweetmeats, others cigarettes. One or two of the visitors smoked curious, long-stemmed pipes and sipped coffee.

Even as I leaned from the platform, surveying that incredible scene (incredible in a street of Soho), another devotee of hashish entered—a tall, distinguished-looking man, wearing a light coat over his evening dress.

"Gad!" whispered Smith, beside me—"Sir Byngham Pyne of the India Office! You see, Petrie! You see! This place is a lure. My God! …"

He broke off, as I clutched wildly at his arm.

The last arrival having taken his seat in a corner of the divan, two heavy curtains draped before an opening at one end of the room parted, and a girl came out, carrying a tray such as already reposed before each of the other men in the room.

She wore a dress of dark lilac-colored gauze, banded about with gold tissue and embroidered with gold thread and pearls; and around her shoulders floated, so ethereally that she seemed to move in a violet cloud; a scarf of Delhi muslin. A white yashmak trimmed with gold tissue concealed the lower part of her face.

My heart throbbed wildly; I seemed to be choking. By the wonderful hair alone I must have known her, by the great, brilliant eyes, by the shape of those slim white ankles, by every movement of that exquisite form. It was Kâramaneh!

I sprang madly back from the rail … and Smith had my arm in an iron grip.

"Where are you going?" he snapped.

"Where am I going?" I cried. "Do you think—"

"What do you propose to do?" he interrupted harshly. "Do you know so little of the resources of Dr. Fu-Manchu that you would throw yourself blindly into that den? Damn it all, man! I know what you suffer!—but wait—wait. We must not act rashly; our plans must be well considered."

He drew me back to my former post and clapped his hand on my shoulder sympathetically. Clutching the rail like a man frenzied, as indeed I was, I looked down into that infamous den again, striving hard for composure.

Kâramaneh listlessly placed the tray upon the little table before Sir Byngham Pyne and withdrew without vouchsafing him a single glance in acknowledgment of his unconcealed admiration.

A moment later, above the dim clamor of London far below, there crept to my ears a sound which completed the magical quality of the scene, rendering that sky platform on a roof of Soho a magical carpet bearing me to the golden Orient. This sound was the wailing of a reed pipe.

"The company is complete," murmured Smith. "I had expected this."

Again the curtains parted, and a *ghazeeyeh* glided out into the room. She wore a white dress, clinging closely to her figure from shoulders to hips, where it was clasped by an ornate girdle, and a skirt of sky-blue gauze which clothed her as Io was clothed of old. Her arms were covered with gold bangles, and gold bands were clasped about her ankles. Her jet-black, frizzy hair was unconfined and without ornament, and she wore a sort of highly colored scarf so arranged that it effectually concealed the greater part of her face, but served to accentuated the brightness of the great flashing eyes. She had unmistakable beauty of a sort, but how different from the sweet witchery of Kâramaneh!

With a bold, swinging grace she walked down the center of the room, swaying her arms from side to side and snapping her fingers.

"Zarmi!" exclaimed Smith.

But his exclamation was unnecessary, for already I had recognized the evil Eurasian who was so efficient a servant of the Chinese doctor.

The wailing of the pipes continued, and now faintly I could detect the throbbing of a *darabûkeh.* This was el Wasr indeed. The dance commenced, its every phase followed eagerly by the motley clientele of the hashish house. Zarmi danced with an insolent nonchalance that nevertheless displayed her barbaric beauty to greatest advantage. She was lithe as a serpent, graceful as a young panther, another Lamia come to damn the souls of men with those arts denounced in a long-dead age by Apolonius of Tyana.

"She seemed, at once, some penanced lady elf, Some demon's mistress, or the demon's self…."

Entranced against my will, I watched the Eurasian until, the barbaric dance completed, she ran from the room, and the curtains concealed her from view. How my mind was torn between hope and fear that I should see Kâramaneh again! How I longed for one more glimpse of her, yet loathed the thought of her presence in that infamous house.

She was a captive; of that there could be no doubt, a captive in the hands of the giant criminal whose wiles were endless, whose resources were boundless, whose intense cunning had enabled him, for years, to weave his nefarious plots in the very heart of civilization, and remain immune. Suddenly—

"That woman is a sorceress!" muttered Nayland Smith. "There is about her something serpentine, at once repelling and fascinating. It would be of interest, Petrie, to learn what State secrets have been filched from the brains of habitués of this den, and interesting to know from what unsuspected spy-hole Fu-Manchu views his nightly catch. If …"

His voice died away, in a most curious fashion. I have since thought that here was a case of true telepathy. For, as Smith spoke of Fu-Manchu's spy-hole, the idea leapt instantly to my mind that *this* was it—this strange platform upon which we stood!

I drew back from the rail, turned, stared at Smith. I read in his face that our suspicions were identical. Then—

"Look! Look!" whispered Weymouth.

He was gazing at the trapdoor—which was slowly rising; inch by inch ... inch by inch ... Fascinatedly, raptly, we all gazed. A head appeared in the opening—and some vague, reflected light revealed two long, narrow, slightly oblique eyes watching us. They were brilliantly green.

"By God!" came in a mighty roar from Weymouth. "It's Dr. Fu-Manchu!"

As one man we leapt for the trap. It dropped, with a resounding bang—and I distinctly heard a bolt shot home.

A guttural voice—the unmistakable, unforgettable voice of Fu-Manchu—sounded dimly from below. I turned and sprang back to the rail of the platform, peering down into the hashish house. The occupants of the divans were making for the curtained doorway. Some, who seemed to be in a state of stupor, were being assisted by the others and by the man, Ismail, who had now appeared upon the scene.

Of Kâramaneh, Zarmi, or Fu-Manchu there was no sign.

Suddenly, the lights were extinguished.

"This is maddening!" cried Nayland Smith—"maddening! No doubt they have some other exit, some hiding-place—and they are slipping through our hands!"

Inspector Weymouth blew a shrill blast upon his whistle, and Smith, running to the rail of the platform, began to shatter the panes of the skylight with his foot.

"That's hopeless, sir!" cried Weymouth. "You'd be torn to pieces on the jagged glass."

Smith desisted, with a savage exclamation, and stood beating his right fist into the palm of his left hand, and glaring madly at the Scotland Yard man.

"I know I'm to blame," admitted Weymouth; "but the words were out before I knew I'd spoken. Ah!"—as an answering whistle came from somewhere in the street below. "But will they ever find us?"

He blew again shrilly. Several whistles replied … and a wisp of smoke floated up from the shattered pane of the skylight.

"I can smell *petrol*!" muttered Weymouth.

An ever-increasing roar, not unlike that of an approaching storm at sea, came from the streets beneath. Whistles skirled, remotely and intimately, and sometimes one voice, sometimes another, would detach itself from this stormy background with weird effect. Somewhere deep in the bowels of the hashish house there went on ceaselessly a splintering and crashing as though a determined assault were being made upon a door. A light shone up through the skylight.

Back once more to the rail I sprang, looked down into the room below—and saw a sight never to be forgotten.

Passing from divan to curtained door, from piles of cushions to stacked-up tables, and bearing a flaming torch hastily improvised out of a roll of newspaper, was Dr. Fu-Manchu. Everything inflammable in the place had been soaked with petrol, and, his gaunt, yellow face lighted by the ever-growing conflagration, so that truly it seemed not the face of a man, but that of a demon of the hells, the Chinese doctor ignited point after point….

"Smith!" I screamed, "we are trapped! that fiend means to burn us alive!"

"And the place will flare like matchwood! It's touch and go this time, Petrie! To drop to the sloping roof underneath would mean almost certain death on the pavement...."

I dragged my pistol from my pocket and began wildly to fire shot after shot into the holocaust below. But the awful Chinaman had escaped—probably by some secret exit reserved for his own use; for certainly he must have known that escape into the court was now cut off.

Flames were beginning to hiss through the skylight. A tremendous crackling and crashing told of the glass destroyed. Smoke spurted up through the cracks of the boarding upon which we stood—and a great shout came from the crowd in the streets....

In the distance—a long, long way off, it seemed—was born a new note in the stormy human symphony. It grew in volume, it seemed to be sweeping down upon us—nearer—nearer—nearer. Now it was in the streets immediately adjoining the Café de l'Egypte and now, blessed sound! It culminated in a mighty surging cheer.

"The fire engines," said Weymouth coolly—and raised himself on to the lower rail, for the platform was growing uncomfortably hot.

Tongues of fire licked out, venomously, from beneath my feet. I leapt for the railing in turn, and sat astride it ... as one end of the flooring burst into flame.

The heat from the blazing room above which we hung suspended was now all but insupportable, and the fumes threatened to stifle us. My head seemed to be bursting; my throat and lungs were consumed by internal fires.

"Merciful heavens!" whispered Smith. "Will they reach us in time?"

"Not if they don't get here within the next thirty seconds!" answered Weymouth grimly—and changed his position, in order to avoid a tongue of flame that hungrily sought to reach him.

Nayland Smith turned and looked me squarely in the eyes. Words trembled on his tongue; but those words were never spoken … for a brass helmet appeared suddenly out of the smoke banks, followed almost immediately by a second….

"Quick, sir! This way! Jump! I'll catch you!"

Exactly what followed I never knew; but there was a mighty burst of cheering, a sense of tension released, and it became a task less agonizing to breathe.

Feeling very dazed, I found myself in the heart of a huge, excited crowd, with Weymouth beside me, and Nayland Smith holding my arm. Vaguely, I heard:—

"They have the man Ismail, but …"

A hollow crash drowned the end of the sentence. A shower of sparks shot up into the night's darkness high above our heads.

"That's the platform gone!"

CHAPTER TWENTY-SEVEN

ROOM WITH THE GOLDEN DOOR

One night early in the following week I sat at work upon my notes dealing with our almost miraculous escape from the blazing hashish house when the clock of St. Paul's began to strike midnight.

I paused in my work, leaning back wearily and wondering what detained Nayland Smith so late. Some friends from Burma had carried him off to a theater, and in their good company I had thought him safe enough; yet, with the omnipresent menace of Fu-Manchu hanging over our heads, always I doubted, always I feared, if my friend should chance to be delayed abroad at night.

What a world of unreality was mine, in those days! Jostling, as I did, commonplace folk in commonplace surroundings, I yet knew myself removed from them, knew myself all but alone in my knowledge of the great and evil man, whose presence in England had diverted my life into these strange channels.

But, despite of all my knowledge, and despite the infinitely greater knowledge and wider experience of Nayland Smith, what did I know, what did he know, of the strange organization called the

Si-Fan, and of its most formidable member, Dr. Fu-Manchu?

Where did the dreadful Chinaman hide, with his murderers, his poisons, and his nameless death agents? What roof in broad England sheltered Kâramaneh, the companion of my dreams, the desire of every waking hour?

I uttered a sigh of despair, when, to my unbounded astonishment, there came a loud rap upon the window pane!

Leaping up, I crossed to the window, threw it widely open and leant out, looking down into the court below. It was deserted. In no other window visible to me was any light to be seen, and no living thing moved in the shadows beneath. The clamor of Fleet Street's diminishing traffic came dimly to my ears; the last stroke from St. Paul's quivered through the night.

What was the meaning of the sound which had disturbed me? Surely I could not have imagined it? Yet, right, left, above and below, from the cloisteresque shadows on the east of the court to the blank wall of the building on the west, no living thing stirred.

Quietly, I reclosed the window, and stood by it for a moment listening. Nothing occurred, and I returned to the writing-table, puzzled but in no sense alarmed. I resumed the seemingly interminable record of the Si-Fan mysteries, and I had just taken up my pen, when … two loud raps sounded upon the pane behind me.

In a trice I was at the window, had thrown it open, and was craning out. Practical joking was not characteristic of Nayland Smith, and I knew of none other likely to take such a liberty. As before, the court below proved to be empty….

Someone was softly rapping at the door of the chambers!

I turned swiftly from the open window; and now, came *fear*. Momentarily, the icy finger of panic touched me, for I thought myself invested upon all sides. Who could this late caller be, this midnight visitor who rapped, ghostly, in preference to ringing the bell?

From the table drawer I took out a Browning pistol, slipped it into my pocket and crossed to the narrow hallway. It was in darkness, but I depressed the switch, lighting the lamp. Toward the closed door I looked—as the soft rapping was repeated.

I advanced; then hesitated, and, strung up to a keen pitch of fearful anticipation, stood there in doubt. The silence remained unbroken for the space, perhaps of half a minute. Then again came the ghostly rapping.

"Who's there?" I cried loudly.

Nothing stirred outside the door, and still I hesitated. To some who read, my hesitancy may brand me childishly timid; but I, who had met many of the dreadful creatures of Dr. Fu-Manchu, had good reason to fear whomsoever or whatsoever rapped at midnight upon my door. Was I likely to forget the great half-human ape, with the strength of four lusty men, which once he had loosed upon us?—had I not cause to remember his Burmese dacoits and Chinese stranglers?

No, I had just cause for dread, as I fully recognized when, snatching the pistol from my pocket, I strode forward, flung wide the door, and stood peering out into the black gulf of the stairhead.

Nothing, no one, appeared!

Conscious of a longing to cry out—if only that the sound of my own voice might reassure me—I stood listening. The silence was complete.

"Who's there?" I cried again, and loudly enough to arrest the attention of the occupant of the chambers opposite if he chanced to be at home.

None replied; and finding this phantom silence more nerve-racking than any clamor, I stepped outside the door—and my heart gave a great leap, then seemed to remain inert, in my breast....

Right and left of me, upon either side of the doorway, stood a dim figure: I had walked deliberately into a trap!

The shock of the discovery paralyzed my mind for one instant. In the next, and with the sinister pair closing swiftly upon me, I stepped back—I stepped into the arms of some third assailant, who must have entered the chambers by way of the open window and silently crept up behind me!

So much I realized, and no more. A bag, reeking of some hashish-like perfume, was clapped over my head and pressed firmly against mouth and nostrils. I felt myself to be stifling—dying—and dropping into a bottomless pit.

When I opened my eyes I failed for some time to realize that I was conscious in the true sense of the word, that I was really awake.

I sat upon a bench covered with a red carpet, in a fair-sized room, very simply furnished, in the Chinese manner, but having a two-leaved, gilded door, which was shut. At the further end of this apartment was a dais some three feet high, also carpeted with red, and upon it was placed a very large cushion covered with a tiger skin.

Seated cross-legged upon the cushion was a Chinaman of most majestic appearance. His countenance was truly noble and gracious and he was dressed in a yellow robe lined with marten-fur. His hair, which was thickly splashed with gray, was confined upon the top of his head by three golden combs, and a large diamond was suspended from his left ear. A pearl-embroidered black cap, surmounted by the red coral ball denoting the mandarin's rank, lay upon a second smaller cushion beside him.

Leaning back against the wall, I stared at his personage with a dreadful fixity, for I counted him the figment of a disarranged mind.

But palpably he remained before me, fanning himself complacently, and watching me with every mark of kindly interest. Evidently perceiving that I was fully alive to my surroundings, the Chinaman addressed a remark to me in a tongue quite unfamiliar.

I shook my head dazedly.

"Ah," he commented in French, "you do not speak my language."

"I do not," I answered, also in French, "but since it seems we have one common tongue, what is the meaning of the outrage to which I have been subjected, and who are you?"

As I spoke the words I rose to my feet, but was immediately attacked by vertigo, which compelled me to resume my seat upon the bench.

"Compose yourself," said the Chinaman, taking a pinch of snuff from a silver vase which stood convenient to his hand. "I have been compelled to adopt certain measures in order to bring about this interview. In China, such measures are not unusual, but I recognize that they are out of accordance with your English ideas."

"Emphatically they are!" I replied.

The placid manner of this singularly imposing old man rendered proper resentment difficult. A sense of futility, and of unreality, claimed me; I felt that this was a dream-world, governed by dream-laws.

"You have good reason," he continued, calmly raising the pinch of snuff to his nostrils, "good reason to distrust all that is Chinese. Therefore, when I despatched my servants to your abode (knowing you to be alone) I instructed them to observe every law of courtesy, compatible with the Sure Invitation. Hence, I pray you, absolve me, for I intended no offense."

Words failed me altogether; wonder succeeded wonder! What was coming? What did it all mean?

"I have selected you, rather than Mr. Commissioner Nayland Smith," continued the mandarin, "as the recipient of those secrets which I am about to impart, for the reason that your friend might possibly be acquainted with my appearance. I will confess there was a time when I must have regarded you with animosity, as one who sought the destruction of the most ancient and potent organization in the world—the Si-Fan."

As he uttered the words he raised his right hand and touched his forehead, his mouth, and finally his breast—a gesture reminiscent of that employed by Moslems.

"But my first task is to assure you," he resumed, "that the activities of that Order are in no way inimical to yourself, your country or your king. The extensive ramifications of the Order have recently been employed by a certain Dr. Fu-Manchu for his own ends, and, since he was (I admit it) a high official, a schism has been created in our ranks. Exactly a month ago, sentence of death was passed upon him by the Sublime Prince, and since I myself must return immediately to China, I look to Mr. Nayland Smith to carry out that sentence."

I said nothing; I remained bereft of the power of speech.

"The Si-Fan," he added, repeating the gesture with his hand, "disown Dr. Fu-Manchu and his servants; do with them what you will. In this envelope"—he held up a sealed package—"is information which should prove helpful to Mr. Smith. I have now a request to make. You were conveyed here in the garments which you wore at the time that my servants called upon you." (I was hatless and wore red leathern slippers.) "An overcoat and a hat can doubtless be found to suit you, temporarily, and my request is that you close your eyes until permission is given to open them."

Is there any one of my readers in doubt respecting my reception of this proposal? Remember my situation, remember the bizarre happening that had led up to it; remember, too, ere judging me, that whilst I could not doubt the unseen presence of Chinamen unnumbered surrounding that strange apartment with the golden door, I had not the remotest clue to guide me in determining where it was situated. Since the duration of my unconsciousness was immeasurable, the place in which I found myself might have been anywhere, within say, thirty miles of Fleet Street!

"I agree," I said.

The mandarin bowed composedly.

"Kindly close your eyes, Dr. Petrie," he requested, "and fear nothing. No danger threatens you."

I obeyed. Instantly sounded the note of a gong, and I became aware that the golden door was open. A soft voice, evidently that of a cultured Chinaman, spoke quite close to my ear—

"Keep your eyes tightly closed, please, and I will help you on with this coat. The envelope you will find in the pocket and here is a tweed cap. Now take my hand."

Wearing the borrowed garments, I was led from the room, along a passage, down a flight of thickly carpeted stairs, and so out of the house into the street. Faint evidences of remote traffic reached my ears as I was assisted into a car and placed in a cushioned corner. The car moved off, proceeded for some distance; then—

"Allow me to help you to descend," said the soft voice. "You may open your eyes in thirty seconds."

I was assisted from the step on to the pavement—and I heard the car being driven back. Having slowly counted to thirty I opened my eyes, and looked about me. This, and not the fevered moment when first I had looked upon the room with the golden door, seemed to be my true awakening, for about me was comprehensible world, the homely streets of London, with deserted Portland Place stretching away on the one hand and a glimpse of midnight Regent Street obtainable on the other! The clock of the neighboring church struck one.

My mind yet dull with wonder of it all, I walked on to Oxford Circus and there obtained a taxi-cab, in which I drove to Fleet Street. Discharging the man, I passed quickly under the time-worn archway into the court and approached our stair. Indeed, I was about to ascend when someone came racing down and almost knocked me over.

"Petrie! Petrie! Thank God you're safe!"

It was Nayland Smith, his eyes blazing with excitement, as I could see by the dim light of the lamp near the archway, and his hands, as he clapped them upon my shoulders, quivering tensely.

"Petrie!" he ran on impulsively, and speaking with extraordinary rapidity, "I was detained by a most ingenious trick and arrived only five minutes ago, to find you missing, the window wide open, and signs of hooks, evidently to support a rope ladder, having been attached to the ledge."

"But where were you going?"

"Weymouth has just rung up. We have indisputable proof that the mandarin Ki-Ming, whom I had believed to be dead, and whom I know for a high official of the Si-Fan, is actually in London! It's neck or nothing this time, Petrie! I'm going straight to Portland Place!"

"To the Chinese Legation?"

"Exactly!"

"Perhaps I can save you a journey," I said slowly. "I have just come from there!"

CHAPTER TWENTY-EIGHT

THE MANDARIN KI-MING

Nayland Smith strode up and down the little sitting-room, tugging almost savagely at the lobe of his left ear. Tonight his increasing grayness was very perceptible, and with his feverishly bright eyes staring straightly before him, he looked haggard and ill, despite the deceptive tan of his skin.

"Petrie," he began in his abrupt fashion, "I am losing confidence in myself."

"Why?" I asked in surprise.

"I hardly know; but for some occult reason I feel afraid."

"Afraid?"

"Exactly; afraid. There is some deep mystery here that I cannot fathom. In the first place, if they had really meant you to remain ignorant of the place at which the episodes described by you occurred, they would scarcely have dropped you at the end of Portland Place."

"You mean ...?"

"I mean that I don't believe you were taken to the Chinese Legation at all. Undoubtedly you saw the mandarin Ki-Ming; I recognize him from your description."

"You have met him, then?"

"No; but I know those who have. He is undoubtedly a very dangerous man, and it is just possible—"

He hesitated, glancing at me strangely.

"It is just possible," he continued musingly, "that his presence marks the beginning of the end. Fu-Manchu's health may be permanently impaired, and Ki-Ming may have superceded him."

"But, if what you suspect, Smith, be only partly true, with what object was I seized and carried to that singular interview? What was the meaning of the whole solemn farce?"

"Its meaning remains to be discovered," he answered; "but that the mandarin is amicably disposed I refuse to believe. You may dismiss the idea. In dealing with Ki-Ming we are to all intents and purposes dealing with Fu-Manchu. To me, this man's presence means one thing: we are about to be subjected to attempts along slightly different lines."

I was completely puzzled by Smith's tone.

"You evidently know more of this man, Ki-Ming, than you have yet explained to me," I said.

Nayland Smith pulled out the blackened briar and began rapidly to load it.

"He is a graduate," he replied, "of the Lama College, or monastery, of Rachë-Churân."

"This does not enlighten me."

Having got his pipe going well—

"What do you know of animal magnetism?" snapped Smith.

The question seemed so wildly irrelevant that I stared at him in silence for some moments. Then—

"Certain powers sometimes grouped under that head are recognized in every hospital today," I answered shortly.

"Quite so. And the monastery of Rache-Churân is entirely devoted to the study of the subject."

"Do you mean that that gentle old man—"

"Petrie, a certain M. Sokoloff, a Russian gentleman whose acquaintance I made in Mandalay, related to me an episode that took place at the house of the mandarin Ki-Ming in Canton. It actually occurred in the presence of M. Sokoloff, and therefore is worthy of your close attention.

"He had had certain transactions with Ki-Ming, and at their conclusion received an invitation to dine with the mandarin. The entertainment took place in a sort of loggia or open pavilion, immediately in front of which was an ornamental lake, with numerous waterlilies growing upon its surface. One of the servants, I think his name was Li, dropped a silver bowl containing orange-flower water for pouring upon the hands, and some of the contents lightly sprinkled M. Sokoloff's garments.

"Ki-Ming spoke no word of rebuke, Petrie; he merely *looked* at Li, with those deceptive, gazelle-like eyes. Li, according to my acquaintance account, began to make palpable and increasingly anxious attempts to look anywhere rather than into the mild eyes of his implacable master. M. Sokoloff, who, up to that moment, had entertained similar views to your own respecting his host, regarded this unmoving stare of Ki-Ming's as a sort of kindly, because silent, reprimand. The behavior of the unhappy Li very speedily served to disabuse his mind of that delusion.

"Petrie—the man grew livid, his whole body began to twitch and shake as though an ague had attacked him; and his eyes protruded hideously from their sockets! M. Sokoloff assured me that he *felt* himself turning pale—when Ki-Ming, very slowly, raised his right hand and pointed to the pond.

"Li began to pant as though engaged in a life-and-death struggle with a physically superior antagonist. He clutched at the posts of the loggia with frenzied hands and a bloody froth came to his lips. He began to move backward, step by step, step by step, all the time striving, with might and main, to *prevent* himself from doing so! His eyes were set rigidly upon Ki-Ming, like the eyes of a rabbit fascinated by a python. Ki-Ming continued to point.

"Right to the brink of the lake the man retreated, and there, for one dreadful moment, he paused and uttered a sort of groaning sob. Then, clenching his fists frenziedly, he stepped back into the water and immediately sank among the lilies. Ki-Ming continued to gaze fixedly—at the spot where bubbles were rising; and presently up came the livid face of the drowning man, still having those glazed eyes turned, immovably, upon the mandarin. For nearly five seconds that hideous, distorted face gazed from amid the mass of blooms, then it sank again … and rose no more."

"What!" I cried, "do you mean to tell me—"

"Ki-Ming struck a gong. Another servant appeared with a fresh bowl of water; and the mandarin calmly resumed his dinner!"

I drew a deep breath and raised my hand to my head.

"It is almost unbelievable," I said. "But what completely passes my comprehension is his allowing me to depart unscathed, having once held me in his power. Why the long harangue and the pose of friendship?"

"That point is not so difficult."

"What!"

"That does not surprise me in the least. You may recollect that Dr. Fu-Manchu entertains for you an undoubted affection, distinctly Chinese in its character, but nevertheless an affection! There is no intention of assassinating *you*, Petrie; *I* am the selected victim."

I started up.

"Smith! what do you mean? What danger, other than that which has threatened us for over two years, threatens us tonight?"

"Now you come to the point which *does* puzzle me. I believe I stated a while ago that I was afraid. You have placed your finger upon the cause of my fear. *What* threatens us tonight?"

He spoke the words in such a fashion that they seemed physically to chill me. The shadows of the room grew menacing; the very silence became horrible. I longed with a terrible longing for company, for the strength that is in numbers; I would have had the place full to overflowing—for it seemed that we two, condemned by the mysterious organization called the Si-Fan, were at that moment surrounded by the entire arsenal of horrors at the command of Dr. Fu-Manchu. I broke that morbid silence. My voice had assumed an unnatural tone.

"Why do you dread this man, Ki-Ming, so much?"

"Because he must be aware that I know he is in London."

"Well?"

"Dr. Fu-Manchu has no official status. Long ago, his Legation denied all knowledge of his existence. But the mandarin Ki-Ming is known to every diplomat in Europe, Asia and America almost. Only *I*, and now yourself, know that he is a high official of the Si-Fan; Ki-Ming is aware that I know. Why, therefore, does he risk his neck in London?"

"He relies upon his national cunning."

"Petrie, he is aware that I hold evidence to hang him, either here or in China! He relies upon one thing; upon striking first and striking surely. Why is he so confident? I do not know. Therefore I am afraid."

Again a cold shudder ran icily through me. A piece of coal

dropped lower into the dying fire—and my heart leapt wildly. Then, in a flash, I remembered something.

"Smith!" I cried, "the letter! We have not looked at the letter."

Nayland Smith laid his pipe upon the mantelpiece and smiled grimly. From his pocket he took out a square piece of paper, and thrust it close under my eyes.

"I remembered it as I passed your borrowed garments—which bear no maker's name—on my way to the bedroom for matches," he said.

The paper was covered with Chinese characters!

"What does it mean?" I demanded breathlessly.

Smith uttered a short, mirthless laugh.

"It states that an attempt of a particularly dangerous nature is to be made upon my life tonight, and it recommends me to guard the door, and advises that you watch the window overlooking the court, and keep your pistol ready for instant employment." He stared at me oddly. "How should you act in the circumstances, Petrie?"

"I should strongly distrust such advice. Yet—what else can we *do*?"

"There are several alternatives, but I prefer to follow the advice of Ki-Ming."

The clock of St. Paul's chimed the half-hour: half-past two.

CHAPTER TWENTY-NINE

LAMA SORCERY

From my post in the chair by the window I could see two sides of the court below; that immediately opposite, with the entrance to some chambers situated there, and that on the right, with the cloisteresque arches beyond which lay a maze of old-world passages and stairs whereby one who knew the tortuous navigation might come ultimately to the Embankment.

It was this side of the court which lay in deepest shadow. By altering my position quite slightly I could command a view of the arched entrance on the left with its pale lamp in an iron bracket above, and of the high blank wall whose otherwise unbroken expanse it interrupted. All was very still; only on occasions the passing of a vehicle along Fleet Street would break the silence.

The nature of the danger that threatened I was wholly unable to surmise. Since, my pistol on the table beside me, I sat on guard at the window, and Smith, also armed, watched the outer door, it was not apparent by what agency the shadowy enemy could hope to come at us.

Something strange I had detected in Nayland Smith's manner,

however, which had induced me to believe that he suspected, if he did not know, what form of menace hung over us in the darkness. One thing in particular was puzzling me extremely: if Smith doubted the good faith of the sender of the message, why had he acted upon it?

Thus my mind worked—in endless and profitless cycles—whilst my eyes were ever searching the shadows below me.

And, as I watched, wondering vaguely why Smith at his post was so silent, presently I became aware of the presence of a slim figure over by the arches on the right. This discovery did not come suddenly, nor did it surprise me; I merely observed without being conscious of any great interest in the matter, that someone was standing in the court below, looking up at me where I sat.

I cannot hope to explain my state of mind at that moment, to render understandable by contrast with the cold fear which had visited me so recently, the utter apathy of my mental attitude. To this day I cannot recapture the mood—and for a very good reason, though one that was not apparent to me at the time.

It was the Eurasian girl Zarmi, who was standing there, looking up at the window! Silently I watched her. Why was I silent?—why did I not warn Smith of the presence of one of Dr. Fu-Manchu's servants? I cannot explain, although later, the strangeness of my behavior may become in some measure understandable.

Zarmi raised her hand, beckoning to me, then stepped back, revealing the presence of a companion, hitherto masked by the dense shadows that lay under the arches. This second watcher moved slowly forward, and I perceived him to be none other than the mandarin Ki-Ming.

This I noted with interest, but with a sort of *impersonal* interest, as I might have watched the entrance of a character upon the stage of a theater. Despite the feeble light, I could see his benign countenance very clearly; but, far from being excited, a dreamy contentment possessed me; I actually found myself hoping that Smith would not intrude upon my reverie!

What a fascinating pageant it had been—the Fu-Manchu drama—from the moment that I had first set eyes upon the Yellow doctor. Again I seemed to be enacting my part in that scene, two years ago and more, when I had burst into the bare room above Shen-Yan's opium den and had stood face to face with Dr. Fu-Manchu. He wore a plain yellow robe, its hue almost identical with that of his gaunt, hairless face; his elbows rested upon the dirty table and his pointed chin upon his long, bony hands.

Into those uncanny eyes I stared, those eyes, long, narrow, and slightly oblique, their brilliant, catlike greenness sometimes horribly filmed, like the eyes of some grotesque bird....

Thus it began; and from this point I was carried on, step by step through every episode, great and small. It was such a retrospect as passes through the mind of one drowning.

With a vividness that was terrible yet exquisite, I saw Kâramaneh, my lost love; I saw her first wrapped in a hooded opera-cloak, with her flower-like face and glorious dark eyes raised to me; I saw her in the gauzy Eastern raiment of a slave-girl, and I saw her in the dress of a gipsy.

Through moments sweet and bitter I lived again, through hours of suspense and days of ceaseless watching; through the long months of that first summer when my unhappy love came to me, and on, on, interminably on. For years I lived again beneath that ghastly Yellow cloud. I searched throughout the land of Egypt for Kâramaneh and knew once more the sorrow of losing her. Time ceased to exist for me.

Then, at the end of these strenuous years, I came at last to my meeting with Ki-Ming in the room with the golden door. At this point my visionary adventures took a new turn. I sat again upon the red-covered couch and listened, half stupefied, to the placid speech of the mandarin. Again I came under the spell of his singular personality, and again, closing my eyes, I consented to be led from the room.

But, having crossed the threshold, a sudden awful doubt passed through my mind, arrow-like. The hand that held my arm was bony and clawish; I could detect the presence of incredibly long finger nails—nails long as those of some buried vampire of the black ages!

Choking down a cry of horror, I opened my eyes—heedless of the promise given but a few moments earlier—and looked into the face of my guide.

It was Dr. Fu-Manchu! …

Never, dreaming or waking, have I known a sensation identical with that which now clutched my heart; I thought that it must be death. For ages, untold ages—aeons longer than the world has known—I looked into that still, awful face, into those unnatural green eyes. I jerked my hand free from the Chinaman's clutch and sprang back.

As I did so, I became miraculously translated from the threshold of the room with the golden door to our chambers in the court adjoining Fleet Street; I came into full possession of my faculties (or believed so at the time); I realized that I had nodded at my post, that I had dreamed a strange dream … but I realized something else. A ghoulish presence was in the room.

Snatching up my pistol from the table I turned. Like some evil jinn of Arabian lore, Dr. Fu-Manchu, surrounded by a slight mist, stood looking at me!

Instantly I raised the pistol, leveled it steadily at the high, dome-like brow—and fired! There could be no possibility of missing at such short range, no possibility whatever ... and in the very instant of pulling the trigger the mist cleared, the lineaments of Dr. Fu-Manchu melted magically. This was not the Chinese doctor who stood before me, at whose skull I still was pointing the deadly little weapon, into whose brain I had fired the bullet; *it was Nayland Smith!*

Ki-Ming, by means of the unholy arts of the Lamas of Rache-Churân, had caused my to murder my best friend!

"Smith!" I whispered huskily—"God forgive me, what have I done? What have I done?"

I stepped forward to support him ere he fell; but utter oblivion closed down upon me, and I knew no more.

"He will do quite well now." said a voice that seemed to come from a vast distance. "The effects of the drug will have entirely worn off when he wakes, except that there may be nausea, and possibly muscular pain for a time."

I opened my eyes; they were throbbing agonizingly. I lay in bed, and beside me stood Murdoch McCabe, the famous toxicological expert from Charing Cross Hospital—and Nayland Smith!

"Ah, that's better!" cried McCabe cheerily. "Here—drink this."

I drank from the glass which he raised to my lips. I was too weak for speech, too weak for wonder. Nayland Smith, his face gray and drawn in the cold light of early morning, watched me anxiously. McCabe in a matter of fact way that acted upon me like a welcome tonic, put several purely medical questions, which at first by dint of a great effort, but, with ever-increasing ease, I answered.

"Yes," he said musingly at last. "Of course it is all but impossible to speak with certainty, but I am disposed to think that you have been drugged with some preparation of hashish. The most likely is that known in Eastern countries as *maagûn* or *barsh*, composed of equal parts of *cannabis indica* and opium, with hellebore and two other constituents, which vary according to the purpose which the *maagûn* is intended to serve. This renders the subject particularly open to subjective hallucination, and a pliable instrument in the hands of a hypnotic operator, for instance."

"You see, old man?" cried Smith eagerly. "You see?"

But I shook my head weakly.

"I shot you," I said. "It is impossible that I could have missed."

"Mr. Smith has placed me in possession of the facts," interrupted McCabe, "and I can outline with reasonable certainty what took place. Of course, it's all very amazing, utterly fantastic in fact, but I have met with almost parallel cases in Egypt, in India, and elsewhere in the East: never in London, I'll confess. You see, Dr. Petrie, you were taken into the presence of a very accomplished hypnotist, having been previously prepared by a stiff administration of *maagûn*. You are doubtless familiar with the remarkable experiments in psycho-therapeutics conducted at the Salpêtrier in Paris, and you will readily understand me when I say that, prior to your recovering consciousness in the presence of the mandarin Ki-Ming, you had received your hypnotic instructions.

"These were to be put into execution either at a certain time (duly impressed upon your drugged mind) or at a given signal...."

"It was a signal," snapped Smith."Ki-Ming stood in the court below and looked up at the window."

"But *I* might not have been stationed at the window," I objected.

"In that event," snapped Smith, "he would have spoken softly, through the letter-box of the door!"

"You immediately resumed your interrupted trance," continued

McCabe, "and by hypnotic suggestion impressed upon you earlier in the evening, you were ingeniously led up to a point at which, under what delusion I know not, you fired at Mr. Smith. I had the privilege of studying an almost parallel case in Simla, where an officer was fatally stabbed by his *khitmatgar* (a most faithful servant) acting under the hypnotic prompting of a certain *fakîr* whom the officer had been unwise enough to chastise. The *fakîr* paid for the crime with his life, I may add. The *khitmatgar* shot him, ten minutes later."

"I had no chance at Ki-Ming," snapped Smith. "He vanished like a shadow. But has played his big card and lost! Henceforth he is a hunted man; and he knows it! Oh!" he cried, seeing me watching him in bewilderment, "I suspected some Lama trickery, old man, and I stuck closely to the arrangements proposed by the mandarin, but kept you under careful observation!"

"But, Smith—I shot you! It was impossible to miss!"

"I agree. But do you recall the *report*?"

"The report? I was too dazed, too horrified, by the discovery of what I had done...."

"There was no report, Petrie. I am not entirely a stranger to Indo-Chinese jugglery, and you had a very strange look in your eyes. Therefore I took the precaution of unloading your Browning!"

CHAPTER THIRTY

MEDUSA

Legal business, connected with the estate of a distant relative, deceased, necessitated my sudden departure from London, within twenty-four hours of the events just narrated; and at a time when London was for me the center of the universe. The business being terminated—and in a manner financially satisfactory to myself—I discovered that with luck I could just catch the fast train back. Amid a perfect whirl of hotel porters and taxi-drivers worthy of Nayland Smith I departed for the station … to arrive at the entrance to the platform at the exact moment that the guard raised his green flag!

"Too late, sir! Stand back, if you please!"

The ticket-collector at the barrier thrust out his arm to stay me. The London express was moving from the platform. But my determination to travel by that train and by no other over-rode all obstacles; if I missed it, I should be forced to wait until the following morning.

I leapt past the barrier, completely taking the man by surprise, and went racing up the platform. Many arms were outstretched to detain me, and the gray-bearded guard stood fully in my path; but I dodged them all, collided with and upset a gigantic negro who wore a chauffeur's uniform—and found myself level with a first-class compartment; the window was open.

Amid a chorus of excited voices, I tossed my bag in at the window, leapt upon the footboard and turned the handle. Although the entrance to the tunnel was perilously near now, I managed to wrench the door open and to swing myself into the carriage. Then, by means of the strap, I reclosed the door in the nick of time, and sank, panting, upon the seat. I had a vague impression that the black chauffeur, having recovered himself, had raced after me to the uttermost point of the platform, but, my end achieved, I was callously indifferent to the outrageous means thereto which I seen fit to employ. The express dashed into the tunnel. I uttered a great sigh of relief.

With Kâramaneh in the hands of the Si-Fan, this journey to the north had indeed been undertaken with the utmost reluctance. Nayland Smith had written to me once during my brief absence, and his letter had inspired a yet keener desire to be back and at grips with the Yellow group; for he had hinted broadly that a tangible clue to the whereabouts of the Si-Fan headquarters had at last been secured.

Now I learnt that I had a traveling companion—a woman. She was seated in the further, opposite corner, wore a long, loose motor-coat, which could not altogether conceal the fine lines of her lithe figure, and a thick veil hid her face. A motive for the excited behavior of the negro chauffeur suggested itself to my mind; a label; "Engaged," was pasted to the window!

I glanced across the compartment. Through the closely woven veil the woman was watching me. An apology clearly was called for.

"Madame," I said, "I hope you will forgive this unfortunate intrusion; but it was vitally important that I should not miss the London train."

She bowed, very slightly, very coldly—and turned her head aside.

The rebuff was as unmistakable as my offense was irremediable. Nor did I feel justified in resenting it. Therefore, endeavoring to dismiss the matter from my mind, I placed my bag upon the rack, and unfolding the newspaper with which I was provided, tried to interest myself in the doings of the world at large.

My attempt proved not altogether successful; strive how I would, my thoughts persistently reverted to the Si-Fan, the evil, secret society who held in their power one dearer to me than all the rest of the world; to Dr. Fu-Manchu, the genius who darkly controlled my destiny; and to Nayland Smith, the barrier between the White races and the devouring tide of the Yellow.

Sighing again, involuntarily, I glanced up ... to meet the gaze of a pair of wonderful eyes.

Never, in my experience, had I seen their like. The dark eyes of Kâramaneh were wonderful and beautiful, the eyes of Dr. Fu-Manchu sinister and wholly unforgettable; but the eyes of this woman were incredible. Their glance was all but insupportable; the were the eyes of a Medusa!

Since I had met; in the not distant past, the soft gaze of Ki-Ming, the mandarin whose phenomenal hypnotic powers rendered him capable of transcending the achievements of the celebrated Cagliostro, I knew much of the power of the human eye. But these were unlike any human eyes I had ever known.

Long, almond-shaped, bordered by heavy jet-black lashes, arched over by finely penciled brows, their strange brilliancy, as of a fire within, was utterly uncanny. They were the eyes of some beautiful wild creature rather than those of a woman.

Their possessor had now thrown back her motor-veil, revealing a face Orientally dark and perfectly oval, with a clustering mass of dull gold hair, small, aquiline nose and full, red lips. Her weird eyes met mine for an instant, and then the long lashes drooped quickly, as she leant back against the cushions, with a graceful languor suggestive of the East rather than of the West.

Her long coat had fallen partly open, and I saw, with surprise, that it was lined with leopard-skin. One hand was ungloved, and lay on the arm-rest—a slim hand of the hue of old ivory, with a strange, ancient ring upon the index finger.

This woman obviously was not a European, and I experienced great difficulty in determining with what Asiatic nation she could claim kinship. In point of fact I had never seen another who remotely resembled her; she was a fit employer for the gigantic negro with whom I had collided on the platform.

I tried to laugh at myself, staring from the window at the moon-bathed landscape; but the strange personality of my solitary companion would not be denied, and I looked quickly in her direction—in time to detect her glancing away; in time to experience the uncanny fascination of her gaze.

The long slim hand attracted my attention again, the green stone in the ring affording a startling contrast against the dull cream of the skin.

Whether the woman's personality, or a vague perfume of which I became aware, were responsible, I found myself thinking of a flower-bedecked shrine, wherefrom arose the smoke of incense to some pagan god.

In vain I told myself that my frame of mind was contemptible, that I should be ashamed of such weakness. Station after station was left behind, as the express sped through moonlit England towards the smoky metropolis. Assured that I was being furtively watched, I became more and more uneasy.

It was with a distinct sense of effort that I withheld my gaze, forcing myself to look out of the window. When, having reasoned against the mad ideas that sought to obsess me, I glanced again across the compartment, I perceived, with inexpressible relief, that my companion had lowered her veil.

She kept it lowered throughout the remainder of the journey; yet during the hour that ensued I continued to experience sensations of which I have never since been able to think without a thrill of fear. It seemed that I had thrust myself, not into a commonplace railway compartment, but into a Cumaean cavern.

If only I could have addressed this utterly mysterious stranger, have uttered some word of commonplace, I felt that the spell might have been broken. But, for some occult reason, in no way associated with my first rebuff, I found myself tongue-tied; I sustained, for an hour (the longest I had ever known), a silent watch and ward over my reason; I seemed to be repelling, fighting against, some subtle power that sought to flood my brain, swamp my individuality, and enslave me to another's will.

In what degree this was actual, and in what due to a mind overwrought from endless conflict with the Yellow group, I know not to this day, but you who read these records of our giant struggle with Fu-Manchu and his satellites shall presently judge for yourselves.

When, at last, the brakes were applied, and the pillars and platforms of the great terminus glided into view, how welcome was the smoky glare, how welcome the muffled roar of busy London!

A huge negro—the double of the man I had overthrown—opened the door of the compartment, bestowing upon me a glance in which enmity and amazement were oddly blended, and the woman, drawing the cloak about her graceful figure, stood up composedly.

She reached for a small leather case on the rack, and her loose sleeve fell back, to reveal a bare arm—soft, perfectly molded, of the even hue of old ivory. Just below the elbow a strange-looking snake bangle clasped the warm flesh; the eyes; dull green, seemed to hold a slumbering fire—a spark—a spark of living light.

Then—she was gone!

"Thank Heaven!" I muttered, and felt like another Dante emerging from the Hades.

As I passed out of the station, I had a fleeting glimpse of a gray figure stepping into a big car, driven by a black chauffeur.

CHAPTER THIRTY-ONE

THE MARMOSET

Half-past twelve was striking as I came out of the terminus, buttoning up my overcoat, and pulling my soft hat firmly down upon my head, started to walk to Hyde Park Corner.

I had declined the services of the several taxi-drivers who had accosted me and had determined to walk a part of the distance homeward, in order to check the fever of excitement which consumed me.

Already I was ashamed of the strange fears which had been mine during the journey, but I wanted to reflect, to conquer my mood, and the midnight solitude of the land of Squares which lay between me and Hyde Park appealed quite irresistibly.

There is a distinct pleasure to be derived from a solitary walk through London, in the small hours of an April morning, provided one is so situated as to be capable of enjoying it. To appreciate the solitude and mystery of the sleeping city, a certain sense of prosperity—a knowledge that one is immune from the necessity of being abroad at that hour—is requisite. The tramp, the night policeman and the coffee-stall keeper know more of London by night than most people—but of the romance of the dark hours they know little. Romance succumbs before necessity.

I had good reason to be keenly alive to the aroma of mystery which pervades the most commonplace thoroughfare after the hum of the traffic has subsided—when the rare pedestrian and the rarer cab alone traverse the deserted highway. With more intimate cares seeking to claim my mind, it was good to tramp along the echoing, empty streets and to indulge in imaginative speculation regarding the strange things that night must shroud in every big city. I have known the solitude of deserts, but the solitude of London is equally fascinating.

He whose business or pleasure had led him to traverse the route which was mine on this memorable night must have observed how each of the squares composing that residential chain which links the outer with the inner Society has a popular and an exclusive side. The angle used by vehicular traffic in crossing the square from corner to corner invariably is rich in a crop of black board bearing house-agent's announcements.

In the shadow of such a board I paused, taking out my case and leisurely selecting a cigar. So many of the houses in the southwest angle were unoccupied, that I found myself taking quite an interest in one a little way ahead; from the hall door and from the long conservatory over the porch light streamed out.

Excepting these illuminations, there was no light elsewhere in the square to show which houses were inhabited and which vacant. I might have stood in a street of Pompeii or Thebes—a street of the dead past. I permitted my imagination to dwell upon this idea as I fumbled for matches and gazed about me. I wondered if a day would come when some savant of a future land, in a future age, should stand where I stood and endeavor to reconstruct, from the crumbling ruins, this typical London square. A slight breeze set the hatchet-board creaking above my head, as I held my gloved hands about the pine-vesta.

At that moment someone or something whistled close beside me!

I turned, in a flash, dropping the match upon the pavement. There was no lamp near the spot whereat I stood, and the gateway and porch of the deserted residence seemed to be empty. I stood there peering in the direction from which the mysterious whistle had come.

The drone of a taxi-cab, approaching from the north, increased in volume, as the vehicle came spinning around the angle of the square, passed me, and went droning on its way. I watched it swing around the distant corner … and, in the new stillness, the whistle was repeated!

This time the sound chilled me. The whistle was pitched in a curious, inhuman key, and it possessed a mocking note that was strangely uncanny.

Listening intently and peering towards the porch of the empty house, I struck a second match, pushed the iron gate open and made for the steps, sheltering the feeble flame with upraised hand. As I did so, the whistle was again repeated, but from some spot further away, to the left of the porch, and from low down upon the ground.

Just as I glimpsed something moving under the lee of the porch, the match was blown out, for I was hampered by the handbag which I carried. Thus reminded of its presence, however, I recollected that my pocket-lamp was in it. Quickly opening the bag, I took out the lamp, and, passing around the corner of the steps, directed a ray of light into the narrow passage which communicated with the rear of the building.

Halfway along the passage, looking back at me over its shoulder, and whistling angrily, was a little marmoset!

I pulled up as sharply as though the point of a sword had been held at my throat. One marmoset is sufficiently like another to deceive the ordinary observer, but unless I was permitting a not unnatural prejudice to influence my opinion, this particular specimen was the pet of Dr. Fu-Manchu!

Excitement, not untinged with fear, began to grow up within me. Hyde Park was no far cry, this was near to the heart of social London; yet, somewhere close at hand, it might be, watching me as I stood—lurked, perhaps, the great and evil being who dreamed of overthrowing the entire white race!

With a grotesque grimace and a final, chattering whistle, the little creature leapt away out of the beam of light cast by my lamp. Its sudden disappearance brought me to my senses and reminded me of my plain duty. I set off along the passage briskly, arrived at a small, square yard ... and was just in time to see the ape leap into a well-like opening before a basement window. I stepped to the brink, directing the light down into the well.

I saw a collection of rotten leaves, waste paper, and miscellaneous rubbish—but the marmoset was not visible. Then I perceived that practically all the glass in the window had been broken. A sound of shrill chattering reached me from the blackness of the underground apartment.

Again I hesitated. What did the darkness mask?

The note of a distant motor-horn rose clearly above the vague throbbing which is the only silence known to the town-dweller.

Gripping the unlighted cigar between my teeth, I placed my bag upon the ground and dropped into the well before the broken window. To raise the sash was a simple matter, and, having accomplished it, I inspected the room within.

The light showed a large kitchen, with torn wallpaper and decorator's litter strewn about the floor, a whitewash pail in one corner, and nothing else.

I climbed in, and, taking from my pocket the Browning pistol without which I had never traveled since the return of the dreadful Chinaman to England, I crossed to the door, which was ajar, and looked out into the passage beyond.

Stifling an exclamation, I fell back a step. Two gleaming eyes stared straightly into mine!

The next moment I had forced a laugh to my lips ... as the marmoset turned and went gamboling up the stairs. The house was profoundly silent. I crossed the passage and followed the creature, which now was proceeding, I thought, with more of a set purpose.

Out into a spacious and deserted hallway it led me, where my cautious footsteps echoed eerily, and ghostly faces seemed to peer down upon me from the galleries above. I should have liked to have unbarred the street door, in order to have opened a safe line of retreat in the event of its being required, but the marmoset suddenly sprang up the main stairway at a great speed, and went racing around the gallery overhead toward the front of the house.

Determined, if possible, to keep the creature in view, I started in pursuit. Up the uncarpeted stairs I went, and, from the rail of the landing, looked down into the blackness of the hallway apprehensively. Nothing stirred below. The marmoset had disappeared between the half-opened leaves of a large folding door. Casting the beam of light ahead of me I followed. I found myself in a long, lofty apartment, evidently a drawing-room.

Of the quarry I could detect no sign; but the only other door of the room was closed; therefore, since the creature had entered, it must, I argued, undoubtedly be concealed somewhere in the apartment. Flashing the light about to right and left, I presently perceived that a conservatory (no doubt facing on the square) ran parallel with one side of the room. French windows gave access to either end of it;

and it was through one of these, which was slightly open, that the questioning ray had intruded.

I stepped into the conservatory. Linen blinds covered the windows, but a faint light from outside found access to the bare, tiled apartment. Ten paces on my right, from an aperture once closed by a square wooden panel that now lay upon the floor, the marmoset was grimacing at me.

Realizing that the ray of my lamp must be visible through the blinds from outside, I extinguished it … and, a moving silhouette against a faintly luminous square, I could clearly distinguish the marmoset watching me.

There was a light in the room beyond!

The marmoset disappeared—and I became aware of a faint, incense-like perfume. Where had I met with it before? Nothing disturbed the silence of the empty house wherein I stood; yet I hesitated for several seconds to pursue the chase further. The realization came to me that the hole in the wall communicated with the conservatory of the corner house in the square, the house with the lighted windows.

Determined to see the thing through, I discarded my overcoat—and crawled through the gap. The smell of burning perfume became almost overpowering, as I stood upright, to find myself almost touching curtains of some semi-transparent golden fabric draped in the door between the conservatory and the drawing-room.

Cautiously, inch by inch, I approached my eyes to the slight gap in the draperies, as, from somewhere in the house below, sounded the clangor of a brazen gong. Seven times its ominous note boomed out. I shrank back into my sanctuary; the incense seemed to be stifling me.

CHAPTER THIRTY-TWO

SHRINE OF SEVEN LAMPS

Never can I forget that nightmare apartment, that efreet's hall. It was identical in shape with the room of the adjoining house through which I had come, but its walls were draped in somber black and a dead black carpet covered the entire floor. A golden curtain—similar to that which concealed me—broke the somber expanse of the end wall to my right, and the door directly opposite my hiding-place was closed.

Across the gold curtain, wrought in glittering black, were seven characters, apparently Chinese; before it, supported upon seven ebony pedestals, burned seven golden lamps; whilst, dotted about the black carpet, were seven gold-lacquered stools, each having a black cushion set before it. There was no sign of the marmoset; the incredible room of black and gold was quite empty, with a sort of stark emptiness that seemed to oppress my soul.

Close upon the booming of the gong followed a sound of many footsteps and a buzz of subdued conversation. Keeping well back in the welcome shadow I watched, with bated breath, the opening of the door immediately opposite.

The outer sides of its leaves proved to be of gold, and one glimpse of the room beyond awoke a latent memory and gave it positive form. I had been in this house before; it was in that room with the golden door that I had had my memorable interview with the mandarin Ki-Ming! My excitement grew more and more intense.

Singly, and in small groups, a number of Orientals came in. All wore European, or semi-European garments, but I was enabled to identify two for Chinamen, two for Hindus and three for Burmans. Other Asiatics there were, also, whose exact place among the Eastern races I could not determine; there was at least one Egyptian and there were several Eurasians; no women were present.

Standing grouped just within the open door, the gathering of Orientals kept up a ceaseless buzz of subdued conversation; then, abruptly, stark silence fell, and through a lane of bowed heads, Ki-Ming, the famous Chinese diplomat, entered, smiling blandly, and took his seat upon one of the seven golden stools. He wore the picturesque yellow robe, trimmed with marten fur, which I had seen once before, and he placed his pearl-encircled cap, surmounted by the coral ball denoting his rank, upon the black cushion beside him.

Almost immediately afterward entered a second and even more striking figure. It was that of a Lama monk! He was received with the same marks of deference which had been accorded the mandarin; and he seated himself upon another of the golden stools.

Silence, a moment of hushed expectancy, and … yellow-robed, immobile, his wonderful, evil face emaciated by illness, but his long, magnetic eyes blazing greenly, as though not a soul but an elemental spirit dwelt within that gaunt, high-shouldered body, Dr. Fu-Manchu entered, slowly, leaning upon a heavy stick!

The realities seemed to be slipping from me; I could not believe that I looked upon a material world. This had been a night of wonders, having no place in the life of a sane, modern man, but belonging to the days of the jinn and the Arabian necromancers.

Fu-Manchu was greeted by a universal raising of hands, but in complete silence. He also wore a cap surmounted by a coral ball, and this he placed upon one of the black cushions set before a golden stool. Then, resting heavily upon his stick, he began to speak—in French!

As one listens to a dream-voice, I listened to that, alternately guttural and sibilant, of the terrible Chinese doctor. He was defending himself! With what he was charged by his sinister brethren I knew not nor could I gather from his words, but that he was rendering account of his stewardship became unmistakable. Scarce crediting my senses, I heard him unfold to his listeners details of crimes successfully perpetrated, and with the results of some of these I was but too familiar; others there were in the ghastly catalog which had been accomplished secretly. Then my blood froze with horror. My own name was mentioned—and that of Nayland Smith! We two stood in the way of the coming of one whom he called the Lady of the Si-Fan, in the way of Asiatic supremacy.

A fantastic legend once mentioned to me by Smith, of some woman cherished in a secret fastness of Hindustan who was destined one day to rule the world, now appeared, to my benumbed senses, to be the unquestioned creed of the murderous, cosmopolitan group known as the Si-Fan! At every mention of her name all heads were bowed in reverence.

Dr. Fu-Manchu spoke without the slightest trace of excitement; he assured his auditors of his fidelity to their cause and proposed to prove to them that he enjoyed the complete confidence of the Lady of the Si-Fan.

And with every moment that passed the giant intellect of the speaker became more and more apparent. Years ago Nayland Smith had assured me that Dr. Fu-Manchu was a linguist who spoke with almost equal facility in any of the civilized languages and in most of the barbaric; now the truth of this was demonstrated. For, following some passage which might be susceptible of misconstruction, Fu-Manchu would turn slightly, and elucidate his remarks, addressing a Chinaman in Chinese, a Hindu in Hindustanee, or an Egyptian in Arabic.

His auditors were swayed by the magnetic personality of the speaker, as reeds by a breeze; and now I became aware of a curious circumstance. Either because they and I viewed the character of this great and evil man from a widely dissimilar aspect, or because, my presence being unknown to him, I remained outside the radius of his power, it seemed to me that these members of the evidently vast organization known as the Si-Fan were dupes, to a man, of the Chinese orator! It seemed to me that he used them as an instrument, playing upon their obvious fanaticism, string by string, as a player upon an Eastern harp, and all the time weaving harmonies to suit some giant, incredible scheme of his own—a scheme over and beyond any of which they had dreamed, in the fruition whereof they had no part—of the true nature and composition of which they had no comprehension.

"Not since the day of the first Yuan Emperor," said Fu-Manchu sibilantly, "has Our Lady of the Si-Fan—to look upon whom, unveiled, is death—crossed the sacred borders. Today I am a man supremely happy and honored above my deserts. You shall all partake with me of that happiness, that honor...."

Again the gong sounded seven times, and a sort of magnetic thrill seemed to pass throughout the room. There followed a faint, musical sound, like the tinkle of a silver bell.

All heads were lowered, but all eyes upturned to the golden curtain. Literally holding my breath, in those moments of intense expectancy, I watched the draperies parted from the center and pulled aside by unseen agency.

A black covered dais was revealed, bearing an ebony chair. And seated in the chair, enveloped from head to feet in a shimmering white veil, was a woman. A sound like a great sigh arose from the gathering. The woman rose slowly to her feet, and raised her arms, which were exquisitely formed, and of the uniform hue of old ivory, so that the veil fell back to her shoulders, revealing the green snake bangle which she wore. She extended her long, slim hands as if in benediction; the silver bell sounded … and the curtain dropped again, entirely obscuring the dais!

Frankly, I thought myself mad; for this "lady of the Si-Fan" was none other than my mysterious traveling companion! This was some solemn farce with which Fu-Manchu sought to impress his fanatical dupes. And he had succeeded; they were inspired, their eyes blazed. Here were men capable of any crime in the name of the Si-Fan!

Every face within my ken I had studied individually, and now slowly and cautiously I changed my position, so that a group of three members standing immediately to the right of the door came into view. One of them—a tall, spare, and closely bearded man whom I took for some kind of Hindu—had removed his gaze from the dais and was glancing furtively all about him. Once he looked in my direction, and my heart leapt high, then seemed to stop its pulsing.

An overpowering consciousness of my danger came to me; a dim envisioning of what appalling fate would be mine in the event of discovery. As those piercing eyes were turned away again, I drew back, step my step.

Dropping upon my knees, I began to feel for the gap in the conservatory wall. The desire to depart from the house of the Si-Fan had become urgent. Once safely away, I could take the necessary steps to ensure the apprehension of the entire group. What a triumph would be mine!

I found the opening without much difficulty and crept through into the empty house. The vague light which penetrated the linen blinds served to show me the length of the empty, tiled apartment. I had actually reached the French window giving access to the drawing-room, when—the skirl of a police whistle split the stillness … and the sound came from the house which I had just quitted!

To write that I was amazed were to achieve the banal. Rigid with wonderment I stood, and clutched at the open window. So I was standing, a man of stone, when the voice, the high-pitched, imperious, unmistakable voice of *Nayland Smith,* followed sharply upon the skirl of the whistle:—

"Watch those French windows, Weymouth! I can hold the door!"

Like a lightning flash it came to me that the tall Hindu had been none other than Smith disguised. From the square outside came a sudden turmoil, a sound of racing feet, of smashing glass, of doors burst forcibly open. Palpably, the place was surrounded; this was an organized raid.

Irresolute, I stood there in the semi-gloom—inactive from amaze of it all—whilst sounds of a tremendous struggle proceeded from the square gap in the partition.

"Lights!" rose a cry, in Smith's voice again—"they have cut the wires!"

At that I came to my senses. Plunging my hand into my pocket, I snatched out the electric lamp … and stepped back quickly into the utter gloom of the room behind me.

Someone was crawling through the aperture into the conservatory!

As I watched I saw him, in the dim light, stoop to replace the movable panel. Then, tapping upon the tiled floor as he walked, the fugitive approached me. He was but three paces from the French window when I pressed the button of my lamp and directed its ray fully upon his face.

"Hands up!" I said breathlessly. "I have you covered, Dr. Fu-Manchu!"

CHAPTER THIRTY-THREE

AN ANTI-CLIMAX

One hour later I stood in the entrance hall of our chambers in the court adjoining Fleet Street. Someone who had come racing up the stairs, now had inserted a key in the lock. Open swung the door—and Nayland Smith entered, in a perfect whirl of excitement.

"Petrie! Petrie!" he cried, and seized both my hands—"you have missed a night of nights! Man alive! we have the whole gang—the great Ki-Ming included!" His eyes were blazing. "Weymouth has made no fewer than twenty-five arrests, some of the prisoners being well-known Orientals. It will be the devil's own work to keep it all quiet, but Scotland Yard has already advised the Press."

"Congratulations, old man," I said, and looked him squarely in the eyes.

Something there must have been in my glance at variance with the spoken words. His expression changed; he grasped my shoulder.

"*She* was not there," he said, "but please God, we'll find her now. It's only a question of time."

But, even as he spoke, the old, haunted look was creeping back into the lean face. He gave me a rapid glance; then:—

"I might as well make a clean breast of it," he rapped. "Fu-Manchu escaped! Furthermore, when we got lights, the woman had vanished, too."

"The woman!"

"There was a woman at this strange gathering, Petrie. Heaven only knows who she really is. According to Fu-Manchu she is that woman of mystery concerning whose existence strange stories are current in the East; the future Empress of a universal empire! But of course I decline to accept the story, Petrie! if ever the Yellow races overran Europe, I am in no doubt respecting the identity of the person who would ascend the throne of the world!"

"Nor I, Smith!" I cried excitedly. "Good God! he holds them all in the palm of his hand! He has welded together the fanatics of every creed of the East into a giant weapon for his personal use! Small wonder that he is so formidable. But, Smith—*who* is that woman?"

"Petrie!" he said slowly, and I knew that I had betrayed my secret, "Petrie—where did you learn all this?"

I returned his steady gaze.

"I was present at the meeting of the Si-Fan," I replied steadily.

"What? What? *You* were present?"

"I was present! Listen, and I will explain."

Standing there in the hallway I related, as briefly as possible, the astounding events of the night. As I told of the woman in the train—

"That confirms my impression that Fu-Manchu was imposing upon the others!" he snapped. "I cannot conceive of a woman recluse from some Lamaserie, surrounded by silent attendants and trained for her exalted destiny in the way that the legendary veiled woman of Tibet is said to be trained, traveling alone in an English railway carriage! Did you observe, Petrie, if her eyes were *oblique* at all?"

"They did not strike me as being oblique. Why do you ask?"

"Because I strongly suspect that we have to do with none other than Fu-Manchu's daughter! But go on."

"By Heavens, Smith! You may be right! I had no idea that a Chinese woman could possess such features."

"She may not have a Chinese mother; furthermore, there are pretty women in China as well as in other countries; also, there are hair dyes and cosmetics. But for Heaven's sake go on!"

I continued my all but incredible narrative; came to the point where I discovered the straying marmoset and entered the empty house, without provoking any comment from my listener. He stared at me with something very like surprised admiration when I related how I had become an unseen spectator of that singular meeting.

"And I thought I had achieved the triumph of my life in gaining admission and smuggling Weymouth and Carter into the roof, armed with hooks and rope-ladders!" he murmured.

Now I came to the moment when, having withdrawn into the empty house, I had heard the police whistle and had heard Smith's voice; I came to the moment when I had found myself face to face with Dr. Fu-Manchu.

Nayland Smith's eyes were on fire now; he literally quivered with excitement, when—

"*Ssh!* what's that?" he whispered, and grasped my arm. "I heard something move in the sitting-room, Petrie!"

"It was a coal dropping from the grate, perhaps," I said—and rapidly continued my story, telling how, with my pistol to his head, I had forced the Chinese doctor to descend into the hallway of the empty house.

"Yes, yes," snapped Smith. "For God's sake go on, man! What have you done with him? Where is he?"

I clearly detected a movement myself immediately behind the half-open door of the sitting-room. Smith started and stared intently across my shoulder at the doorway; then his gaze shifted and became fixed upon my face.

"He bought his life from me, Smith."

Never can I forget the change that came over my friend's tanned features at those words; never can I forget the pang that I suffered to see it. The fire died out of his eyes and he seemed to grow old and weary in a moment. None too steadily I went on:—

"He offered a price that I could not resist, Smith. Try to forgive me, if you can. I know that I have done a dastardly thing, but—perhaps a day may come in your own life when you will understand. He descended with me to a cellar under the empty house, in which someone was locked. Had I arrested Fu-Manchu this poor captive must have died there of starvation; for no one would ever have suspected that the place had an occupant...."

The door of the sitting-room was thrown open, and, wearing my great-coat over the bizarre costume in which I had found her, with her bare ankles and little red slippers peeping grotesquely from below, and her wonderful cloud of hair rippling over the turned-up collar, Kâramaneh came out!

Her great dark eyes were raised to Nayland Smith's with such an appeal in them—an appeal for *me*—that emotion took me by the throat and had me speechless. I could not look at either of them; I turned aside and stared into the lighted sitting-room.

How long I stood so God knows, and I never shall; but suddenly I found my hand seized in a vice-like grip, I looked around and Smith, holding my fingers fast in that iron grasp, had his left arm about Kâramaneh's shoulders, and his gray eyes were strangely soft, whilst hers were hidden behind her upraised hands.

"Good old Petrie!" said Smith hoarsely. "Wake up, man; we have to get her to a hotel before they all close, remember. *I* understand, old man. That day came in my life long years ago!"

CHAPTER THIRTY-FOUR

GRAYWATER PARK

"This is a singular situation in which we find ourselves," I said, "and one that I'm bound to admit I don't appreciate."

Nayland Smith stretched his long legs, and lay back in his chair.

"The sudden illness of Sir Lionel is certainly very disturbing," he replied, "and had there been any possibility of returning to London tonight, I should certainly have availed myself of it, Petrie. I share your misgivings. We are intruders at a time like this."

He stared at me keenly, blowing a wreath of smoke from his lips, and then directing his attention to the cone of ash which crowned his cigar. I glanced, and not for the first time, toward the quaint old doorway which gave access to a certain corridor. Then—

"Apart from the feeling that we intrude," I continued slowly, "there is a certain sense of unrest."

"Yes," snapped Smith, sitting suddenly upright—"yes! You experience this? Good! You are happily sensitive to this type of impression, Petrie, and therefore quite as useful to me as a cat is useful to a physical investigator."

He laughed in his quick, breezy fashion.

"You will appreciate my meaning," he added; "therefore I offer no excuse for the analogy. Of course, the circumstances, as we know them, may be responsible for this consciousness of unrest. We are neither of us likely to forget the attempt upon the life of Sir Lionel Barton two years ago or more. Our attitude toward sudden illness is scarcely that of impartial observers."

"I suppose not," I admitted, glancing yet again at the still vacant doorway by the foot of the stairs, which now the twilight was draping in mysterious shadows.

Indeed, our position was a curious one. A welcome invitation from our old friend, Sir Lionel Barton, the world-famous explorer, had come at a time when a spell of repose, a glimpse of sea and awakening countryside, and a breath of fair, untainted air were very desirable. The position of Kâramaneh, who accompanied us, was sufficiently unconventional already, but the presence of Mrs. Oram, the dignified housekeeper, had rendered possible her visit to this bachelor establishment. In fact it was largely in the interests of the girl's health that we had accepted.

On our arrival at Graywater Park we had learnt that our host had been stricken down an hour earlier by sudden illness. The exact nature of his seizure I had thus far been unable to learn; but a local doctor, who had left the Park barely ten minutes before our advent, had strictly forbidden visitors to the sick-room. Sir Lionel's man, Kennedy, who had served him in many strange spots in the world, was in attendance.

So much we had gathered from Homopoulo, the Greek butler (Sir Lionel's household had ever been eccentric). Furthermore, we learned that there was no London train that night and no accommodation in the neighboring village.

"Sir Lionel urgently requests you to remain," the butler had assured us, in his flawless, monotonous English. "He trusts that you will not be dull, and hopes to be able to see you tomorrow and to make plans for your entertainment."

A ghostly, gray shape glided across the darkened hall—and was gone. I started involuntarily. Then remote, fearsome, came muted howling to echo through the ancient apartments of Graywater Park. Nayland Smith laughed.

"That was the civet cat, Petrie!" he said. "I was startled, for a moment, until the lamentations of the leopard family reminded me of the fact that Sir Lionel had transferred his menagerie to Graywater!"

Truly, this was a singular household. In turn, Graywater Park had been a fortress, a monastery, and a manor-house. Now, in the extensive crypt below the former chapel, in an atmosphere artificially raised to a suitably stuffy temperature, were housed the strange pets brought by our eccentric host from distant lands. In one cage was an African lioness, a beautiful and powerful beast, docile as a cat. Housed under other arches were two surly hyenas, goats from the White Nile, and an antelope of Kordofan. In a stable opening upon the garden were a pair of beautiful desert gazelles, and near to them, two cranes and a marabou. The leopards, whose howling now disturbed the night, were in a large, cell-like cage immediately below the spot where of old the chapel alter had stood.

And here were we an odd party in odd environment. I sought to make out the time by my watch, but the growing dusk rendered it impossible. Then, unheralded by any sound, Kâramaneh entered by the door which during the past twenty minutes had been the focus of my gaze. The gathering darkness precluded the possibility of my observing with certainty, but I think a soft blush stole to her cheeks as those glorious dark eyes rested upon me.

The beauty of Kâramaneh was not of the type which is enhanced by artificial lighting; it was the beauty of the palm and the pomegranate blossom, the beauty which flowers beneath merciless suns, which expands, like the lotus, under the skies of the East. But there, in the dusk, as she came towards me, she looked exquisitely lovely, and graceful with the grace of the desert gazelles which I had seen earlier in the evening. I cannot describe her dress; I only know that she seemed very wonderful—so wonderful that a pang; almost of terror, smote my heart, because such sweetness should belong to *me*.

And then, from the shadows masking the other side of the old hall, emerged the black figure of Homopoulo, and our odd trio obediently paced into the somber dining-room.

A large lamp burned in the center of the table; a shaded candle was placed before each diner; and the subdued light made play upon the snowy napery and fine old silver without dispersing the gloom about us. Indeed, if anything, it seemed to render it more remarkable, and the table became a lighted oasis in the desert of the huge apartment. One could barely discern the suits of armor and trophies which ornamented the paneled walls; and I never failed to start nervously when the butler appeared, somber and silent, at my elbow.

Sir Lionel Barton's *penchant* for strange visitors, of which we had had experience in the past, was exemplified in the person of Homopoulo. I gathered that the butler (who, I must admit, seemed thoroughly to comprehend his duties) had entered the service of Sir Lionel during the time that the latter was pursuing his celebrated excavations upon the traditional site of the Daedalian Labyrinth in Crete. It was during this expedition that the death of a distant relative had made him master of Graywater Park; and the event seemingly had inspired the eccentric baronet to engage a suitable factotum.

His usual retinue of Malay footmen, Hindu grooms and Chinese cooks, was missing apparently, and the rest of the household, including the charming old housekeeper, had been at the Park for periods varying from five to five-and-twenty years. I must admit that I welcomed the fact; my tastes are essentially insular.

But the untimely illness of our host had cast a shadow upon the party. I found myself speaking in a church-whisper, whilst Kâramaneh was quite silent. That curious dinner party in the shadow desert of the huge apartment frequently recurs in my memories of those days because of the uncanny happening which terminated it.

Nayland Smith, who palpably had been as ill at ease as myself, and who had not escaped the contagious habit of speaking in a hushed whisper, suddenly began, in a loud and cheery manner, to tell us something of the history of Graywater Park, which in his methodical way he had looked up. It was a desperate revolt, on the part of his strenuous spirit, against the phantom of gloom which threatened to obsess us all.

Parts of the house, it appeared, were of very great age, although successive owners had added portions. There were fascinating traditions connected with the place; secret rooms walled up since the Middle Ages, a private stair whose entrance, though undiscoverable, was said to be somewhere in the orchard to the west of the ancient chapel. It had been built by an ancestor of Sir Lionel who had flourished in the reign of the eighth Henry. At this point in his reminiscences (Smith had an astonishing memory where recondite facts were concerned) there came an interruption.

The smooth voice of the butler almost made me leap from my chair, as he spoke out of the shadows immediately behind me.

"The '45 port, sir," he said—and proceeded to place a crusted bottle upon the table. "Sir Lionel desires me to say that he is with you in spirit and that he proposes the health of Dr. Petrie and his fiancée, whom he hopes to have the pleasure of meeting in the morning."

Truly it was a singular situation, and I am unlikely ever to forget the scene as the three of us solemnly rose to our feet and drank our host's toast, thus proposed by proxy, under the eye of Homopoulo, who stood a shadowy figure in the background.

The ceremony solemnly performed and the gloomy butler having departed with a suitable message to Sir Lionel—

"I was about to tell you," resumed Nayland Smith, with a gaiety palpably forced, "of the traditional ghost of Graywater Park. He is a black-clad priest, said to be the Spanish chaplain of the owner of the Park in the early days of the Reformation. Owing to some little misunderstanding with His Majesty's commissioners, this unfortunate churchman met with an untimely death, and his shade is said to haunt the secret room—the site of which is unknown—and to clamor upon the door, and upon the walls of the private stair."

I thought the subject rather ill chosen, but recognized that my friend was talking more or less at random and in desperation; indeed, failing his reminiscences of Graywater Park, I think the demon of silence must have conquered us completely.

"Presumably," I said, unconsciously speaking as though I feared the sound of my own voice, "this Spanish priest was confined at some time in the famous hidden chamber?"

"He was supposed to know the secret of a hoard of church property, and tradition has it, that he was put to the question in some gloomy dungeon …"

He ceased abruptly; in fact the effect was that which must have resulted had the speaker been suddenly stricken down. But the deadly silence which ensued was instantly interrupted. My heart seemed to be clutched as though by fingers of ice; a stark and supernatural horror held me riveted in my chair.

For as though Nayland Smith's words had been heard by the ghostly inhabitant of Graywater Park, as though the tortured priest sought once more release from his age-long sufferings—there came echoing, hollowly and remotely, as if from a subterranean cavern, the sound of *knocking*.

From whence it actually proceeded I was wholly unable to determine. At one time it seemed to surround us, as though not one but a hundred prisoners were beating upon the paneled walls of the huge, ancient apartment.

Faintly, so faintly, that I could not be sure if I heard aright, there came, too, a stifled cry. Louder grew the frantic beating and louder … then it ceased abruptly.

"Merciful God!" I whispered—"what was it? What was it?"

CHAPTER THIRTY-FIVE

THE EAST TOWER

With a cigarette between my lips I sat at the open window, looking out upon the skeleton trees of the orchard; for the buds of early spring were only just beginning to proclaim themselves.

The idea of sleep was far from my mind. The attractive modern furniture of the room could not deprive the paneled walls of the musty antiquity which was their birthright. This solitary window deeply set and overlooking the orchard upon which the secret stair was said to open, struck a note of more remote antiquity, casting back beyond the carousing days of the Stuart monarchs to the troublous time of the Middle Ages.

An air of ghostly evil had seemed to arise like a miasma within the house from the moment that we had been disturbed by the unaccountable rapping. It was at a late hour that we had separated, and none of us, I think, welcomed the breaking up of our little party. Mrs. Oram, the housekeeper, had been closely questioned by Smith—for Homopoulo, as a newcomer, could not be expected to know anything of the history of Graywater Park. The old lady admitted the existence of the tradition which Nayland Smith had in some way unearthed, but assured us that never, in her time, had the uneasy spirit declared himself. She was ignorant (or, like the excellent retainer that she was, professed to be ignorant) of the location of the historic chamber and staircase.

As for Homopoulo, hitherto so irreproachably imperturbable, I had rarely seen a man in such a state of passive panic. His dark face was blanched to the hue of dirty parchment and his forehead dewed with cold perspiration. I mentally predicted an early resignation in the household of Sir Lionel Barton. Homopoulo might be an excellent butler, but his superstitious Greek nature was clearly incapable of sustaining existence beneath the same roof with a family ghost, hoary though the specter's antiquity might be.

Where the skeleton shadows of the fruit trees lay beneath me on the fresh green turf my fancy persistently fashioned a black-clad figure flitting from tree to tree. Sleep indeed was impossible. Once I thought I detected the howling of the distant leopards.

Somewhere on the floor above me, Nayland Smith, I knew, at that moment would be restlessly pacing his room, the exact situation of which I could not identify, because of the quaint, rambling passages whereby one approached it. It was in regard to Kâramaneh, however, that my misgivings were the keenest. Already her position had been strange enough, in those unfamiliar surroundings, but what tremors must have been hers now in the still watches of the night, following the ghostly manifestations which had so dramatically interrupted Nayland Smith's story, I dared not imagine. She had been allotted an apartment somewhere upon the ground floor, and Mrs. Oram, whose motherly interest in the girl had touched me deeply, had gone with her to her room, where no doubt her presence had done much to restore the girl's courage.

Graywater Park stood upon a well-wooded slope, and, to the

southwest, starting above the trees almost like a giant Spanish priest, showed a solitary tower. With a vague and indefinite interest I watched it. It was Monkswell, an uninhabited place belonging to Sir Lionel's estate and dating, in part, to the days of King John. Flicking the ash from my cigarette, I studied the ancient tower wondering idly what deeds had had their setting within its shadows, since the Angevin monarch, in whose reign it saw the light, had signed the Magna Carta.

This was a perfect night, and very still. Nothing stirred, within or without Graywater Park. Yet I was conscious of a definite disquietude which I could only suppose to be ascribable to the weird events of the evening, but which seemed rather to increase than to diminish.

I tossed the end of my cigarette out into the darkness, determined to turn in, although I had never felt more wide awake in my life. One parting glance I cast into the skeleton orchard and was on the point of standing up, when—although no breezed stirred—a shower of ivy leaves rained down upon my head!

Brushing them away irritably, I looked up—and a second shower dropped fully upon my face and filled my eyes with dust. I drew back, checking an exclamation. What with the depth of the embrasure, due to the great thickness of the wall, and the leafy tangle above the window, I could see for no great distance up the face of the building; but a faint sound of rustling and stumbling which proceeded from somewhere above me proclaimed that someone, or something, was climbing either up or down the wall of the corner tower in which I was housed!

Partially removing the dust from my smarting eyes, I returned to the embrasure, and stepping from the chair on to the deep ledge, I grasped the corner of the quaint, diamond-paned window, which I had opened to its fullest extent, and craned forth.

Now I could see the ivy-grown battlements surmounting the tower (the east wing, in which my room was situated, was the oldest part of Graywater Park). Sharply outlined against the cloudless sky they showed ... and the black silhouette of a man's head and shoulders leant over directly above me!

I drew back sharply. The climber, I thought, had not seen me, although he was evidently peering down at my window. What did it mean?

As I crouched in the embrasure, a sudden giddiness assailed me, which at first I ascribed to a sympathetic nervous action due to having seen the man poised there at that dizzy height. But it increased, I swayed forward, and clutched at the wall to save myself. A deadly nausea overcame me ... and a deadly doubt leapt to my mind.

In the past, Sir Lionel Barton had had spies in his household; what if the dark-faced Greek, Homopoulo, were another of these? I thought of the '45 port, of the ghostly rapping; and I thought of the man who crouched upon the roof of the tower above my open window.

My symptoms now were unmistakable; my head throbbed and my vision grew imperfect; there had to be an opiate in the wine!

I almost fell back into the room. Supporting myself by means of the chair, the chest of drawers, and finally, the bed-rail, I got to my grip, and with weakening fingers, extracted the little medicine-chest which was invariably my traveling companion.

Grimly pitting my will against the drug, but still trembling weakly from the result of the treatment, internal and subcutaneous, which I had adopted, I staggered to the door, out into the corridor and up the narrow, winding stairs to Smith's room. I carried an electric pocket-lamp, and by its light I found my way to the triangular, paneled landing.

I tried the handle. As I had expected, the door was locked. I beat upon it with my fist.

"Smith!" I cried—"Smith!"

There was no reply.

Again I clamored; awaking ancient echoes within the rooms and all about me. But nothing moved and no answering voice rewarded my efforts; the other rooms were seemingly unoccupied, and Smith—was drugged!

My senses in disorder, and a mist dancing before my eyes, I went stumbling down into the lower corridor. At the door of my own room I paused; a new fact had suddenly been revealed to me, a fact which the mazy windings of the corridors had hitherto led me to overlook. Smith's room was also in the east tower, and must be directly above mine!

"My God!" I whispered, thinking of the climber—"he has been murdered!"

I staggered into my room and clutched at the bed-rail to support myself, for my legs threatened to collapse beneath me. How should I act? That we were victims of a cunning plot, that the deathful Si-Fan had at last wreaked its vengeance upon Nayland Smith I could not doubt.

My brain reeled, and a weakness, mental and physical, threatened to conquer me completely. Indeed, I think I must have succumbed, sapped as my strength had been by the drug administered to me, if the sound of a creaking stair had not arrested my attention and by the menace which it conveyed afforded a new stimulus.

Someone was creeping down from the landing above—coming to my room! The creatures of the Yellow doctor, having despatched

Nayland Smith, were approaching stealthily, stair by stair, to deal with *me*!

From my grip I took out the Browning pistol. The Chinese doctor's servants should have a warm reception. I burned to avenge my friend, who I was persuaded, lay murdered in the room above. I partially closed the door and took up a post immediately behind it. Nearer came the stealthy footsteps—nearer.... Now the one who approached had turned the angle of the passage....

Within sight of my door he seemed to stop; a shaft of white light crept through the opening, across the floor and on to the wall beyond. A moment it remained so—then was gone. The room became plunged in darkness.

Gripping the Browning with nervous fingers I waited, listening intently; but the silence remained unbroken. My gaze set upon the spot where the head of this midnight visitant might be expected to appear, I almost held my breath during the ensuing moments of frightful suspense.

The door was opening; slowly—slowly—by almost imperceptible degrees. I held the pistol pointed rigidly before me and my gaze remained fixed intently on the dimly seen opening. I suppose I acted as ninety-nine men out of a hundred would have done in like case. Nothing appeared.

Then a voice—a voice that seemed to come from somewhere under the floor snapped:—

"Good God! it's Petrie!"

I dropped my gaze instantly ... and there, looking up at me from the floor at my feet, I vaguely discerned the outline of a human head!

"Smith!" I whispered.

Nayland Smith—for indeed it was none other—stood up and entered the room.

"Thank God you are safe, old man," he said. "But in waiting for one who is stealthily entering a room, don't, as you love me, take it for granted that he will enter *upright*. I could have shot you from the floor with ease! But, mercifully, even in the darkness, I recognized your Arab slippers!"

"Smith," I said, my heart beating wildly, "I thought you were drugged—murdered. The port contained an opiate."

"I guessed as much!" snapped Smith. "But despite the excellent tuition of Dr. Fu-Manchu, I am still childishly trustful; and the fact that I did not partake of the crusted '45 was not due to any suspicions which I entertained at that time."

"But, Smith, I saw you drink some port."

"I regret to contradict you, Petrie, but you must be aware that the state of my liver—due to a long residence in Burma—does not permit me to indulge in the luxury of port. My share of the '45 now reposes amid the moss in the tulip-bowl, which you may remember decorated the dining table! Not desiring to appear churlish, by means of a simple feat of legerdemain I drank your health and future happiness in claret!"

"For God's sake what is going on, Smith? Someone climbed from your window."

"I climbed from my window!"

"What!" I said dazedly—"it was you! But what does it all mean? Kâramaneh—"

"It is for her I fear, Petrie, now. We have not a moment to waste!"

He made for the door.

"Sir Lionel must be warned at all cost!" I cried.

"Impossible!" snapped Smith.

"What do you mean?"

"Sir Lionel has disappeared!"

CHAPTER THIRTY-SIX

THE DUNGEON

We were out in the corridor now, Smith showing the way with the light of his electric pocket-lamp. My mind was clear enough, but I felt as weak as a child.

"You look positively ghastly, old man," rapped Smith, "which is no matter for wonder. I have yet to learn how it happened that you are not lying insensible, or dead, as a result of the drugged wine. When I heard someone moving in your room, it never occurred to me that it was *you*."

"Smith," I said—"the house seems as still as death."

"You, Kâramaneh, and myself are the only occupants of the east wing. Homopoulo saw to that."

"Then he—"

"He is a member of the Si-Fan, a creature of Dr. Fu-Manchu—yes, beyond all doubt! Sir Lionel is unfortunate—as ever—in his choice of servants. I blame my own stupidity entirely, Petrie; and I pray that my enlightenment has not come too late."

"What does it all mean?—what have you learnt?"

"Mind these three steps," warned Smith, glancing back. "I found my mind persistently dwelling upon the matter of that weird rapping, Petrie, and I recollected the situation of Sir Lionel's room, on the southeast front. A brief inspection revealed the fact that, by means of a kindly branch of ivy, I could reach the roof of the east tower from my window."

"Well?"

"One may walk from there along the roof of the southeast front, and by lying face downwards at the point where it projects above the main entrance look into Sir Lionel's room!"

"I saw you go!"

"I feared that someone was watching me, but that it was you I had never supposed. Neither Barton nor his man are in that room, Petrie! They have been spirited away! This is Kâramaneh's door."

He grasped me by the arm, at the same time directing the light upon a closed door before which we stood. I raised my fist and beat upon the panels; then, every muscle tensed and my heart throbbing wildly, I listened for the girl's voice.

Not a sound broke that deathly stillness except the beating of my own heart, which, I thought, must surely be audible to my companion. Frantically I hurled myself against the stubborn oak, but Smith thrust me back.

"Useless, Petrie!" he said—"useless. This room is in the base of the east tower, yours is above it and mine at the top. The corridors approaching the three floors deceive one, but the fact remains. I have no positive evidence, but I would wager all I possess that there is a stair in the thickness of the wall, and hidden doors in the paneling of the three apartments. The Yellow group has somehow obtained possession of a plan of the historic secret passages and chambers of Graywater Park. Homopoulo is the spy in the household; and Sir Lionel, with his man Kennedy, was removed directly the invitation to us had been posted. The group will know by now that we have escaped them, but Kâramaneh …."

"Smith!" I groaned, "Smith! What can we do? What has befallen her? …"

"This way!" he snapped. "We are not beaten yet!"

"We must arouse the servants!"

"Why? It would be sheer waste of priceless time. There are only three men who actually sleep in the house (excepting Homopoulo) and these are in the northwest wing. No, Petrie; we must rely upon ourselves."

He was racing recklessly along the tortuous corridors and up the oddly placed stairways of that old-world building. My anguish had reinforced the atropine which I had employed as an antidote to the opiate in the wine, and now my blood, that had coursed sluggishly, leapt through my veins like fire and I burned with a passionate anger.

Into a large and untidy bedroom we burst. Books and papers littered about the floor; curios, ranging from mummied cats and ibises to Turkish yataghans and Zulu assegais, surrounded the place in riotous disorder. Beyond doubt this was the apartment of Sir Lionel Barton. A lamp burned upon a table near to the disordered bed, and a discolored Greek statuette of Orpheus lay overturned on the carpet close beside it.

"Homopoulo was on the point of leaving this room at the moment that I peered in at the window," said Smith, breathing heavily. "From here there is another entrance to the secret passages. Have your pistol ready."

He stepped across the disordered room to a little alcove near the foot of the bed, directing the ray of the pocket-lamp upon the small, square paneling.

"Ah!" he cried, a note of triumph in his voice—"he has left the door ajar! A visit of inspection was not anticipated tonight, Petrie! Thank God for an Indian liver and a suspicious mind."

He disappeared into a yawning cavity which now I perceived to exist in the wall. I hurried after him, and found myself upon roughly fashioned stone steps in a very low and narrow descending passage. Over his shoulder—

"Note the direction," said Smith breathlessly. "We shall presently find ourselves at the base of the east tower."

Down we went and down, the ray of the electric lamp always showing more steps ahead, until at last these terminated in a level, arched passage, curving sharply to the right. Two paces more brought us to a doorway, less, than four feet high, approached by two wide steps. A blackened door, having a most cumbersome and complicated lock, showed in the recess.

Nayland Smith bent and examined the mechanism intently.

"Freshly oiled!" he commented. "You know into whose room it opens?"

Well enough I knew, and, detecting that faint, haunting perfume which spoke of the dainty personality of Kâramaneh, my anger blazed up anew. Came a faint sound of metal grating upon metal, and Smith pulled open the door, which turned outward upon the steps, and bent further forward, sweeping the ray of light about the room beyond.

"Empty, of course!" he muttered. "Now for the base of these damned nocturnal operations."

He descended the steps and began to flash the light all about the arched passageway wherein we stood.

"The present dining-room of Graywater Park lies almost due south of this spot," he mused. "Suppose we try back."

We retraced our steps to the foot of the stair. In the wall on their left was an opening, low down against the floor and little more than three feet high; it reminded me of some of the entrances to those seemingly interminable passages whereby one approaches the sepulchral chambers of the Egyptian Pyramids.

"Now for it!" snapped Smith. "Follow me closely."

Down he dropped, and, having the lamp thrust out before him, began to crawl into the tunnel. As his heels disappeared, and only a faint light outlined the opening, I dropped upon all fours in turn, and began laboriously to drag myself along behind him. The atmosphere was damp, chilly, and evil-smelling; therefore, at the end of some ten or twelve yards of this serpentine crawling, when I saw Smith, ahead of me, to be standing erect, I uttered a stifled exclamation of relief. The thought of Kâramaneh having been dragged through this noisome hole was one I dared not dwell upon.

A long, narrow passage now opened up, its end invisible from where we stood. Smith hurried forward. For the first thirty of forty paces the roof was formed of massive stone slabs; then its character changed; the passage became lower, and one was compelled frequently to lower the head in order to avoid the oaken beams which crossed it.

"We are passing under the dining-room," said Smith. "It was from here the sound of beating first came!"

"What do you mean?"

"I have built up a theory, which remains to be proved, Petrie. In my opinion a captive of the Yellow group escaped tonight and sought to summon assistance, but was discovered and overpowered."

"Sir Lionel?"

"Sir Lionel, or Kennedy—yes, I believe so."

Enlightenment came to me, and I understood the pitiable

condition into which the Greek butler had been thrown by the phenomenon of the ghostly knocking. But Smith hurried on, and suddenly I saw that the passage had entered upon a sharp declivity; and now both roof and walls were composed of crumbling brickwork. Smith pulled up, and thrust back a hand to detain me.

"*Ssh!*" he hissed, and grasped my arm.

Silent, intently still, we stood and listened. The sound of a guttural voice was clearly distinguishable from somewhere close at hand!

Smith extinguished the lamp. A faint luminance proclaimed itself directly ahead. Still grasping my arm, Smith began slowly to advance toward the light. One—two—three—four—five paces we crept onward … and I found myself looking through an archway into a medieval torture-chamber!

Only a part of the place was visible to me, but its character was unmistakable. Leg-irons, boots and thumb-screws hung in racks upon the fungi-covered wall. A massive, iron-studded door was open at the further end of the chamber, and on the threshold stood Homopoulo, holding a lantern in his hand.

Even as I saw him, he stepped through, followed by one of those short, thick-set Burmans of whom Dr. Fu-Manchu had a number among his entourage; they were members of the villainous robber bands notorious in India as the dacoits. Over one broad shoulder, slung sackwise, the dacoit carried a girl clad in scanty white drapery….

Madness seized me, the madness of sorrow and impotent wrath. For, with Kâramaneh being borne off before my eyes, I dared not fire at her abductors lest I should strike *her*!

Nayland Smith uttered a loud cry, and together we hurled ourselves into the chamber. Heedless of what, of whom, else it might shelter, we sprang for the group in the distant doorway. A memory is mine of the dark, white face of Homopoulo, peering, wild-eyed, over the lantern, of the slim, white-clad form of the lovely captive seeming to fade into the obscurity of the passage beyond.

Then, with bleeding knuckles, with wild imprecations bubbling from my lips, I was battering upon the mighty door—which had been slammed in my face at the very instant that I had gained it.

"Brace up, man!—Brace up!" cried Smith, and in his strenuous, grimly purposeful fashion, he shouldered me away from the door. "A battering ram could not force that timber; we must seek another way!"

I staggered, weakly, back into the room. Hand raised to my head, I looked about me. A lantern stood in a niche in one wall, weirdly illuminating that place of ghastly memories; there were braziers, branding-irons, with other instruments dear to the Black Ages, about me—and gagged, chained side by side against the opposite wall, lay Sir Lionel Barton and another man unknown to me!

Already Nayland Smith was bending over the intrepid explorer, whose fierce blue eyes glared out from the sun-tanned face madly, whose gray hair and mustache literally bristled with rage long repressed. I choked down the emotions that boiled and seethed within me, and sought to release the second captive, a stockily built, clean-shaven man. First I removed the length of toweling which was tied firmly over his mouth; and—

"Thank you, sir," he said composedly. "The keys of these irons are on the ledge there beside the lantern. I broke the first ring I was chained to, but the Yellow devils overhauled me, all manacled as I was, halfway along the passage before I could attract your attention, and fixed me up to another and stronger ring!"

Ere he had finished speaking, the keys were in my hands, and I had unlocked the gyves from both the captives. Sir Lionel Barton, his gag removed, unloosed a torrent of pent-up wrath.

"The hell-fiends drugged me!" he shouted. "That black villain Homopoulo doctored my tea! I woke in this damnable cell, the secret of which has been lost for generations!" He turned blazing blue eyes upon Kennedy. "How did *you* come to be trapped?" he demanded unreasonably. "I credited you with a modicum of brains!"

"Homopoulo came running from your room, sir, and told me you were taken suddenly ill and that a doctor must be summoned without delay."

"Well, well, you fool!"

"Dr. Hamilton was away, sir."

"A false call beyond doubt!" snapped Smith.

"Therefore I went for the new doctor, Dr. Magnus, in the village. He came at once and I showed him up to your room. He sent Mrs. Oram out, leaving only Homopoulo and myself there, except yourself."

"Well?"

"Sandbagged!" explained the man nonchalantly. "Dr. Magnus, who is some kind of dago, is evidently one of the gang."

"Sir Lionel!" cried Smith—"where does the passage lead to beyond that doorway?

"God knows!" was the answer, which dashed my last hope to the ground. "I have no more idea than yourself. Perhaps …"

He ceased speaking. A sound had interrupted him, which, in those grim surroundings, lighted by the solitary lantern, translated my thoughts magically to Ancient Rome, to the Rome of Tigellinus, to the dungeons of Nero's Circus. Echoing eerily along the secret passages it came—the roaring and snarling of the lioness and the leopards.

Nayland Smith clapped his hand to his brow and stared at me almost frenziedly, then—

"God guard her!" he whispered. "Either their plans, wherever they got them, are inaccurate, or in their panic they have mistaken the way." Wild cries now were mingling with the snarling of the beasts…. "They have blundered into the old crypt!"

How we got out of the secret labyrinth of Graywater Park into the grounds and around the angle of the west wing to the ivy-grown, pointed door, where once the chapel had been, I do not know. Light seemed to spring up about me, and half-clad servants to appear out of the void. Temporarily I was insane.

Sir Lionel Barton was behaving like a madman too, and like a madman he tore at the ancient bolts and precipitated himself into the stone-paved cloister barred with the moon-cast shadows of the Norman pillars. From behind the iron bars of the home of the leopards came now a fearsome growling and scuffling.

Smith held the light with a steady hand, whilst Kennedy forced the heavy bolts of the crypt door.

In leapt the fearless baronet among his savage pets, and in the ray of light from the electric lamp I saw that which turned me sick with horror. Prone beside a yawning gap in the floor lay Homopoulo, his throat torn indescribably and his white shirt-front smothered in blood. A black leopard, having its fore-paws upon the dead man's breast, turned blazing eyes upon us; a second crouched beside him.

Heaped up in a corner of the place, amongst the straw and litter of the lair, lay the Burmese dacoit, his sinewy fingers embedded in the throat of the third and largest leopard—which was dead—whilst the creature's gleaming fangs were buried in the tattered flesh of the man's shoulder.

Upon the straw beside the two, her slim, bare arms outstretched and her head pillowed upon them, so that her rippling hair completely concealed her face, lay Kâramaneh.

In a trice Barton leapt upon the great beast standing over Homopoulo, had him by the back of the neck and held him in his powerful hands whining with fear and helpless as a rat in the grip of a terrier. The second leopard fled into the inner lair.

So much I visualized in a flash; then all faded, and I knelt alone beside her whose life was my life, in a world grown suddenly empty and still.

Through long hours of agony I lived, hours contained within the span of seconds, the beloved head resting against my shoulder, whilst I searched for signs of life and dreaded to find ghastly wounds.... At first I could not credit the miracle; I could not receive the wondrous truth.

Kâramaneh was quite uninjured and deep in drugged slumber!

"The leopards thought her dead," whispered Smith brokenly, "and never touched her!"

CHAPTER THIRTY-SEVEN

THREE NIGHTS LATER

"Listen!" cried Sir Lionel Barton.

He stood upon the black rug before the massive, carven mantelpiece, a huge man in an appropriately huge setting.

I checked the words on my lips, and listened intently. Within Graywater Park all was still, for the hour was late. Outside, the rain was descending in a deluge, its continuous roar drowning any other sound that might have been discernible. Then, above it, I detected a noise that at first I found difficult to define.

"The howling of the leopards!" I suggested.

Sir Lionel shook his tawny head with impatience. Then, the sound growing louder, suddenly I knew it for what it was.

"Someone shouting!" I exclaimed—"someone who rides a galloping horse!"

"Coming here!" added Sir Lionel. "Hark! he is at the door!"

A bell rang furiously, again and again sending its brazen clangor echoing through the great apartments and passages of Graywater.

"There goes Kennedy."

Above the sibilant roaring of the rain I could hear someone

releasing heavy bolts and bars. The servants had long since retired, as also had Kâramaneh; but Sir Lionel's man remained wakeful and alert.

Sir Lionel made for the door, and I, standing up, was about to follow him, when Kennedy appeared, in his wake a bedraggled groom, hatless, and pale to the lips. His frightened eyes looked from face to face.

"Dr. Petrie?" he gasped interrogatively.

"Yes!" I said, a sudden dread assailing me. "What is it?"

"Gad! it's Hamilton's man!" cried Barton.

"Mr. Nayland Smith, sir," continued the groom brokenly—and all my fears were realized. "He's been attacked, sir, on the road from the station, and Dr. Hamilton, to whose house he was carried—"

"Kennedy!" shouted Sir Lionel, "get the Rolls-Royce out! Put your horse up here, my man, and come with us!"

He turned abruptly … as the groom, grasping at the wall, fell heavily to the floor.

"Good God!" I cried—"What's the matter with him?"

I bent over the prostrate man, making a rapid examination.

"His head! A nasty blow. Give me a hand, Sir Lionel; we must get him on to a couch."

The unconscious man was laid upon a Chesterfield, and, ably assisted by the explorer, who was used to coping with such hurts as this, I attended to him as best I could. One of the men-servants had been aroused, and, just as he appeared in the doorway, I had the satisfaction of seeing Dr. Hamilton's groom open his eyes, and look about him, dazedly.

"Quick," I said. "Tell me—what hurt you?"

The man raised his hand to his head and groaned feebly.

"Something came *whizzing*, sir," he answered. "There was no report, and I saw nothing. I don't know what it can have been—"

"Where did this attack take place?"

"Between here and the village, sir; just by the coppice at the cross-roads on top of Raddon Hill."

"You had better remain here for the present," I said, and gave a few words of instruction to the man whom we had aroused.

"This way," cried Barton, who had rushed out of the room, his huge frame reappearing in the doorway; "the car is ready."

My mind filled with dreadful apprehensions, I passed out on to the carriage sweep. Sir Lionel was already at the wheel.

"Jump in, Kennedy," he said, when I had taken a seat beside him; and the man sprang into the car.

Away we shot, up the narrow lane, lurched hard on the bend—and were off at ever growing speed toward the hills, where a long climb awaited the car.

The headlight picked out the straight road before us, and Barton increased the pace, regardless of regulations, until the growing slope made itself felt and the speed grew gradually less; above the throbbing of the motor, I could hear, now, the rain in the overhanging trees.

I peered through the darkness, up the road, wondering if we were near to the spot where the mysterious attack had been made upon Dr. Hamilton's groom. I decided that we were just passing the place, and to confirm my opinion, at that moment Sir Lionel swung the car around suddenly, and plunged headlong into the black mouth of a narrow lane.

Hitherto, the roads had been fair, but now the jolting and swaying became very pronounced.

"Beastly road!" shouted Barton—"and stiff gradient!"

I nodded.

That part of the way which was visible in front had the appearance of a muddy cataract, through which we must force a path.

Then, as abruptly as it had commenced, the rain ceased; and at almost the same moment came an angry cry from behind.

The canvas hood made it impossible to see clearly in the car, but, turning quickly, I perceived Kennedy, with his cap off, rubbing his close-cropped skull. He was cursing volubly.

"What is it, Kennedy?

"Somebody sniping!" cried the man. "Lucky for me I had my cap on!"

"Eh, sniping?" said Barton, glancing over his shoulder. "What d'you mean? A stone, was it?"

"No, sir," answered Kennedy. "I don't know what it was—but it wasn't a stone."

"Hurt much?" I asked.

"No, sir! nothing at all." But there was a note of fear in the man's voice—fear of the unknown.

Something struck the hood with a dull drum-like thud.

"There's another, sir!" cried Kennedy. "There's someone following us!"

"Can you see anyone?" came the reply. "I thought I saw something then, about twenty yards behind. It's so dark."

"Try a shot!" I said, passing my Browning to Kennedy.

The next moment, the crack of the little weapon sounded sharply, and I thought I detected a vague, answering cry.

"See anything?" came from Barton.

Neither Kennedy nor I made reply; for we were both looking back down the hill. Momentarily, the moon had peeped from the cloud-banks, and where, three hundreds yards behind, the bordering trees were few, a patch of dim light spread across the muddy road—and melted away as a new blackness gathered.

But, in the brief space, three figures had shown, only for an instant—but long enough for us both to see that they were those of three gaunt men, seemingly clad in scanty garments. What weapons they employed I could not conjecture; but we were pursued by three of Dr. Fu-Manchu's dacoits!

Barton growled something savagely, and ran the car to the left of the road, as the gates of Dr. Hamilton's house came in sight.

A servant was there, ready to throw them open; and Sir Lionel swung around on to the drive, and drove ahead, up the elm avenue to where the light streamed through the open door on to the wet gravel. The house was a blaze of lights, every window visible being illuminated; and Mrs. Hamilton stood in the porch to greet us.

"Doctor Petrie?" she asked, nervously, as we descended.

"I am he," I said. "How is Mr. Smith?"

"Still insensible," was the reply.

Passing a knot of servants who stood at the foot of the stairs like a little flock of frightened sheep—we made our way into the room where my poor friend lay.

Dr. Hamilton, a gray-haired man of military bearing, greeted Sir Lionel, and the latter made me known to my fellow practitioner, who grasped my hand, and then went straight to the bedside, tilting the lampshade to throw the light directly upon the patient.

Nayland Smith lay with his arms outside the coverlet and his fists tightly clenched. His thin, tanned face wore a grayish hue, and a white bandage was about his head. He breathed stentoriously.

"We can only wait," said Dr. Hamilton, "and trust that there will be no complications."

I clenched my fists involuntarily, but, speaking no word, turned and passed from the room.

Downstairs in Dr. Hamilton's study was the man who had found Nayland Smith.

"We don't know when it was done, sir," he said, answering my first question. "Staples and me stumbled on him in the dusk, just by the big beech—a good quarter-mile from the village. I don't know how long he'd laid there, but it must have been for some time, as the last rain arrived an hour earlier. No, sir, he hadn't been robbed; his money and watch were on him but his pocketbook lay open beside him;—though, funny as it seems, there were three five-pound notes in it!"

"Do you understand, Petrie?" cried Sir Lionel. "Smith evidently obtained a copy of the old plan of the secret passages of Graywater and Monkswell, sooner than he expected, and determined to return tonight. They left him for dead, having robbed him of the plans!"

"But the attack on Dr. Hamilton's man?"

"Fu-Manchu clearly tried to prevent communication with us tonight! He is playing for time. Depend on it, Petrie, the hour of his departure draws near and he is afraid of being trapped at the last moment."

He began taking huge strides up and down the room, forcibly reminding me of a caged lion.

"To think," I said bitterly, "that all our efforts have failed to discover the secret—"

"The secret of my own property!" roared Barton—"and one known to that damned, cunning Chinese devil!"

"And in all probability now known also to Smith—"

"And he cannot speak! ..."

"*Who* cannot speak?" demanded a hoarse voice.

I turned in a flash, unable to credit my senses—and there, holding weakly to the doorpost, stood Nayland Smith!

"Smith!" I cried reproachfully—"you should not have left your room!"

He sank into an armchair, assisted by Dr. Hamilton.

"My skull is fortunately thick!" he replied, a ghostly smile playing around the corners of his mouth—"and it was a physical impossibility for me to remain inert considering that Dr. Fu-Manchu proposes to leave England tonight!"

CHAPTER THIRTY-EIGHT

THE MONK'S PLAN

"My inquiries in the Manuscript Room of the British Museum," said Nayland Smith, his voice momentarily growing stronger and some of the old fire creeping back into his eyes, "have proved entirely successful."

Sir Lionel Barton, Dr. Hamilton, and myself hung upon every word; and often I found myself glancing at the old-fashioned clock on the doctor's mantelpiece.

"We had very definite proof," continued Smith, "of the fact that Fu-Manchu and company were conversant with that elaborate system of secret rooms and passages which forms a veritable labyrinth, in, about, and beneath Graywater Park. Some of the passages we explored. That Sir Lionel should be ignorant of the system was not strange, considering that he had but recently inherited the property, and that the former owner, his kinsman, regarded the secret as lost. A starting-point was discovered, however, in the old work on haunted manors unearthed in the library, as you remember. There was a reference, in the chapter dealing with Graywater, so a certain monkish manuscript said to repose in the national collection and to contain a plan of these passages and stairways.

"The Keeper of the Manuscripts at the Museum very courteously assisted me in my inquiries, and the ancient parchment was placed in my hands. Sure enough, it contained a carefully executed drawing of the hidden ways of Graywater, the work of a monk in the distant days when Graywater was a priory. This monk, I may add—a certain Brother Anselm—afterwards became Abbot of Graywater."

"Very interesting!" cried Sir Lionel loudly; "very interesting indeed."

"I copied the plan," resumed Smith, "with elaborate care. That labor, unfortunately, was wasted, in part, at least. Then, in order to confirm my suspicions on the point, I endeavored to ascertain if the monk's manuscript had been asked for at the Museum recently. The Keeper of the Manuscripts could not recall that any student had handled the work, prior to my own visit, during the past ten years.

"This was disappointing, and I was tempted to conclude that Fu-Manchu had blundered on to the secret in some other way, when the Assistant Keeper of Manuscripts put in an appearance. From him I obtained confirmation of my theory. Three months ago a Greek gentleman—possibly, Sir Lionel, your late butler, Homopoulo—obtained permission to consult the manuscript, claiming to be engaged upon a paper for some review or another.

"At any rate, the fact was sufficient. Quite evidently, a servant of Fu-Manchu had obtained a copy of the plan—and this within a day or so of the death of Mr. Brangholme Burton—whose heir, Sir Lionel, you were! I became daily impressed anew with the omniscience, the incredible genius, of Dr. Fu-Manchu.

"The scheme which we know of to compass the death, or captivity, of our three selves and Kâramaneh was put into operation, and failed. But, with its failure, the utility of the secret chambers was by no means terminated. The local legend, according to which a passage exists, linking Graywater and Monkswell, is confirmed by the monk's plan."

"What?" cried Sir Lionel, springing to his feet—"a passage between the Park and the old tower! My dear sir, it's impossible! Such a passage would have to pass under the River Starn! It's only a narrow stream, I know, but—"

"It *does*, or *did*, pass under the River Starn!" said Nayland Smith coolly. "That it is still practicable I do not assert; what interests me is the spot at which it terminates."

He plunged his hand into the pocket of the light overcoat which he wore over the borrowed suit of pyjamas in which the kindly Dr. Hamilton had clothed him. He was seeking his pipe!

"Have a cigar, Smith!" cried Sir Lionel, proffering his case—"if you *must* smoke; although I think I see our medical friends frowning!"

Nayland Smith took a cigar, bit off the end, and lighted up. He began to surround himself with odorous clouds, to his evident satisfaction.

"To resume," he said; "the Spanish priest who was persecuted at Graywater in early Reformation days and whose tortured spirit is said to haunt the Park, held the secret of this passage, and of the subterranean chamber in Monkswell, to which it led. His confession—which resulted in his death at the stake!—enabled the commissioners to recover from his chamber a quantity of church ornaments. For these facts I am indebted to the author of the work on haunted manors.

"Our inquiry at this point touches upon things sinister and incomprehensible. In a word, although the passage and a part of the underground room are of unknown antiquity, it appears certain that they were improved and enlarged by one of the abbots of Monkswell—at a date much later than Brother Anselm's abbotship—and the place was converted to a secret chapel—"

"A *secret* chapel!" said Dr. Hamilton.

"Exactly. This was at a time in English history when the horrible cult of Asmodeus spread from the Rhine monasteries and gained proselytes in many religious houses of England. In this secret chapel, wretched Churchmen, seduced to the abominable views of the abbot, celebrated the Black Mass!"

"My God!" I whispered—"small wonder that the place is reputed to be haunted!"

"Small wonder," cried Nayland Smith, with all his old nervous vigor, "that Dr. Fu-Manchu selected it as an ideal retreat in times of danger!"

"What! the chapel?" roared Sir Lionel.

"Beyond doubt! Well knowing the penalty of discovery, those old devil-worshipers had chosen a temple from which they could escape in an emergency. There is a short stair from the chamber into the cave which, as you may know, exists in the cliff adjoining Monkswell."

Smith's eyes were blazing now, and he was on his feet, pacing the floor, an odd figure, with his bandaged skull and inadequate garments, biting on the already extinguished cigar as though it had been a pipe.

"Returning to our rooms, Petrie," he went on rapidly, "who should I run into but Summers! You remember Summers, the Suez Canal pilot whom you met at Ismailia two years ago? He brought the yacht through the Canal, from Suez, on which I suspect Ki-Ming came to England. She is a big boat—used to be on the Port Said and Jaffa route before a wealthy Chinaman acquired her—through an Egyptian agent—for his personal use.

"All the crews, Summers told me, were Asiatics, and little groups of natives lined the Canal and performed obeisances as the vessel passed. Undoubtedly they had that woman on board, Petrie, the Lady of the Si-Fan, who escaped, together with Fu-Manchu, when we raided the meeting in London! Like a fool I came racing back here without advising you; and, all alone, my mind occupied with the tremendous import of these discoveries, started, long after dusk, to walk to Graywater Park."

He shrugged his shoulders whimsically, and raised one hand to his bandaged head.

"Fu-Manchu employs weapons both of the future and of the past," he said. "My movements had been watched, of course; I was mad. Someone, probably a dacoit, laid me low with a ball of clay propelled from a sling of the Ancient Persian pattern! I actually saw him … then saw, and knew, no more!"

"Smith!" I cried—whilst Sir Lionel Barton and Dr. Hamilton stared at one another, dumbfounded—"you think *he* is on the point of flying from England—"

"The Chinese yacht, *Chanak-Kampo*, is lying two miles off the coast and in the sight of the tower of Monkswell!"

CHAPTER THIRTY-NINE

THE SHADOW ARMY

The scene of our return to Graywater Park is destined to live in my memory for ever. The storm, of which the violet rainfall had been a prelude, gathered blackly over the hills. Ebon clouds lowered upon us as we came racing to the gates. Then the big car was spinning around the carriage sweep, amid a deathly stillness of Nature indescribably gloomy and ominous. I have said, a stillness of nature; but, as Kennedy leapt out and ran up the steps to the door, from the distant cages wherein Sire Lionel kept his collection of rare beasts proceeded the angry howling of the leopards and such a wild succession of roars from the African lioness that I stared at our eccentric host questioningly.

"It's the gathering storm," he explained. "These creatures are peculiarly susceptible to atmospheric disturbances."

Now the door was thrown open, and, standing in the lighted hall, a picture fair to look upon in her dainty kimono and little red, high-heeled slippers, stood Kâramaneh!

I was beside her in a moment; for the lovely face was pale and there was a wildness in her eyes which alarmed me.

"*He* is somewhere near!" she whispered, clinging to me. "Some great danger threatens. Where have you been?—what has happened?"

"Smith was attacked on his way back from London," I replied. "But, as you see, he is quite recovered. We are in no danger; and I insist that you go back to bed. We shall tell you all about it in the morning."

Rebellion blazed up in her wonderful eyes instantly—and as quickly was gone, leaving them exquisitely bright. Two tears, like twin pearls, hung upon the curved black lashes. It made my blood course faster to watch this lovely Eastern girl conquering the barbaric impulses that sometimes flamed up within, her, because *I* willed it; indeed this was a miracle that I never tired of witnessing.

Mrs. Oram, the white-haired housekeeper, placed her arm in motherly fashion about the girl's slim waist.

"She wants to stay in my room until the trouble is all over," she said in her refined, sweet voice.

"You are very good, Mrs. Oram," I replied. "Take care of her."

One long, reassuring glance I gave Kâramaneh, then turned and followed Smith and Sir Lionel up the winding oak stair. Kennedy came close behind me, carrying one of the acetylene headlamps of the car. And—

"Just listen to the lioness, sir!" he whispered. "It's not the gathering storm that's making her so restless. Jungle beasts grow quiet, as a rule, when there's thunder about."

The snarling of the great creature was plainly audible, distant though we were from her cage.

"Through your room, Barton!" snapped Nayland Smith, when we gained the top corridor.

He was his old, masterful self once more, and his voice was

vibrant with that suppressed excitement which I knew well. Into the disorderly sleeping apartment of the baronet we hurried, and Smith made for the recess near the bed which concealed a door in the paneling.

"Cautiously here!" cried Smith. "Follow immediately behind me, Kennedy, and throw the beam ahead. Hold the lamp well to the left."

In we filed, into that ancient passage which had figured in many a black deed but had never served the ends of a more evil plotter than the awful Chinaman who so recently had rediscovered it.

Down we marched, and down, but not to the base of the tower, as I had anticipated. At a point which I judged to be about level with the first floor of the house, Smith—who had been audibly counting the steps—paused, and began to examine the seemingly unbroken masonry of the wall.

"We have to remember," he muttered, "that this passage may be blocked up or otherwise impassable, and that Fu-Manchu may know of another entrance. Furthermore, since the plan is lost, I have to rely upon my memory for the exact position of the door."

He was feeling about in the crevices between the stone blocks of which the wall was constructed.

"Twenty-one steps," he muttered; "I feel certain."

Suddenly it seemed that his quest had proved successful.

"Ah!" he cried—"the ring!"

I saw that he had drawn out a large iron ring from some crevice in which it had been concealed.

"Stand back, Kennedy!" he warned.

Kennedy moved on to a lower step—as Smith, bringing all his weight to bear upon the ring, turned the huge stone slab upon its hidden pivot, so that it fell back upon the stair with a reverberating boom.

We all pressed forward to peer into the black cavity. Kennedy moving the light, a square well was revealed, not more than three feet across. Footholes were cut at intervals down the further side.

"H'm!" said Smith—"I was hardly prepared for this. The method of descent that occurs to me is to lean back against one side and trust one's weight entirely to the footholes on the other. A shaft appeared in the plan, I remember, but I had formed no theory respecting the means provided for descending it. Tilt the lamp forward, Kennedy. Good! I can see the floor of the passage below; only about fifteen feet or so down."

He stretched his foot across, placed it in the niche and began to descend.

"Kennedy next!" came his muffled voice, "with the lamp. Its light will enable you others to see the way."

Down went Kennedy without hesitation, the lamp swung from his right arm.

"I will bring up the rear," said Sir Lionel Barton.

Whereupon I descended. I had climbed down about halfway when, from below, came a loud cry, a sound of scuffling, and a savage exclamation from Smith. Then—

"We're right, Petrie! This passage was recently used by Fu-Manchu!"

I gained the bottom of the well, and found myself standing in the entrance to an arched passage. Kennedy was directing the light of the lamp down upon the floor.

"You see, the door was guarded," said Nayland Smith.

"What!"

"Puff adder!" he snapped, and indicated a small snake whose head was crushed beneath his heel.

Sir Lionel now joined us; and, a silent quartette, we stood staring from the dead reptile into the damp and evil-smelling tunnel. A distant muttering and rumbling rolled, echoing awesomely along it.

"For Heaven's sake what was that, sir?" whispered Kennedy.

"It was the thunder," answered Nayland Smith. "The storm is breaking over the hills. Steady with the lamp, my man."

We had proceeded for some three hundred yards, and, according to my calculation, were clear of the orchard of Graywater Park and close to the fringe of trees beyond; I was taking note of the curious old brickwork of the passage, when—

"Look out, sir!" cried Kennedy—and the light began dancing madly. "Just under your feet! Now it's up the wall!—mind your hand, Dr. Petrie!"

The lamp was turned, and, since it shone fully into my face, temporarily blinded me.

"On the roof over your head, Barton!"—this from Nayland Smith. "What can we kill it with?"

Now my sight was restored to me, and looking back along the passage, I saw, clinging to an irregularity in the moldy wall, the most gigantic scorpion I had ever set eyes upon! It was fully as large as my open hand.

Kennedy and Nayland Smith were stealthily retracing their steps, the former keeping the light directed upon the hideous insect, which now began running about with that horrible, febrile activity characteristic of the species. Suddenly came a sharp, staccato report.... Sir Lionel had scored a hit with his Browning pistol.

In waves of sound, the report went booming along the passage. The lamp, as I have said, was turned in order to shine back upon us, rendering the tunnel ahead a mere black mouth—a veritable inferno, held by inhuman guards. Into that black cavern I stared, gloomily fascinated by the onward rolling sound storm; into that blackness I looked … to feel my scalp tingle horrifically, to know the crowning horror of the horrible journey.

The blackness was spangled with watching, diamond eyes!—with tiny insect eyes that moved; upon the floor, upon the walls, upon the ceiling! A choking cry rose to my lips.

"Smith! Barton! for God's sake, look! The place is *alive* with scorpions!"

Around we all came, panic plucking at our hearts, around swept the beam of the big lamp; and there, retreating before the light, went a veritable army of venomous creatures! I counted no fewer than three of the giant red centipedes whose poisonous touch, called "the zayat kiss," is certain death; several species of scorpion were represented; and some kind of bloated, unwieldy spider, so gross of body that its short, hairy legs could scarce support it, crawled, hideous, almost at my feet.

What other monstrosities of the insect kingdom were included in that obscene host I know not; my skin tingled from head to feet; I experienced a sensation as if a million venomous things already clung to me—unclean things bred in the malarial jungles of Burma, in the corpse-tainted mud of China's rivers, in the fever spots of that darkest East from which Fu-Manchu recruited his shadow army.

I was perilously near to losing my nerve when the crisp, incisive tones of Nayland Smith's voice came to stimulate me like a cold douche.

"This wanton sacrifice of horrors speaks eloquently of a forlorn hope! Sweep the walls with light, Kennedy; all those filthy things are nocturnal and they will retreat before us as we advance."

His words proved true. Occasioning a sort of *rustling* sound—a faint sibilance indescribably loathsome—the creatures gray and black and red darted off along the passage. One by one, as we proceeded, they crept into holes and crevices of the ancient walls, sometimes singly, sometimes in pairs—the pairs locked together in deadly embrace.

"They cannot live long in this cold atmosphere," cried Smith. "Many of them will kill one another—and we can safely leave the rest to the British climate. But see that none of them drops upon you in passing."

Thus we pursued our nightmare march, on through that valley of horror. Colder grew the atmosphere and colder. Again the thunder boomed out above us, seeming to shake the roof of the tunnel fiercely, as with Titan hands. A sound of falling water, audible for some time, now grew so loud that conversation became difficult. All the insects had disappeared.

"We are approaching the River Starn!" roared Sir Lionel. "Note the dip of the passage and the wet walls!"

"Note the type of brickwork!" shouted Smith.

Largely as a sedative to the feverish excitement which consumed me, I forced myself to study the construction of the tunnel; and I became aware of an astonishing circumstance. Partly the walls were natural, a narrow cavern traversing the bed of rock which upcropped on this portion of the estate, but partly, if my scanty knowledge of archaeology did not betray me, they were *Phoenician*!

"This stretch of passage," came another roar from Sir Lionel, "dates back to Roman days or even earlier! By God! It's almost incredible!"

And now Smith and Kennedy, who lid, were up to their knees in a running tide. An icy shower-bath drenched us from above; ahead was a solid wall of falling water. Again, and louder, nearer, boomed and rattled the thunder; its mighty voice was almost lost in the roar of that subterranean cataract. Nayland Smith, using his hands as a megaphone, cried;—

"Failing the evidence that others have passed this way, I should not dare to risk it! But the river is less than forty feet wide at the point below Monkswell; a dozen paces should see us through the worst!"

I attempted no reply. I will frankly admit that the prospect appalled me. But, bracing himself up as one does preparatory to a high dive, Smith, nodding to Kennedy to proceed, plunged into the cataract ahead....

CHAPTER FORTY

THE BLACK CHAPEL

Of how we achieved that twelve or fifteen yards below the rocky bed of the stream the Powers that lent us strength and fortitude alone hold record. Gasping for breath, drenched, almost reconciled to the end which I thought was come—I found myself standing at the foot of a steep flight of stairs roughly hewn in the living rock.

Beside me, the extinguished lamp still grasped in his hand, leant Kennedy, panting wildly and clutching at the uneven wall. Sir Lionel Barton had sunk exhausted upon the bottom step, and Nayland Smith was standing near him, looking up the stairs. From an arched doorway at their head light streamed forth!

Immediately behind me, in the dark place where the waters roared, opened a fissure in the rock, and into it poured the miniature cataract; I understood now the phenomenon of minor whirlpools for which the little river above was famous. Such were my impressions of that brief breathing-space; then—

"Have your pistols ready!" cried Smith. "Leave the lamp, Kennedy. It can serve us no further."

Mustering all the reserve that remained to us, we went, pell-mell, a wild, bedraggled company, up that ancient stair and poured into the room above....

One glance showed us that this was indeed the chapel of Asmodeus, the shrine of Satan where the Black Mass had been sung in the Middle Ages. The stone altar remained, together with certain Latin inscriptions cut in the wall. Fu-Manchu's last home in England had been within a temple of his only Master.

Save for nondescript litter, evidencing a hasty departure of the occupants, and a ship's lantern burning upon the altar, the chapel was unfurnished. Nothing menaced us, but the thunder hollowly crashed far above. To cover his retreat, Fu-Manchu had relied upon the noxious host in the passage and upon the wall of water. Silent, motionless, we four stood looking down at that which lay upon the floor of the unholy place.

In a pool of blood was stretched the Eurasian girl, Zarmi. Her picturesque finery was reft into tatters and her bare throat and arms were covered with weals and bruises occasioned by ruthless, clutching fingers. Of her face, which had been notable for a sort of devilish beauty, I cannot write; it was the awful face of one who had did from strangulation.

Beside her, with a Malay *krîs* in his heart—a little, jeweled weapon that I had often seen in Zarmi's hand—sprawled the obese Greek, Samarkan, a member of the Si-Fan group and sometime manager of a great London hotel!

It was ghastly, it was infinitely horrible, that tragedy of which the story can never be known, never be written; that fiendish fight to the death in the black chapel of Asmodeus.

"We are too late!" said Nayland Smith. "The stair behind the altar!"

He snatched up the lantern. Directly behind the stone altar was a narrow, pointed doorway. From the depths with which it communicated proceeded vague, awesome sounds, as of waves breaking in some vast cavern....

We were more than halfway down the stair when, above the muffled roaring of the thunder, I distinctly heard the voice of *Dr. Fu-Manchu*!

"My God!" shouted Smith, "perhaps they are trapped! The cave is only navigable at low tide and in calm weather!"

We literally fell down the remaining steps ... and were almost precipitated into the water!

The light of the lantern showed a lofty cavern tapering away to a point at its remote end, pear-fashion. The throbbing of an engine and churning of a screw became audible. There was a faint smell of petrol.

"Shoot! shoot!"—the frenzied voice was that of Sir Lionel—"Look! they can just get through! ..."

Crack! Crack! Crack!

Nayland Smith's Browning spat death across the cave. Then followed the report of Barton's pistol; then those of mine and Kennedy's.

A small motorboat was creeping cautiously out under a low, natural archway which evidently gave access to the sea! Since the tide was incoming, a few minutes more of delay had rendered the passage of the cavern impossible....

The boat disappeared.

"We are not beaten!" snapped Nayland Smith. "The *Chanak-Kampo* will be seized in the Channel!"

"There were formerly steps, in the side of the well from which this place takes its name," declared Nayland Smith dully. "This was the means of access to the secret chapel employed by the devil-worshipers."

"The top of the well (alleged to be the deepest in England)," said Sir Lionel, "is among a tangle of weeds close by the ruined tower."

Smith, ascending three stone steps, swung the lantern out over the yawning pit below; then he stared long and fixedly upwards.

Both thunder and rain had ceased; but even in those gloomy depths we could hear the coming of the tempest which followed upon that memorable storm.

"The steps are here," reported Smith; "but without the aid of a rope from above, I doubt if they are climbable."

"It's that or the way we came, sir!" said Kennedy. "I was five years at sea in wind-jammers. Let me swarm up and go for a rope to the Park."

"Can you do it?" demanded Smith. "Come and look!"

Kennedy craned from the opening, staring upward and downward; then—

"I can do it, sir," he said quietly.

Removing his boots and socks, he swung himself out from the opening into the well and was gone.

The story of Fu-Manchu, and of the organization called the Si-Fan which he employed as a means to further his own vast projects, is almost told.

Kennedy accomplished the perilous climb to the lip of the well, and sped barefooted to Graywater Park for ropes. By means of these we all escaped from the strange chapel of the devil-worshipers. Of how we arranged for the removal of the bodies which lay in the place I need not write. My record advances twenty-four hours.

The great storm which burst over England in the never-to-be-forgotten spring when Fu-Manchu fled our shores has become historical. There were no fewer than twenty shipwrecks during the day and night that it raged.

Imprisoned by the elements in Graywater Park, we listened to the wind howling with the voice of a million demons around the ancient manor, to the creatures of Sir Lionel's collection swelling the unholy discord. Then came the news that there was a big steamer on the Pinion Rocks—that the lifeboat could not reach her.

As though it were but yesterday I can see us, Sir Lionel Barton, Nayland Smith and I, hurrying down into the little cove which sheltered the fishing-village; fighting our way against the power of the tempest….

Thrice we saw the rockets split the inky curtain of the storm; thrice saw the gallant lifeboat crew essay to put their frail craft out to sea … thrice the mighty rollers hurled them contemptuously back….

Dawn—a gray, eerie dawn—was creeping ghostly over the iron-bound shore, when the fragments of wreckage began to drift in. Such are the currents upon those coasts that bodies are rarely recovered from wrecks on the cruel Pinion Rocks.

In the dim light I bent over a battered and torn mass of timber—that once had been the bow of a boat; and in letters of black and gold I read: "S. Y. *Chanak-Kampo.*"

ABOUT THE AUTHOR

Sax Rohmer was born Arthur Henry Ward in 1883, in Birmingham, England, adding "Sarsfield" to his name in 1901. He was four years old when Sherlock Holmes appeared in print, five when the Jack the Ripper murders began, and sixteen when H.G. Wells' Martians invaded.

Initially pursuing a career as a civil servant, he turned to writing as a journalist, poet, comedy sketch writer, and songwriter in British music halls. At age 20 he submitted the short story "The Mysterious Mummy" to *Pearson's* magazine and "The Leopard-Couch" to *Chamber's Journal*. Both were published under the byline "A. Sarsfield Ward."

Ward's Bohemian associates Cumper, Bailey, and Dodgson gave him the nickname "Digger," which he used as his byline on several serialized stories. Then, in 1908, the song "Bang Went the Chance of a Lifetime" appeared under the byline "Sax Rohmer." Becoming immersed in theosophy, alchemy, and mysticism, Ward decided the name was appropriate to his writing, so when "The Zayat Kiss" first appeared in *The Story-Teller* magazine in October,

1912, it was credited to Sax Rohmer.

That was the first story featuring Fu-Manchu, and the first portion of the novel *The Mystery of Dr. Fu-Manchu.* Novels such as *The Yellow Claw*, *Tales of Secret Egypt*, *Dope*, *The Dream Detective*, *The Green Eyes of Bast*, and *Tales of Chinatown* made Rohmer one of the most successful novelists of the 1920s and 1930s.

There are fourteen Fu-Manchu novels, and the character has been featured in radio, television, comic strips, and comic books. He first appeared in film in 1923, and has been portrayed by such actors as Boris Karloff, Christopher Lee, John Carradine, Peter Sellers, and Nicolas Cage.

Rohmer died in 1959, a victim of an outbreak of the type A influenza known as the Asian flu.

APPRECIATING DOCTOR FU-MANCHU

BY LESLIE S. KLINGER

The "yellow peril"—that stereotypical threat of Asian conquest—seized the public imagination in the late nineteenth century, in political diatribes and in fiction. While several authors exploited this fear, the work of Arthur Henry Sarsfield Ward, better known as Sax Rohmer, stood out.

Dr. Fu-Manchu was born in Rohmer's short story "The Zayat Kiss," which first appeared in a British magazine in 1912. Nine more stories quickly appeared and, in 1913, the tales were collected as *The Mystery of Dr. Fu-Manchu* (*The Insidious Dr. Fu-Manchu* in America). The Doctor appeared in two more series before the end of the Great War, collected as *The Devil Doctor* (*The Return of Dr. Fu-Manchu*) and *The Si-Fan Mysteries* (*The Hand of Fu-Manchu*).

After a fourteen-year absence, the Doctor reappeared in 1931, in *The Daughter of Fu-Manchu*. There were nine more novels, continuing until Rohmer's death in 1959, when *Emperor Fu-Manchu* was published. Four stories, which had previously appeared only in magazines, were published in 1973 as *The Wrath of Fu-Manchu*.

The Fu-Manchu stories also have been the basis of numerous

motion pictures, most famously the 1932 MGM film *The Mask of Fu-Manchu*, featuring Boris Karloff as the Doctor.

In the early stories, Fu-Manchu and his cohorts are the "yellow menace," whose aim is to establish domination of the Asian races. In the 1930s Fu-Manchu foments political dissension among the working classes. By the 1940s, as the wars in Europe and Asia threaten terrible destruction, Fu-Manchu works to depose other world leaders and defeat the Communists in Russia and China.

Rohmer undoubtedly read the works of Conan Doyle, and there is a strong resemblance between Nayland Smith and Holmes. There are also marked parallels between the four doctors, Petrie and Watson as the narrator-comrades, and Dr. Fu-Manchu and Professor Moriarty as the arch-villains.

The emphasis is on fast-paced action set in exotic locations, evocatively described in luxuriant detail, with countless thrills occurring to the unrelenting ticking of a tightly wound clock. Strong romantic elements and sensually described, sexually attractive women appear throughout the tales, but ultimately it is the *fantastic* nature of the adventures that appeal.

This is the continuing appeal of Dr. Fu-Manchu, for despite his occasional tactic of alliance with the West, he unrelentingly pursued his own agenda of world domination. In the long run, Rohmer's depiction of Fu-Manchu rose above the fears and prejudices that may have created him to become a picture of a timeless and implacable creature of menace.

A complete version of this essay can be found in *The Mystery of Fu-Manchu*, also available from Titan Books.

ALSO AVAILABLE FROM TITAN BOOKS

THE COMPLETE FU-MANCHU SERIES

Sax Rohmer

THE RETURN OF DR. FU-MANCHU

THE HAND OF FU-MANCHU

DAUGHTER OF FU-MANCHU

THE MASK OF FU-MANCHU

THE BRIDE OF FU-MANCHU

THE TRAIL OF FU-MANCHU

PRESIDENT FU-MANCHU

THE DRUMS OF FU-MANCHU

THE ISLAND OF FU-MANCHU

THE SHADOW OF FU-MANCHU

RE-ENTER: FU-MANCHU

EMPEROR FU-MANCHU

THE WRATH OF FU-MANCHU AND OTHER STORIES

WWW.TITANBOOKS.COM

SÉANCE FOR A VAMPIRE

by Fred Saberhagen

THE SEVENTH BULLET

by Daniel D. Victor

THE WHITECHAPEL HORRORS

by Edward B. Hanna

DR. JEKYLL AND MR. HOLMES

by Loren D. Estleman

THE ANGEL OF THE OPERA

by Sam Siciliano

THE GIANT RAT OF SUMATRA

by Richard L. Boyer

THE PEERLESS PEER

by Philip José Farmer

THE STAR OF INDIA

by Carole Buggé

THE TITANIC TRAGEDY

by Sam Siciliano

SHERLOCK HOLMES VS. DRACULA

by Loren D. Estleman

THE GRIMSWELL CURSE

by Sam Siciliano

THE DEVIL'S PROMISE

by David Stuart Davies

THE ALBINO'S TREASURE

by Stuart Douglas

Coming soon:

MURDER AT SORROW'S CROWN

by Steven Savile & Robert Greenberger

THE WHITE WORM

by Sam Siciliano

THE RIPPER LEGACY

by David Stuart Davies

THE COUNTERFEIT DETECTIVE

by Stuart Douglas

ALSO AVAILABLE FROM TITAN BOOKS

THE HARRY HOUDINI MYSTERIES

Daniel Stashower

THE DIME MUSEUM MURDERS
THE FLOATING LADY MURDER
THE HOUDINI SPECTER

In turn-of-the-century New York, the Great Houdini's confidence in his own abilities is matched only by the indifference of the paying public. Now the young performer has the opportunity to make a name for himself by attempting the most amazing feats of his fledgling career—solving what seem to be impenetrable crimes. With the reluctant help of his brother Dash, Houdini must unravel murders, debunk frauds and escape from danger that is no illusion…

A thrilling series from the author of *The Further Adventures of Sherlock Holmes: The Ectoplasmic Man*.

For more fantastic fiction, author events, exclusive excerpts, competitions, limited editions and more

VISIT OUR WEBSITE

titanbooks.com

LIKE US ON FACEBOOK

facebook.com/titanbooks

FOLLOW US ON TWITTER

@TitanBooks

EMAIL US

readerfeedback@titanemail.com